Praise for Stephen D. Cork, Jenny O'Shane and *Sir, I Can Explain*

"Jenny O'Shane at her finest. I liked her in Knight Time and absolutely love her in *Sir, I Can Explain*... irch in

USNR (RET), USNA 1957

"I love Jenny O'Shane...where has she been? More importantly, this is a story that needs to be told..."

—Charley Richards, COL, US Army (Ret), former Florida Sarasota County Commissioner and President of the Florida County Commissioners Association.

"Fantastic story…truly authentic in descriptions…awesome intrigue… super well written…"

—LTC (P) Ron Birchall US Army (Ret), former 'A' Team Special Forces Commander, SOCOM. Former High Altitude, Low Opening (HALO) parachute Team Chief

"This is a super book with a storylines that speak to our social fiber – it should be read by everybody. I truly enjoyed. Fantastic action…I love Jenny O'Shane…"

—Joann Tiffany, DVM, former Captain, US Army

"I thoroughly enjoyed *Sir, I Can Explain*… The plot and subplots are woven together masterfully…What a wild ride…"

—Bob Clancy, CEO, Clancy Financial Group, Inc.

"I read it straight through...I loved *Sir, I Can Explain*...The human trafficking plot line is scary ...a fantastic story."

—Roberto Mei, owner and executive chef, Café Baci, Sarasota, Florida

"Great read! Action packed...a page turner. Jenny O'Shane is a new breed of warrior. Can't wait for her future exploits."

—Commander Tim Leighton, USN (Ret), Naval Aviator and retired airline pilot. USCG Licensed 100 Ton Captain

"*Sir, I Can Explain* is a great book...couldn't put it down...well written...intense and exciting... non-stop action. Jenny O'Shane is a female James Bond."

—Jennings Lyon, Senior Safety Engineer (Ret), Newport News Shipbuilding. USCG 100 Ton Captain

Sir, I Can Explain
Stephen D. Cork

© Copyright 2013 by Stephen D. Cork

ISBN 9781938467554

All rights reserved. No part of this publication may be reproduced, stored in a retrieval system, or transmitted in any form or by any means – electronic, mechanical, photocopy, recording, or any other – except for brief quotations in printed reviews, without the prior written permission of the author.

This is a work of fiction. All the characters in this book are fictitious, or are used fictitiously, and any resemblance to actual persons, living or dead, is purely coincidental. The names, incidents, dialogue, and opinions expressed are products of the author's imagination and are not to be construed as real.

Published by

an imprint of Morgan James Publishing

5 Penn Plaza, 23rd floor
c/o Morgan James Publishing
New York, NY 10001
212-574-7939
www.koehlerbooks.com

Publisher
John Köehler

Executive Editor
Joe Coccaro

In an effort to support local communities, raise awareness and funds, Morgan James Publishing donates a percentage of all book sales for the life of each book to Habitat for Humanity Peninsula and Greater Williamsburg.
Get involved today, visit www.MorganJamesBuilds.com

Also by Stephen D. Cork

Take That (short story)
Knight Moves

Coming Soon,
Next in the Jenny O'Shane Series,
This is a Goat Rope

To my wife, Peggy,

and daughters, Gina and Joann,

whom I love more than words can describe.

Sir, I Can Explain

Stephen D. Cork

NEW YORK
VIRGINIA

Citrus County Library System

Chapter One

The soft leather of the chair felt cool against Jenny O'Shane's arms. She was alone; the whir of air conditioning the only sound. Summoned to a security meeting at the Saudi National Guard Headquarters, she was drumming her fingers on a large conference table while admiring the panorama of downtown Riyadh. Her ears were still ringing from the call to prayer broadcast from a minaret of a nearby mosque. She'd been waiting thirty minutes. She knew that the Saudis were being rude to express their annoyance at having to meet with a woman.

Trickles of sweat rolled down the small of her back. Despite the building's cooled air, the U.S. Army's combat uniform was too warm in the ovenlike Saudi summer.

Jenny stood when the room's double doors swung open—a habit from her military upbringing. An older man bustled in with an arrogant air of royalty. He wore a Saudi dishdasha robe and a flowing shora headdress. Gold stitching hemmed the edges of the dazzling white silk robe and formed an intricate pattern on the chest.

She stifled a smile when a small retinue hovered about him like butterflies in a flower garden, each trying to outdo the other in servicing their charge. There were two younger men wearing similar, less ornate dishdashas, and a young, pretty Caucasian girl in an ivory colored ankle-length abaya dress and hijab scarf. The slim girl placed a coffee service on the polished conference table and then backed out of the room, bowing low.

The two men adjusted blinds and set out the coffee cups and condiments. Jenny got a good look at the older man as his entourage scurried about. He had a ready-to-smile kind of face, but the grey eyes that returned her look were as hard as granite.

"Good evening, Major O'Shane," he said in fluent English. "I'm Prince Allaweh Kaliq, Minister of Security, and first cousin to Crown Prince Fahd." He ignored her offered hand and didn't bother introducing the others.

She figured the others were aides in that one of them poured from a copper-trimmed crystal coffeepot into two matching tumblers. He stirred cream and sugar into both without asking for preferences. He gave one cup to Kaliq and the other to Jenny.

Kaliq sat in a chair at the center position of the table. Motioning Jenny to a seat opposite him, he raised his cup, slurped loudly and sighed with appreciative pleasure. The aide immediately refilled his cup.

Briefed on Middle Eastern culture, Jenny knew that it was customary for hosts to exhibit a gesture of hospitality and to exchange pleasantries prior to discussing business. And she knew that she was expected to follow Kaliq's example. She slurped and was rewarded with a mouthful of bitter, high-octane espresso. The jolt of caffeine went directly into her bloodstream. Her hands and feet tingled.

Barely suppressing a cough, she sighed in pretended pleasure. The aide started to serve her more. She placed her hand over her cup to indicate she was satisfied. With a slight nod of his head, Kaliq seemed to acknowledge her correct protocol and to indicate that obligations of hospitality had been met.

The same aide gathered the cups and placed them on the service tray. He snapped his fingers, and the girl reentered the room, picked up the tray and bowed out. Only when the doors closed did Kaliq speak again.

"So, the Americans sent a woman to coordinate security for the Commanding General of Central Command. Some would interpret that as a sign of weakness by General Penfant."

"Yes, Excellency. But many more would see it as recognition of the modern times in which we live." *So much for pleasantries,* she thought.

"Harrumph. Perhaps." He paused, and then added, "I hope I didn't keep you waiting long?"

"Thirty minutes isn't long with a view like this, Excellency." She detected a faint smile. She figured he knew her meaning.

He opened a folder one of his aides placed in front of him. "Thank you, Mohammed," Kaliq said to the aide. Jenny noticed that Mohammed was staring at her. There was an unpleasantness about his demeanor that made her skin feel itchy. She ignored his stare and refocused her attention on Kaliq.

She recognized the paper he was looking at in the folder. It was the bio she'd been told to provide as an introduction. It was hard to miss the bold letters at the top:

U.S. Army Major Jennifer O'Shane, Military Police

"We already know a lot about you," Kaliq said without more preambles. "You recommended against having your General Penfant attend the reception we've planned during his visit to thank him for helping us with the Somalian pirates." He held up the palm of his hand to indicate she needn't respond.

Jenny watched his long fingernail trail down the list of bullet points on the bio. His lips moved as if he were reading the information out loud. He passed over the first bullets that talked about her graduation from West Point and early promotion to major. His finger paused on the third bullet that indicated her title as the Chief of Security for the Commanding General of CENTCOM. "How long have you had this job?"

"Nearly one year," she answered, suppressing the urge to say more.

Kaliq's finger rested on another bullet point: her list of awards. He turned the resumé over and dismissively pushed it aside. "There won't be any need for your heroics at the reception. The palace is impregnable."

He looked her over as if for the first time; an eyebrow rose when his eyes glanced at the parachutist airborne badge over the left pocket of her ACU jacket and shifted briefly to the combat patch velcroed to her right shoulder.

With a sniff and a lift of his hawklike nose, he seemed to challenge her to question his assertion about palace security. She didn't rise to the bait and stared back.

Mohammed snapped his fingers. The Caucasian girl slipped back through the double doors as if by magic. Jenny noticed for the first time how out of place she looked among the dark features of the Saudis. Jenny could see a pale face peeking out from under the girl's headscarf. She bowed low to the aide and handed him a folder.

She appeared afraid of Mohammed, cowering. She didn't even glance toward Jenny. The aide snapped his fingers again, and the girl hurried back out the doors. Jenny registered the fear but pushed it to the back of her mind. *It's none of your business. Focus.*

Kaliq took the folder from the aide and slid it toward Jenny. He motioned with a backhanded wave that the folder was for her. His minimal effort caused Jenny to have to stand and reach across the table. She ignored his intentional slight.

In the folder, Jenny found a copy of a letter containing three short paragraphs on heavy bond paper. The Saudi royal family seal was embossed at the top. The subject line read: "Guidelines for U.S. Participation in Security at the Reception Honoring General Penfant." It was dated two days earlier, addressed directly to the Commanding General, and was signed by the Crown Prince.

Her jaw clenched. *Crap, this meeting's a sham. Everything's done.* By having the Crown Prince write directly to the CG, Kaliq had done an end run. She swallowed her anger. She was going to have to be extra clever to negotiate any change with this cagey old man.

She scanned the first paragraph, then looked up, careful to keep her voice respectful. "Excellency, your *request* that General Penfant's protection detail not display weapons is unusual." She watched to see if he got her point. A sly, crooked smile indicated that he understood. She added, "But, we can live with it. We'll wear jackets." It felt good appearing as if she'd compromised. She'd planned to have the staff wear sport jackets anyway.

She read on, and then asked, "Why do you *request* that only four people be on the detail in the reception hall? I usually bring at least a squad of nine inside for big events."

Kaliq examined his manicured nails and didn't look at her when he responded. "As I said, the palace is impregnable. And we'll have ample guards. Mohammed has made the necessary arrangements. He manages all social affairs for the Crown Prince."

Jenny simmered over Kaliq's cavalier attitude but decided against arguing about security inside the palace. She was more concerned with areas outside the palace where warrens of tiny alleyways and higher elevations of multiple buildings made ambushes easy. She had recommendations for securing those areas that she wanted his agreement on.

Then she read the last paragraph of the letter. It was a deal breaker.

"What's this about no females on the protection detail?"

"Women don't carry weapons in Saudi Arabia," Kaliq answered, disdain in every syllable.

"Well, I intend to lead this detail. That's nonnegotiable." She locked eyes with him. She wasn't backing down.

It was Kaliq's turn to blink. Then he smiled as if he'd tricked her. "Very well," he said. "You may accompany your team. But there will only be three others, and *you* will be unarmed." He looked pleased with himself.

Jenny stared at him. *This is impossible.*

Kaliq pulled at the side of his flowing shora headdress and straightened the fancy egal on its top. If he detected her anger, he ignored it and added with another sniff, "I believe our exposure is minimal. We see no reason for special measures given the low-threat level in Saudi Arabia."

Jenny had enough. She blurted out an exclamation of disbelief. "Excellency, terrorists attacked a U.S. civilian compound in Riyadh last year. Eight people were killed and hundreds were injured. We all know it happened. That's a big reason why the U.S. lists Saudi Arabia as a level orange security risk for VIPs and why I recommended against the CG attending this event."

Taking a deep, calming breath, Jenny lowered her voice. Pasting on her most engaging smile, she pointed to a diagram she'd brought to demonstrate her ideas. "Sir, I have two companies of military police to help beef up security on the outside of the palace. Here are the locations I'd recommend they be positioned."

Kaliq didn't even glance at the diagram. Instead he said, "We won't require additional staff for security. Thank you. Our meeting is over." He stalked out with his entourage close behind.

Jenny stared at the closing door of the conference room, open-mouthed. "What? No discussion? That's it?" She threw her hands in the air in exasperation and then gave Kaliq the finger in absentia.

Chapter Two

Too fidgety to sit, Jenny paced Penfant's outer office at the King Khalid International Airport. It was seven, the morning after her meeting with Minister Kaliq. Biting a thumbnail, she worried about being summoned to see Penfant on such short notice.

"The Commanding General wants to see you right away," his aide told her on the phone and then hung up without waiting for questions.

Jenny figured she knew the subject and thought she had a reasonable explanation. She tried not to think about Penfant's reputation as a hard-ass.

She occupied her mind by looking at the various miniature flags and unit crests mounted in a glass-covered credenza. They represented the Army, Air Force, Navy and Marine units assigned to Central Command. Jenny recalled hearing estimates of nearly three hundred and fifty thousand troops in the command, most engaged in anti-terrorist operations in Iraq and Afghanistan.

Being an Army brat, she'd seen dozens of military offices as her dad moved from job to job. He'd been given a fancy one in the Pentagon when promoted to a three-star general.

Most offices she'd seen had a personal touch. Even temporary ones, like those set up for Penfant's one-week visit to Saudi Arabia, had some attempt at décor. Not this one. The light-brown walls were unadorned. Wooden straight-backed chairs were lined up like soldiers around the edges. The room reflected the personality of its occupant. George Penfant was all business.

A Marine gunnery sergeant sitting at the receptionist desk interrupted her thoughts. He waved Jenny into the inner sanctum.

Penfant glared at her when she walked in. She had a sinking feeling in the pit of her stomach as she stood at attention six inches in front of his desk, snapping her best parade-ground salute. "Sir, Major O'Shane reporting as ordered."

He returned her salute and didn't mince words. "You need to listen to this, and listen good," he said with his clipped New England accent. He pressed a button on a phone.

Jenny had seldom seen him wear anything but an impeccable Marine camouflage uniform with four stars sparkling on the collar points. Today was no exception. She wondered if he wore a uniform to bed.

"Good morning, Mr. Ambassador," Penfant said. "I have Major O'Shane with me, listening on speakerphone."

Penfant's greeting jolted Jenny as she began to sweat.

"Thanks, General," the ambassador replied. "Good morning, Major. I don't have much time, so let me get to the point. Minister Kaliq called me personally and strongly objected to your statement that terrorists attacked the U.S. Riyadh compound. He restated the Saudis' official position, claiming that it wasn't terrorists, but feuding Bedouin tribes. The attack was aimed at a visiting tribal sheik."

Taking an audible breath, the voice continued, "Although we have intelligence that contradicts the Saudis, the State Department has chosen to ignore the disagreement to keep our relations positive. We don't need some uninformed maverick scraping the scab off this issue."

"You're right, Mr. Ambassador," Penfant responded. "We apologize. We shouldn't have offered an opinion on the matter. I can assure you that it won't happen again." He looked at Jenny with narrowed eyes that dared her to contradict him.

She nodded her head. "Yes, sir," she said. She felt her own eyes widen. Penfant and the ambassador disconnected.

Jenny started talking as soon as the CG hung up the phone. "Sir, I, uhhh ... I can explain. Those comments are taken out of context. Kaliq was rude and ..."

Penfant's face paled and his lips thinned. In that second, Jenny realized that the pressures of command gave him zero patience for junior officers when he thought that they screwed up. It was apparent that he wasn't going to cut her any slack.

"Save it, O'Shane. Minister Kaliq called me too. He's the Crown Prince's number two man. In his eyes, you violated Muslim custom. In their world, women don't disagree with men in a public setting. He was embarrassed. And don't offer your personal opinions to high ranking Saudi officials about circumstances in this country. Use that bright mind of yours before opening your big mouth. You can't have *everything* your way. Now get your ass out of my office!"

Penfant turned his back and began speaking on another telephone before she could respond. Her "Yes, sir" went unheard as she saluted and left the office. She overheard a snatch of the conversation. Something about sex slaves, but it was white noise. She was too chagrined at being chewed out to pay much heed.

Chapter Three

Ten hours after being reamed out in his office, Jenny escorted Penfant from the Central Command headquarters building with three members of his Military Police protection detail. They were headed to the Saudi reception.

She watched heat waves ripple off the airport tarmac from the supercharged desert sun. Wind blew. Not a breeze, but a sand-filled wind—a gritty-tooth, gummy-lipped, eye-stinging kind of desert blow.

The boiling late afternoon heat, the unrelenting wind and an inexplicable foreboding caused her stomach to churn. Jenny felt as if she were about to implode.

Penfant didn't utter a word. She wanted to tell him he looked good in his suit and tie, but his demeanor made it clear that he was still angry. She'd hoped he might offer some comment about her outfit. She felt stylish in a modest full-length green and gold skirt, topped by a long-sleeve white satin blouse and a matching headscarf. If he noticed, she couldn't tell.

On arrival at the royal palace in Riyadh, Jenny was dazzled by the sparkle of diamonds, rubies, emeralds and gold hanging off the highrollers. Although she wanted to gawk open-mouthed at the ostentatious display, she was even more astonished by the palace decor.

Thick Persian carpets; bright, intricate wall tapestries in various lengths hanging from fifty-foot ceilings; aromas of exotic Middle Eastern spices; servants dressed in white pantaloons and red embroidered vests waving ostrich-feather fans. Despite the beautiful people and stunning décor, Jenny felt even more anxious when she escorted Penfant to a short flight of stairs leading down into the main reception hall.

Saudi security arrangements were far less than she expected. "Only ten men in here," she muttered to herself, counting the visible guards from her vantage point at the top of the stairs. Kaliq had clearly implied more. Also, there was no central entry point for weapons detection. Nor did the Saudi guards display weapons; they carried ceremonial swords.

Combined with the fact that she'd seen no traffic checkpoints during the drive to the palace, Jenny vacillated between being flabbergasted and being worried sick. She bit a thumbnail, her mind reeling. Surveying the hundreds of diplomats and civilians in the ornate hall, she kicked herself for being bullied by Kaliq into decisions that were contrary to her better judgment. *I should have insisted on a larger detail ... demanded an opportunity to review the overall security plan.* She gritted her teeth at her own naiveté.

Seeing the security arrangements, or lack thereof, Jenny was now glad she'd ignored Kaliq's instructions about being armed. Her Beretta was strapped to her inner thigh and a throwing knife was holstered behind her neck.

It was only a minor victory in the scheme of things. Penfant's safety was her prime concern and given the poor security, the potential for failure felt real. Her gut knotted at the thought.

They crossed an arched threshold into the main reception hall. Penfant's arrival caused a stir among the guests. Several stared. Jenny detected more than one look that was less than friendly.

Crown Prince Fahd greeted Penfant as a longtime friend, and seemed oblivious to any hostility. He hugged Penfant and kissed him on both cheeks. "Allah has indeed smiled on us by sending you, General," Fahd said. He held his hand, pulling him toward an area that was set up for a receiving line to introduce Penfant as the guest of honor.

Jenny had been briefed on the Crown Prince. Fahd was next in succession to be crowned king, an event that appeared more imminent every day as the health of the current king continued to deteriorate. Fahd was the antithesis of his father—U.S. friendly, and a charismatic, popular leader. He appeared carefree with a ready smile.

His leanings toward increasing democracy and improving women's rights were unpopular among the upper levels of the Royal Family, and his initiatives weren't popular among the Saudi Muslim community either. Jollying his guests to begin the receiving line, Jenny detected little concern in Fahd's behavior. "Come, come. You all know what to do," he said, speaking with a chuckle. His voice was naturally loud and penetrating.

Obediently, all the other guests lined up to be introduced. Jenny crowded close by. She knew that she was irritating Penfant, but she was determined to do her job even at the risk of being irritating. She posted the other members of the protection detail to help take the measure of every guest.

All was smooth until the end of the line. A fat, disheveled man approached. Sweat dripped off his round black face in rivulets. He was the only guest in uniform—a long-sleeve tan jacket with matching trousers. Wet stains seeped out from under the arms. His rumpled jacket front bulged from a large potbelly and was covered in medals, badges, cords and colored ribbons. He was introduced as the Sudanese Army Chief of Staff.

"So you're the mighty General," he said. He appeared drunk and was slurring his words. Mean, beady eyes focused on Penfant. "You wouldn't be so big in my country."

Jenny tensed, instantly alert. She stepped in front of Penfant. Others on the detail heard the exchange and moved in, surrounding him.

Kaliq was also nearby. He pushed the Sudanese away, saying, "Come, General. We have some interesting artifacts for you to view." A man in front of the General, who had been introduced by the name of Esquedas, assisted in pulling the big man onward. Kaliq, Esquedas and the Sudanese struggled briefly, pushing and shoving.

"You're not helping," Jenny heard Esquedas say in a hoarse whisper.

As he and the Sudanese general moved away, they both gave a backward glance, locking eyes with Jenny. Esquedas's look appeared curious, as if he was assessing her for some reason. The General, on the other hand, licked his fat lips, wetting them in an obscenelike gesture, and then he grinned. Jenny's temper flared. *I wish you would try something with me, Porky!* Jenny eyed the big Sudanese until he disappeared into the crowd.

Chapter Four

Prince Fahd ignored the disruption and made a short, eloquent speech thanking the CG for his commitment to regional security.

He ended with, "General Penfant, as I've said before, you are a blessing from Allah."

Afterward, over polite applause, the Crown Prince added, "Come. Let us enjoy a meal together."

Jenny followed the dignitaries when Fahd led them into another ornate hall. Inside men and women were shown to separate waist-high tables. Unnerved at first by the separation from Penfant, she was relieved when she saw that his table was within arm's reach.

A Saudi dressed as a maître d' stepped up and welcomed the guests. "Ladies and gentlemen, you undoubtedly noticed that there are no chairs, plates, napkins or silverware. Although unconventional, this meal will be served in the tradition of our Bedouin forefathers. I promise you a fun-filled, enjoyable meal.

"On the tables before you are three entrées that are specialties of our culture: pit-baked goat, shish kebab and stuffed grape leaves. Each entrée is layered over a bed of rice and vegetables infused overnight in goat's milk."

During the maître d's introduction, servants circulated offering Jenny and the others bowls of scented water and towels to wash their hands. All who wanted were provided plastic aprons similar to those used in U. S. restaurants for eating lobster.

As the guests were attending to preparations, the host said, "Let me demonstrate how you will be eating dinner tonight." He pulled off a small chunk of goat meat with his right hand, dug the hand into the thick mounds of rice and vegetables, and with one hand, formed a ball of food. To appreciative "ohhs and ahhhs," he then popped the morsel into his mouth.

Jenny couldn't help but grin when he explained the Middle Eastern custom of eating with only the right hand. "For Muslims, it is considered impolite to eat food with the left hand." To a few embarrassed twitters and shared glances between guests, he further explained, "We use the left hand to cleanse ourselves after using the bathroom."

After the guests quieted, he explained more procedure. "It is also customary for you to exchange places between other guests at your tables so that you may have samples of each entrée." He paused, and then added, "Those are your instructions, ladies and gentlemen. Enjoy your meal."

Jenny gradually relaxed, watching the guests having a good time. The Saudi guards appeared attentive and her own detail was alert.

She didn't normally eat at official functions, but it was obvious that the Saudis expected her to participate. *Don't want to do anything else to piss 'em off,* she thought, visually surveying the room. *What the hell.* She grabbed a handful of rice and vegetables and braced her mouth for a dose of hot and spicy. Instead, she was surprised with tastes of bay leaves, basil and something similar to cilantro. The spices were blended with rice, onion and sweet peppers in a delicious combination.

She next pulled off a piece of goat meat. It wasn't gamy or greasy as she'd anticipated. It reminded her of the moist, dark turkey meat she loved on Thanksgiving. With that introduction, even keeping one eye on Penfant, she managed to eat her fair share of the meal.

As fun as the experience was, Jenny noticed one woman

who didn't seem to be enjoying herself. Her eyes were downcast and she barely ate. Only a sad and beautiful olive-skinned face showed out of a light-brown silk hijab worn over a fancy black, embroidered abaya.

The woman moved to Jenny's side. She whispered out of the side of her mouth, "You American?"

Caught with a mouthful of food, Jenny could only nod her head. Before she could say anything, the woman was jostled away by the other guests sampling the various entrées.

Jenny let it pass, and a few minutes later gratefully accepted a wet towel from a white-coated servant to wash her hands. Sipping on a glass of iced pineapple juice that the server also provided, she used the opportunity to again scan the room to verify security conditions. All seemed calm.

Then the woman reappeared. She looked at Jenny with mournful, saucer-sized brown eyes brimming with tears. She said in broken English, "Me Italian. Somalia ... help. Please?"

Interrupting the Italian's plea, the Crown Prince's voice boomed out, "Everyone. Follow me. I have a surprise. We have after-dinner entertainment arranged especially for General Penfant. Another area is prepared." He started to lead the main party away.

Jenny felt torn between staying with Penfant and seeking out the anguished Italian. She followed close behind Penfant, glancing back to see the woman. She was gone. Jenny surveyed the room. On the edge of the crowd she spotted the brown hijab. The woman was being spirited away by a fat, dark-skinned man. He wore a tan uniform—the Sudanese general.

The Italian glanced back once and then disappeared out the doors. *What was that all about?*

Jenny flashed back to a briefing by the task force commander who'd led the takedown of the Somalian pirates. He'd described a small prison filled with women and children that his team had uncovered. *Italian ... Somalia ... there's a connection.*

She shrugged off the fleeting thought. *Stay in your lane.* She returned her mind to the business at hand. The distraction had caused Jenny to fall behind the dignitaries, so she hurried to catch up. Prince Fahd led them into a giant white tent erected behind the palace. Fahd said, gesturing toward a raised platform, "Have a seat, General. I've invited a troupe of Pakistani performers who had an unexpected opening on their schedule. They've been entertaining U.S. forces in Kuwait."

Kaliq stepped in front of Jenny when she moved to join Penfant on the raiser. Kaliq had a pleased, superior smile on his face. "This is for the Royal Party, young lady." He pointed to nearby bleachers. "Your seat is over there."

Jenny gave him a sharp elbow in the ribs, shouldering her way onto the platform. Signaling one of her MP team members to follow, she ignored Kaliq's glare and shook off his hand when he grabbed to restrain her.

She moved close on the heels of General Penfant so that Kaliq couldn't stop her without embarrassing the Crown Prince. She sighed in relief when Fahd ignored the jostling staff and motioned for the Pakistani performance to begin.

Standing to one side, leaning against the rail of the platform, Jenny watched the troupe begin a Cirque du Soleil-style event. Trapeze artists, contortionists, magicians, jugglers and clowns all performed. Their outfits were the brightest colors of the rainbow, and one daredevil act followed another. Acrobats soared through the air. A strong beat of music filled the tent. Flashing lights lit every corner. The entertainers soon captivated the audience.

It was hard not to watch the show, but Jenny's eyes were drawn to three men circling among the troupe members. They were out of sync and on the fringes. They were dressed like the performers, but not participating.

Alarmed, Jenny scanned the tented arena to determine if there were other hangers-on. There were none she could identify. She refocused on the three men.

Their eyes fixed on the dignitary area. The men did not have entertainers' professional smiles.

She raised her arm to speak into her cuff microphone to alert the other staff.

It was then that she noticed a glint of steel under the robes of the nearest man. Instead of the simple alert she'd intended, she yelled into the mike, "Gun!! Gun!!"

She launched herself at Penfant, who stared at her in disbelief.

Chapter Five

Jenny hit Penfant in the chest with her shoulder in a tackle that she figured any NFL linebacker would take pride in. She didn't count on him grabbing for a handhold to stop his fall. His hands closed on the robes of Crown Prince Fahd.

"What's going—?" she heard.

In a domino effect, Jenny, Penfant and Fahd crashed to the floor; people, cushions and chairs tumbled across the space.

Jenny soon knew she'd guessed right. The three men she'd spotted in the midst of the entertainment troupe had AK-47 assault rifles hidden in their robes. They began firing into the dignitary area over the top of the railing.

Her move surprised the shooters, throwing off their timing. Their first bursts were high and wide. Bullets ripped the air in the space that she'd been standing.

She saw the MP on the platform draw his pistol. The assassins dispensed with him with a quick burst; the soldier's body jerked like a puppet when a line of bullets stitched his midsection. Leveraging her hand and knee against the back of the CG, she drew and threw her knife in one fluid motion. She opted against her pistol to avoid shooting toward the screaming and stampeding spectators.

Even over the sound of the panicked mass, she heard the nearest assailant.

"Nnnnhhh!" he gagged. Her knife was imbedded in his throat.

Jenny rolled away from Penfant and Fahd and yanked her pistol from its holster. The crowd behind the second assassin cleared. Kneeling, she snapped off two rounds.

The man staggered backward, arms flailing as if to catch his balance. He then collapsed with a bullet through an eye and a hole punched in his forehead.

Jenny dove to the platform as a decoy to distract the third assassin, landing awkwardly on her stomach, knocking her windless; her gun hand smacked the floor. The Beretta spun from her grasp.

Breathless, scrambling to retrieve her weapon, Jenny could only watch the rest of the action. In those seconds, movement came into sharper focus.

The muzzle of the third assassin's rifle centered on her chest. She saw his finger squeeze the trigger. The man's mouth twisted in a sneer.

Just as the staccato of automatic-weapon fire echoed once more, Jenny felt a tug on her sleeve and something tear at the waist of her skirt. Splinters from the platform's wooden floor whirled through the air.

In the same instance, she saw Minister Kaliq moving fast. Then she saw a flash of light glittering off the steel blade of his ceremonial sword. Folds of his purple robe danced in the candlelight.

Both forearms of the assassin were severed in a single blow of the sword. The assailant's AK-47 clattered to the platform floor with his dirty hands still clutching the rifle.

"Ahieee!" he screamed a primal sound. Kaliq's sword descended again. The man's head spun from his shoulders. It bounced off the platform railing and rolled to within inches of Jenny's face.

For a gruesome second, lying on the platform, she was face-to-face with the assassin's frozen look of agony. His mouth opened wide in mid-scream; his pale lips locked in a grimace;

his stained, crooked teeth exposed.

Jenny recoiled in disgust. She barely swallowed back the gorge that rose in her throat. Her hands couldn't find a purchase on the platform's surface, slipping and sliding in a pool of the man's blood.

His dying heart had pumped fountains onto the platform from his neck and severed arms. Revulsion intensified. She became frenetic trying to scuttle away.

A shadow crossed her vision. She glanced up, half-expecting to find something else to add to the macabre scene. Instead, the Crown Prince was standing above her.

She'd never seen him up-close. In that split second, she registered a handsome, kind face. A crinkle of laugh creases around his eyes deepened when he smiled at her from under his flowing white silk shora headdress.

Appearing unfazed, he ignored the blood that seeped up the embroidered, floor-length hem of his purple silk dishdasha robe when it brushed over the pooled blood.

He took Jenny's arm and helped her to stand. She knew that his gesture was monumental in the traditions of the Kingdom. The law of the land was that the Crown Prince never touched a woman in public, let alone an infidel foreigner. She was even more amazed that he used the loose sleeve of his garment to help wipe the blood from her hands.

"You saved my life, Major. Thank you. I'm in your debt," he said to her over the noise of the scrambling spectators. He had a majestic charisma; a pair of intelligent jade-green eyes drew her into their depths.

His calm, regal carriage helped Jenny regain her senses. She lowered her eyes and bowed her head in respect and appreciation for his gesture. *Do I curtsy or what?*

"You're welcome, Your Highness," she said instead. "But I think we should head back to our compound. Would you excuse us?" She looked at Penfant, who nodded. He'd taken a hard fall and had just risen to his feet.

"Of course, young lady, I understand. *Assalumu alaikum,*" Crown Prince Fahd responded. "Peace be with you."

"*Wa alaikum assalaam,* Your Highness," she and Penfant answered simultaneously. "May peace also be with you."

Chapter Six

On an Argentinean estancia, Francisco Gutierrez heard the distant chime of a wall clock striking four p.m. He gazed out his office bay windows, watching the early twilight envelop his ranch. He munched on M&M's chocolate peanuts waiting for a report. Lamenting his addiction to the candy, knowing its effect on his already large girth, he was unable to resist the urge when under pressure.

Although he was eagerly anticipating a call, he jumped when his phone rang. "Hola," he answered. As expected, it was his agent reporting from Saudi Arabia about the assassination attempt.

Gutierrez flopped into his chair in shock when he heard the report of failure. He detected terror in the man's voice; the cost of failure in the criminal network in which they worked was well known. The Saudi relayed the bad news.

"Our team is dead. The O'Shane woman was a whirling dervish ... she wasn't supposed to be armed. It was as if she knew we were coming. Please tell El Toro I did everything I could. She's possessed." Gutierrez didn't let the Saudi finish. Slamming the receiver down, he faintly heard, "... she's a witch."

Pacing back and forth across an exquisite parquet floor, he puffed on an expensive Cuban cigar he'd planned to smoke as a celebration. Now it tasted funereal. A bottle of champagne in a nearby bucket was going flat. Utter failure was not only unexpected, it was a disaster. Hundreds of thousands of dollars spent hiring and training the team and bribing officials—wasted. He grabbed another handful of M&M's.

"The hell with the Saudi," he said, muttering to himself. "How do I explain away the collapse of what was supposed to be a perfect plan?" The cigar burned halfway before he sighed in resignation.

He sat in a high-backed, handcrafted chair behind his red oak desk and brushed at a speck of dust on its spotless, polished top. His fingers felt slippery with sweat dialing the phone. He noticed a tremble in his hand when he knocked ashes off the cigar into a crystal ashtray. He hung up. *Come on hombre ... steady*, he tried to reassure himself.

For a moment, Gutierrez reflected on the man whose number he'd dialed—the man known as El Toro. He considered the nickname well deserved. The man brought new definition to the word meanspirited, a replica of what one would envision of a rutting bull. The slightest perceived insult or provocation could throw El Toro into a spit-spraying rage; his cruelty in dealing with enemies was renowned.

Shuddering, Gutierrez remembered another man who'd failed El Toro; staked spread-eagled on his back, naked over a giant anthill, honey dripped in his eyes and between his legs.

Flashing back over the many years he'd helped El Toro become capo de capo of an international crime syndicate, murders, extortion and bribery were commonplace. As capo, El Toro had accumulated massive wealth and power—first in Argentina, and then worldwide. Drug cartels in Mexico and Colombia reported to him. Illicit diamond mines in the Congo and weapons smuggling into virtually every continent brought enormous profits.

"Come on, get your head together," Gutierrez said out loud, briskly wiping his hands on his trousers. "He won't take it out on you. Not with your job." Human trafficking and the sex-slave trade was a current mainstay of the syndicate's operations.

Profits were astronomical, and its management was Gutierrez's primary responsibility.

Forming the assassination plan was a secondary mission: Infiltrate the Pakistani entertainment troupe, and include the show in the itinerary for the CENTCOM commander's visit to Riyadh. Everything had worked to perfection, except ...

"Bullshit," he muttered, dialing El Toro's number. "The man doesn't know the word mercy. I'll be lucky to live through the day."

Standing while the security system engaged and the number connected, he sucked on more candy as he stared again out the large bay window. During his pacing the sun had set, and he now watched shadows darken distant mountains. He wondered if his father, who'd built and willed him the giant estate, was spinning in his grave given his son's chosen profession.

He heard the phone ring only once before being answered. There was no greeting.

"You're an incompetent fool!" El Toro screamed. "I don't understand how men with automatic weapons could miss their target from a range of twenty feet! Where did you find those buffoons?"

"El Toro ... Señor, por favor." Gutierrez heard a whine come into his voice. It made him furious that he couldn't better control himself. He was an established crime boss himself, surrounded by an army of hired thugs on a secluded ranch. But, he was unnerved. How could El Toro know?

"Señor, no one could have anticipated this result. Those men were the best that money could buy. It was a good plan ... perfect place. I'll find out what happened."

"You idiot! I don't want excuses. I want results." El Toro paused to take a breath. "I told you that this was not someone to trifle with. I knew I should have taken a more direct role. I thought I could depend on you."

"Por favor, El Toro. I am your man. I'll make other arrangements, and I won't fail you again. I know this is important to you. I will succeed." Sweat formed on his brow.

The voice on the phone chilled him to the bone. "You'd better not miss again, or the next death will be yours. The hundreds of gauchos you have on your estancia won't be enough to protect you. And tell your friend in Saudi that he has a choice. His way or my way. He's got twenty-four hours."

Gutierrez had no doubt that his threats were real. A picture of the spread-eagled man flashed through his memory again. "I understand," he said. *This man is the Devil.*

Silence followed. The static on the long-distance line buzzed in his ear. The receiver slipped in his wet hand.

"Fine. I'll await hearing of your next plan." Gutierrez heard a dial tone and breathed a sigh of relief. He'd felt the cold breeze of death on his neck. He pulled the bowl of M&M's closer.

Chapter Seven

Jenny O'Shane and General Penfant sped away from the reception in Riyadh in the CENTCOM command Humvee toward the compound at the King Khalid International Airport. The evening quiet was blasted by flashing lights and wailing sirens from two Saudi police motorcycle escorts. Jenny also heard the whoop-whoop of a helicopter circling overhead.

She alerted the main security force at the airport compound over the Humvee radio. "Code Black," she said into the microphone. "We're en route to your location."

By the time the vehicle squealed through the airport gates, the entire security force was deployed in armored Humvees around the lighted cantonment area. Sharpshooters lined rooftops. A sandbagged bunker blockaded the entry. Everyone wore Kevlar vests and helmets.

The CG put his hand on Jenny's shoulder when they exited the Humvee. "You lived up to your reputation tonight, O'Shane. Good job. And, what the hell ...?" He was pointing at Jenny's sleeve. "There's fresh blood all over the side of your blouse." A drop dripped off a finger of her hand. "Corpsman!" Penfant yelled.

"Sir, it's a nick on my arm. I thought it was the terrorist's blood. It doesn't even hurt. I ..." She leaned against the side of the Humvee, dizzy, lightheaded and feeling a sting. She didn't realize she'd been hit.

With Penfant beside her, a medic cleaned and bandaged her arm and gave her a shot for the pain. As the shock wore off, she looked around the cantonment area on the airport. Temporary headquarters office buildings were already being disassembled.

"General, given the events, I recommend we move up the departure time. If the bad guys have anymore surprises for us, a change in schedule will screw them up."

Penfant looked at her for a moment and said, "Good point. You get some rest. I'll tell the Chief."

Two hours later, after she'd cleaned up and changed into uniform, she was in Admiral Jim Bryan's office. He was her boss, first in her chain of command. More importantly, he was the Central Command chief of staff. Called "Chief," he was a rail-thin, tall, grey-haired Navy rear admiral. She ventured that the rumors were correct that he'd been handpicked for the job by Penfant, a fellow Naval Academy graduate. Bryan had chosen Navy; Penfant, the Marines.

She was in Bryan's office intending to brief him on her security plan for the CG's departure early the next morning. It was routine for them to review arrival and departure plans, and with the recent assassination attempt, she felt this event deserved special attention.

"I thought you were supposed to take some time?" the Chief asked with a raised eyebrow.

"Sir, I got a nap. I'm fine."

The eyebrow arched higher. "I think the Commanding General meant something more than a twenty-minute nap." His retort was interrupted by a voice on the intercom.

"Sorry to bother you, Chief," his assistant said. "It's a call from Minister Kaliq. I thought you'd want to take it."

Picking up his phone, Bryan said, "Your Excellency, how are you and the Crown Prince?"

Bryan listened for a few seconds and then responded, "We're fine, thank you." There was another pause, and then he said, "Yes, sir. The soldier is in serious condition, but his prognosis is good. He's been evacuated to the Army hospital in Landstuhl, Germany."

After listening for a shorter period, Bryan said, "Yes, sir. She happens to be right in front of me. She says she's fine too. Of course I can make her available. Wa alaikum assalaam."

On arrival at the palace, she girded herself for a "royal" ass chewing for carrying weapons to the reception. It hadn't helped her uneasy feelings when the driver took a circuitous route back to the palace that added at least ten minutes to the drive.

She noticed several other U.S. military Humvees parked nearby. *That's strange—this time of night?*

Kaliq appeared at the main entrance. His demeanor was changed, and he even smiled at her.

"Good evening," he said. "Thank you for returning on short notice. Please follow me." He led Jenny down a long corridor covered by a thick red carpet and lined on both sides with what she estimated to be a hundred soldiers in dress uniform: green vests stitched with gold thread, high-buttoned white satin shirts, and pantaloons bloused loosely from buff-colored combat boots.

The soldiers were also in ceremonial-green turban headdresses, and had bright, glistening swords drawn, held in the overhead honor position of present arms. Jenny was guided under the arch of swords.

Kaliq led her into a large room. Except for a spotlight in its center, the entire room was lit by candles. On a table standing alone and spotlighted were a medal and a dagger in a jeweled scabbard. Crown Prince Fahd was standing beside the table. He picked up a large medallion attached to a red, white and blue pendant. The gold and bronze disk sparkled in the candlelight.

Admiral Bryan and several members of her MP security team stepped out of the shadows to stand beside her. *What the hell?*

"Please come forward and participate in a small ceremony with me," Fahd said. When Jenny was close, he draped the medallion around her neck. "This is the Saudi Arabian Medal of Honour. It is awarded for deeds of great bravery. This medal has never been awarded to a person not of Saudi Arabia. But this one is yours." He held up a hand to silence her when Jenny started to comment.

Fahd then picked up the scabbard off the table and

unsheathed the dagger. He drew its sharp edge across his wrist. A thin line of blood was visible.

Motioning for her to move closer, he gripped her wrist and made a similar small cut. Jenny winced at the tingling pinprick. But Fahd's grip was firm, and she sensed the serious solemnity of the occasion. She resisted the natural urge to pull back.

Without further hesitation, Fahd pressed his wrist against hers. He said, "I know small boys do this in your country in meaningless games. However, in Saudi Arabia, this is a ceremony handed down through generations of Bedouin ancestors. For us it symbolizes that you are now of royal blood."

He then hugged her and handed her the dagger and scabbard. Although beautiful, Jenny could tell by feel and weight that the dagger was perfectly balanced, crafted by a master. It was a throwing knife.

"We are now brother and sister," the Prince continued. "Your possession of this ancient dagger indicates that you have all the rights and privileges of a princess of the Kingdom of Saudi Arabia."

She was stunned. Tears welled up in her eyes. "Thank you so much, Your Highness. This gesture ... I don't deserve—"

"Nonsense, young lady," interrupted Kaliq. "We believe you saved the life of our Crown Prince. The royal family feels honor-bound to recognize your bravery. I humbly apologize for not being more attentive to your suggestions."

He bowed deeply and smiled at her. "Remember that in this matter, the Crown Prince commands. You are now a royal princess. Here is my business card. Call that number anytime, day or night if we can ever help you. And please, call me Allaweh."

She heard applause, and her teammates swarmed around to shake her hand.

Chapter Eight

Jenny stood at the top of the stairway leading into the CENTCOM commander's airplane parked at the King Khalid airport. She'd only had six hours to craft their departure plan. She stifled a yawn of exhaustion. The power nap the previous evening had been the sum of her rest for two days. Her arm was throbbing from the assassin's bullet.

She spoke to her sniper team leader through her earpiece radio. "Tiger One, what's your status?"

After a brief pause, she heard her radio call sign in her ear, "Tiger Six, both sniper teams are in place. If anyone pays a call tonight it'll cost 'em big time."

"Roger," Jenny responded. "Tiger Two, report status." She heard a prompt response from her second team leader.

"Roger Six. The airfield perimeter is secure. There are Saudi guards every ten feet along the fence and my guys are in six roving vehicles. We're covered here."

She didn't think there was much more they could do. She spoke into the radio one more time, "Transport one, two and three, standby."

"Roger, Roger, Roger," she heard in quick succession.

Jenny walked the length of the cabin in the specially modified Air Force EC-135 one last time to verify only the aircrew was on board.

Jenny recalled her orientation on the aircraft when she was assigned to CENTCOM. The EC-135 is normally a midair refueling aircraft. The specially configured version for the CENTCOM commander can still perform limited refueling, but instead of fuel tanks, most of the interior is configured as a VIP office/communications/command center/conference room and as sleep areas for passengers. Its mission is long-distance transport of senior military and civilian leaders.

She found the steward in the galley. She said, "Put the coffee on. Backpack's on his way." Backpack was the security code name for Penfant.

She stepped back onto the top of the stairway and said into her hand mike, "Convoy teams, on my count. Five, four, three, two, one, go!"

On her command "go," Jenny watched from the stairway. In the distance, three identical vehicles emerged from different airplane hangars nearby the CENTCOM headquarters. Each vehicle was an up-armored Humvee with a manned fifty-caliber machine gun. Two Apache helicopters lifted off and began circling the airport, spotlights splaying over empty spaces.

The Humvees traveled from the hangars to the headquarters in seconds. They squealed to a stop in front.

Six men exited the building all dressed in Marine Camouflage Uniform, and outfitted in high-collared Kevlar vests and combat helmets; they were unrecognizable running to the vehicles.

The Humvees accelerated toward the plane at a breakneck pace, hardly pausing to load their passengers. They braked adjacent to the airplane stairway with tires and wheel wells boiling with smoke. The six men jumped from the Humvees and ran onto the plane. One of them was Penfant. Another was Bryan.

Jenny said into her hand mike, "Nice job, Tiger team. Stand down. Regroup at the assembly area. Load on the transport aircraft, and prepare for departure."

As she hustled across the threshold of the EC-135 doorway, the stairway was pulled away, and the plane started its roll. She helped the steward secure the door. He then headed toward the galley.

Jenny moved to do the same, but instead bumped into the large frame of Backpack's new aide-de-camp, Colonel Jack Everett.

She looked up to make eye contact. Her nose only reached the third button on his shirt.

Besides being tall, Everett was also wide, with extremely broad shoulders. His face had a chiseled, Slavic appearance.

She'd been told that he'd graduated number two in his class at West Point, and his career was on a fast track. He'd been selected for the aide job after being commander of an airmobile brigade in Afghanistan. At the moment, it was clear that he was pissed at her. *Guess I'm about to find out why.*

He said, "Major, if you ever take it upon yourself to change the CG's schedule again without checking with me first, I'm going to be an unhappy camper. Understand?"

Jenny tried not to let her face betray her true feelings, but she could feel her lip curl slightly. "Yes, sir … I understand." She kept her voice even.

She felt the plane speeding down the runway. She knew it would rotate up at any second. She was wedged against a seat back and the door handle and was prepared for the sharp turn. Everett wasn't. *Warn him or not? Ahh, screw it. Serves the dunce right.*

The plane began a steep climb and bank. Gravitational force took over. Everett tumbled backward and bounced against a bulkhead and one of the conference tables. He fell into the first starboard seat. Feeling some guilt, Jenny moved to help him.

He wasn't having any and pushed her hand away. Wincing in pain, he pointed to the seat across from his, "Sit over there." Jenny sat and fastened the seat belt.

Everett did the same. He punched the intercom button to the galley and said, "Bring me some ice water when we level out." Turning his attention back to Jenny, he continued, "Major, the change caught me off-guard … no notice to me at all until departure time. How about keeping me in the loop in the future. I might have some suggestions."

Jenny was running on fumes and her patience was thin. She

also sensed a condescending attitude that was annoying. He might be the new kid on the block, but that attitude had to go. Her voice went up an octave.

Leaning forward in her seat, she said, "Colonel, you just arrived yesterday. You weren't at the reception. Men were killed. The departure plan was impromptu and a rush job. If you—"

She clipped her response as Admiral Bryan moved into a seat across the aisle from her's. She felt a blush percolate up her neck and face, embarrassed that he'd witnessed their exchange. But she pushed herself back into her seat, her body language conveying her angst at Everett's attitude.

Bryan eyed her folded arms and clenched jaw and glanced at Everett's reddening face. He asked in a neutral tone, "Do you guys think you could ratchet it down? Backpack is trying to catch some shuteye."

Then he turned to Everett and said, "Jack, you should know that General Penfant and I think O'Shane's doing a bang-up job. She averted a disaster a few hours ago.

"And the idea to change the schedule was a good one from a security standpoint. You weren't info'd on the change because you're new and not in the loop yet." He paused until he got a nod of acknowledgement from Everett.

"More importantly," Bryan continued, "we need to realize that yesterday's attack took major pre-planning. Given that, we're going to change scheduling procedures. The CG's calendar will go with less-advertised planning. That will only add to an already high-stress level. Knowing that, let's try harder to keep things civil among his personal staff. Understood?"

Jenny's anger dissipated listening to Bryan. She responded with a quick, "Yes, sir."

Everett wasn't quite as prompt, but gave a good political smile and said, "Of course, Chief. I was just giving O'Shane some coaching."

He turned his eyes toward Jenny, his look anything but pleasant. She said nothing and returned his gaze with a steady look of her own.

Bryan ignored the continued tension and said to Jenny, "Let's go get a cup of coffee and review the security for landing in Maryland."

He headed toward the galley. Jenny unbuckled and started to join him. Everett gripped her arm and whispered, "At least try to give me a heads-up next time."

Jenny leaned close to his ear. Speaking as quietly, she said, "Of course, Colonel. But you're hurting my arm. Please don't put your hands on me again."

"Sorry already," Everett said with little apparent sincerity. But his head cocked. A dim light of respect seemed to be reflected in his face; perhaps he detected a warrior ethos he could identify with. He nodded a fraction and loosened his grip. "Don't push your luck. Your Taekwondo black belt and those kickboxing exercises you do most mornings mean—"

"Coming, O'Shane?" Bryan asked.

She pulled her arm free without further comment and followed him to the galley.

"Steer clear of Everett for a few days," Bryan said as he poured a cup of coffee. "He's still very new and has some rough edges. For now, get some rest. The steward made up the starboard settee."

As an afterthought, he added, "Here's a report I'd like your take on. It'll be a good sleep potion."

Jenny nodded, asleep on her feet. Stretching out on the settee, she started to glance through the report. It was titled "Slavery in the U.S.—Fact or Urban Legend." An INTERPOL investigator named Tavares had authored it. *What does this have to do with me?*

Chapter Nine

Francisco Gutierrez stood on the wraparound porch of the main house of his Argentine estancia. The sprawling fifteen-thousand-square-foot, three-story mansion was built on a rise that overlooked the western reaches of the ranch, abutting low hills edging the Andes Mountains. Afternoon breezes blew through the pampas grass that stretched for miles. The undulation of the tall green stalks reminded Gutierrez of the rise and fall of ocean waters.

Two gauchos on pinto horses crested a distant hill driving a small herd of cattle toward a collection corral. This view of his ranch at work usually brought Gutierrez peace of mind. Not today.

He was still stunned by the news from his Saudi agent and the subsequent tongue lashing from El Toro. A ring of his desk phone jangled his already frayed nerves. He saw the blinking green light through the study window that indicated it was his secure line.

He rushed inside. "Hola," he answered, hoping it wasn't El Toro with another dose of venom. It wasn't. He breathed a sigh of relief as he heard from his southeastern U.S. sector manager who reported meeting his quota again. Combined with an earlier report of success from the northeast, his day brightened considerably.

Gutierrez dialed the secure number for El Toro. Some good news for a change. *He'll want to know.* His palms started sweating. He shook his head in irritation. "Why am I so intimidated?"

After only two rings, he heard, "Hola?"

"Buenos días, El Toro. ¿Cómo estás?"

"You don't care how I am. Tell me why you called. I've better things to do than pass the time of day."

Gutierrez wanted to say, "You're a horse's ass." Of course he didn't say that. Instead, he said, "Sí, señor. I called to inform you that all pick-ups for the eastern U.S. are complete. We even picked up the special requests for our Cuban friends."

"Ahhh, that is good. I thought you might have difficulty. That will make them happy, which is important to us all. By the way, my new passport is causing hardly a glance. I'm sorry I waited so long to use it."

"It's just as well, señor. We needed the time to establish your bona fides and let the plastic surgery heal. You're now a married, successful businessman. No one remembers an obscure prison break in the backwaters of Argentina."

"True. That was some of your best work. However, we need to remain alert. We've been fortunate so far. What about the condition of the new merchandise?"

"Good," Gutierrez answered. "In fact, I'm told that one operative disobeyed your orders. He paid with his life."

"Well, killing isn't always the answer, but we receive a premium for unblemished merchandise. It's our trademark, and it's one of the key reasons for customer satisfaction. The previous eastern sector leader didn't understand, and it's why I gave you that temporary responsibility. Maybe if he'd been more careful with that girl in Aruba ..."

"Comprendo, señor," Gutierrez answered. He understood completely. *You enjoyed every minute*, he couldn't help but think. *You cut him with that little knife of yours.*

"We need to find a replacement sector leader," El Toro continued in a dismissive tone. "But that's for another time.

What about the other sectors?"

"The European report is due tomorrow and the western U.S. the day after. I'll call you."

"Bien. Keep emphasizing clean merchandise. And don't mingle resources. Separation of activities remains paramount for security."

"It will be as you say, El Toro. This operation has worked like clockwork for two years. Our last container transport ship was launched from Rosario two weeks ago, fully modified."

"Excellent. But overconfidence is unhealthy, my friend. I'm concerned about the European sector. Their technique is unnerving our sources. Inform the leader that I'm watching him."

"Sí, señor. The ex-KGB and East German Stassi agents on the snatch teams are, uhhh ..."

"Impatient. The network that provides information to the Women's Resources organization does so because they believe that we will help. Rushing to grab the identified targets too soon puts the whole operation at risk."

"I'll get right on it, señor."

"Fine. On a different subject, you know I'm going to D.C. tomorrow?"

"Sí, señor. I have that on your calendar."

Four thousand miles north of the Argentinean estancia, a derelict trawler sat docked. Paint and rust flaked from its sides in equal amounts. The dock was located in an isolated waterway off Tampa Bay.

Two things were invisible to the idle observer: girls being held captive below deck and a pair of new four-hundred-horsepower Cummins diesels in the rebuilt engine room.

"Shush, Isabella," a girl named Crystal said over the soft sobs of her bunkmate. "We must be strong. We'll get out of this."

Seventeen-year-old Crystal Tavares spoke with more bravery than she felt. She was petrified. She was from New Mexico—a runaway trying to escape her parents. The battle had been ongoing for her entire senior year of high school—her dad insisting she go to college at the University of New Mexico in Albuquerque. She wanted to go to New York City to follow her dream of becoming a model. Now it seemed trivial. Her mind screamed *Daddyyyy! Please find me. I'm so sorry.*

Another nearby girl whispered, "You two keep it down. We don't need another visit."

The girl was speaking about their last warning. A man named Frankel had squeezed unannounced into the boat's tiny hold. He warned the fifteen girls crammed on bunks stacked floor-to-ceiling against the bulkheads to stay quiet.

He'd said, "I warned you to keep quiet. I won't tell you again." He'd then placed a stun gun high in the hairlines of two of the girls and pulled the trigger. Neither made a sound as they convulsed from the shock. Thirty minutes later they still quietly groaned in pain.

Chapter Ten

Jenny stepped off the CENTCOM command aircraft and stretched. It had been a long flight—nonstop from Riyadh to Washington D.C. Even with the VIP accommodations on board, the journey was wearing. Admiral Bryan joined her at the bottom of the plane's stairway.

"Well, this isn't exactly as we planned it," he said, stretching and touching his toes, blinking in the bright cobalt sky. "Getting diverted from Andrews put a few wrinkles in things."

"Yes, sir. Do we know what happened yet?" Jenny asked.

"Apparently the Andrews base commander thought that there was a credible bomb threat and canceled all flights in and out. So they diverted us to Reagan National. The transport aircraft with the security team should be here in a few minutes."

"Yes, sir. I heard our aircrew talking about them being twenty minutes out."

"Good," he said, handing her some papers. "Once they gas up the plane and change aircrews, send them on to MacDill. These orders should help smooth the way for you to make the necessary arrangements."

"Yes, sir." She glanced through the paperwork. It gave her

authority to use any and all military resources necessary to move the team to their destination. "Wow. I guess this will do the trick."

"General Penfant didn't want anybody to give you grief. There's a lot of big brass in this area, and they won't take kindly to a lowly Army major telling them what to do. Try not to piss anybody off. Please.

"Also, we were informed in the air that he and I are wanted for some meetings in D.C. You'll stay here with us after the protection detail heads out. Colonel Everett has to go back to MacDill to move into his new quarters, so you'll fill in as the CG's aide."

"From what I've seen of Everett so far, that should be easy."

"Knock off the wiseass comments." He gave her a hard look.

"Sorry, sir."

"Pay attention. There's a couple of issues here we wouldn't have at Andrews. The big one is customs. There's a VIP suite that the airport has for dignitaries. They've given us permission to use it for the security team's inspection. Get the luggage and troops through and transferred back onto the plane as quickly as possible. Keep an eye out to be sure customs doesn't hassle the staff. Meet us at the Chairman's quarters on Ft. McNair when you're done."

"Got it, sir. When will we be headed back to MacDill?"

"You'll be traveling back alone. The CG and I both plan to take a few days off with family in the local area after our meetings here. When you get back to MacDill, you take some downtime yourself."

Jenny interrupted his instructions: "Sir, I don't need time off." She got another frigid stare.

"O'Shane, I'm unaccustomed to interruptions from junior officers. Now put a lid on it!"

"Sorry, sir."

"Listen for a change. As I was saying, once you get the team stood down and secure at MacDill, take some time. I saw you twisting and turning in your sleep. And you woke in a cold sweat. It's been a traumatic few days. I want you to make an appointment with the CENTCOM staff psychologist. Any questions?"

"Uhhh ... no, sir. No questions. Time off. Counseling. As soon as the team is secure. Got it, Admiral."

"Dammit, O'Shane," Bryan responded. "I should know that bright mind of yours would twist this. And you can knock off the sarcasm. I meant what I said."

He made eye contact. "You will take at least five days in a row when you return. Spend time with your fiancé. Don't come to the office. Don't call or e-mail any of us. And you will see our staff psychologist before our next overseas trip. Now, tell me you understand my orders."

"Awww, sir. You're taking all the fun out of it."

"Knock it off, O'Shane. You've been working nonstop for over a month. I'm waiting for your answer. In the Navy, you would respond, 'Aye, aye, sir.' That means, 'I understand my orders, and I will comply.'"

Jenny could tell by his arched eyebrow that he was serious. She answered, "Aye, aye, sir."

"Good. I'll look for your leave papers. On a different tack, what did you make of the report I gave you about the slave trade?"

"It was scary. I had no idea that the problem was so extensive, or that the U.S. was a prime source. Illegal immigration seems to be a major contributor to the problem."

"Yeah. But it's the trading in the sex-slave business that has all the attention. It's bad and getting worse. The girl that we think was kidnapped in Aruba about blew the lid off. The whole issue is the subject of one of our meetings in Washington. CENTCOM may play a future role."

"Wow. That's a switch in mission. How would that work?" Jenny asked.

"We're not sure at this point. I'll let you know if it impacts security. For now, get the troops through customs and back on that plane without mishap. See you at McNair."

Fifteen minutes later, Jenny was standing to the side watching members of her MP security team pull their bags off a conveyor belt along one wall of the room. They then lined up for the customs and TSA officers who had temporary stations at counters in the middle. She knew that the process had potential for fireworks in that one arm of law enforcement was inspecting another. Plus it was mixing civilians with military—not always a good scenario.

She'd already pre-briefed her soldiers to avoid letting any resentment translate into a confrontation. "Show a copy of the orders and your ID card. They'll inspect your bags. It's a formality. Keep any comments to yourself."

With the extensive background checks that the team members had to undergo prior to assignment to the MPs, and an even more in-depth check prior to being allowed on her elite protection detail, she expected no ID or contraband issues. But it had been a long flight on a transport aircraft not built for comfort. Her senior noncommissioned officer said it best: "These soldiers are tired and cranky. It's asking for trouble."

Jenny nodded her head in agreement.

"Sorry for the inconvenience," the senior customs officer told her when he introduced himself. "We're just doing our job."

"Right. We understand," she replied. Her feelings were different. *This is unnecessary bureaucratic BS.*

Jenny stood alone at the end of the carousel. When she'd relaxed and began to believe the unpleasantness was going to be over without a hitch, a man walked into the VIP lounge and grabbed one of the last bags.

"This is mine," he said in a brusque manner.

"I'm sorry, sir," Jenny responded. "That's got a CENTCOM sticker on it. You must be mistaken." She reached to take back the piece of luggage.

"Bullshit," he said. He struck her hand away. Then a look of astonishment flashed across his face. "You!" he exclaimed.

Jenny vaguely recognized the man. His eyes looked familiar. *How do I know this guy?*

Before recognition registered, a penlike device appeared in the man's hand. She glimpsed a tiny razor protruding from the end. He closed to within striking distance with menacing intent.

She shifted her stance, balancing to kick him in the groin. But before she could, the customs official shouted, "Hey. What's going on?" He started around the counter.

Jenny's senior NCO also reacted. "Ma'am, do you need some help?" He began to briskly walk toward her.

Before either of the two men could reach her, a woman

hooked the arm of Jenny's assailant and began pulling him toward the exit. "Come, Papa," she said. "This is not the time. Have a porter bring our luggage to the main customs station." She leveled a venomous glare at Jenny. "We'll see you soon," she hissed.

Who the hell are you? Jenny thought as the couple hustled out the door.

"What was that all about?" the customs official asked as he reached Jenny's side, breathless.

She recalled the Chief's guidance to stay out of trouble. Reluctantly, she responded, "It was a misunderstanding about baggage. It's over. Let's get this job done so the transport plane can be reloaded."

She promised herself to review airport security tapes and customs records. At least she'd get a name.

A short while later, another scene unfolded on the fringes of the Reagan airport. The man and woman who had confronted Jenny in the VIP lounge stood in front of an old, empty warehouse. The scream of jet engines from nearby runways battered their ears.

The man looked over the scene trying to take a mental picture of every detail: the rusted metal walls, a door hanging off its hinges, broken windows and weeds bursting through seams in the surrounding concrete pads.

He clasped the hand of his daughter, who stood at his side. Rivulets of tears filled the creases in his face.

"You don't have to do this," his daughter said. "We should go back to the apartment."

"No. I need to see," the man said as he pushed through faded police tape surrounding the abandoned building.

"Papa, it's been over two years. We have new identities. Marriage ... a business. We can't be seen here."

"I owe it to Esteban. I should have protected him."

"We've been over this a dozen times. No one could have known."

"Be silent, Carlotta," the man called El Toro said. He could feel the vein on his forehead throb. She'd grown up learning the signs of his anger, and she'd experienced firsthand the wrath of his explosive temper. As he expected, she held her tongue.

They walked down a narrow corridor to a steel door recessed into a brick wall. The door creaked on its hinges as he pushed it open. He pointed with the beam of his flashlight to a brown stain on the near wall, and then he touched the spot as if caressing skin.

"Here," he said, his voice choked with emotion. "My son died here." It didn't matter to El Toro that the man he was referring to was dealing in stolen weapons, and that he was killed by a person he had tortured.

Pausing briefly, El Toro spoke as if his son was standing in the room. "I will avenge your death, Esteban."

Chapter Eleven

After enduring two presidential elections together, Harold Fisher and his chief of staff, Stephen Augusta, behaved more like a contentious old married couple than esteemed dignitaries. President Fisher was starting to get bored with the job and, in Augusta's eyes, a bit careless

"Mr. President, I'm still nervous about this award to Louis Esquedas," said Augusta. "I know he's married to the First Lady's friend, but—"

"Steve, look," said Fisher, already tired of the subject. "I've known Vanessa a long time. She was maid of honor for Betty at our wedding, for Christ's sake. They've been friends since college. Louis is rich and generous. He's been vetted by the FBI. So what if we get backlash from the Cubanistas because he doesn't cater to them or run in their circles. I've already been reelected. What's to worry?"

Augusta frowned. Most people became leery when his frown appeared. Fisher grinned at the intimidating figure: six-four and three hundred pounds.

"Don't give me that look. Your worst enemy acknowledges your political brilliance, and we all know you got me reelected.

But I want to do this. Sorry."

"Sir, with respect, this guy came out of nowhere. He made a one hundred thousand dollar contribution to the party two years ago, and that's the first time he popped up on the radar."

"Yeah, and he doubled his donation this year. He's a Cuban refugee and a self-made billionaire. More importantly, he's been appointed chairman of the Women's Resource International Charity. They help thousands of abused and abandoned women. The charity is worldwide for crying out loud." He felt his face flush. He was getting hot. "This is a prerogative of the office, dammit."

"I know," responded Augusta, not backing down. "I went with you to the black-tie affair last year. I even wrote the charity a big check. But I still don't like him, or the fact that he seems to have insinuated himself into high levels of government in a short time. Where did he get his money?"

Fisher took a deep breath. He knew Augusta had great instincts for sniffing out potential hot buttons with the media. He'd learned to give him a lot of leeway. "OK, OK. I hear you. Let's not give the newshounds a free shot at rumors about his wealth. Keep it low-key. Make it a standard photo op. Can you live with that?"

"Of course, Mr. President. I just want to insulate us and our party from potential problems. We do want to keep the White House."

"I do too, Steve. All I want to do is give a small award to a loyal supporter and an international philanthropist. It's an innocent gesture. Make it happen."

"Yes, Mr. President."

Chapter Twelve

Louis Esquedas stood in front of a mirror in an open armoire at the Mayflower in Washington, D.C. He was listening on his cell speakerphone to Francisco Gutierrez as he adjusted the knot in his necktie.

He smoothed his graying hair and checked out his profile. He smiled at what he saw: a handsome, flat-bellied, middle-aged executive, impeccable in a blue pin-striped, hand-tailored suit. Perfect creases in his trousers led to freshly shined shoes. His smile broadened as he recognized the unembarrassed vanity as he checked his appearance.

"You look beautiful, Papa," Carlotta said. She came into the room without knocking and plopped into a wingtip chair near the window overlooking DuPont Circle. She wiped her sweaty face with a towel from the fitness center and began nibbling on a croissant from a breakfast tray that sat on a nearby table.

Esquedas put a finger over his lips and shook his head. "That's great news, Gutierrez," he said into the phone. "But fill me in on the details later. I have to go. I'll be late for my appointment." His voice cracked watching Carlotta take off the top of her sweat suit. She was an eyeful. The brief top she wore under the sweatshirt left little to the imagination.

"Yes, I know," Esquedas said, looking away, trying to concentrate on the conversation. "I'm supposed to get a humanitarian award. If they only knew ..." He chortled.

Carlotta yawned loudly to get his attention again. She stretched her arms, arched her back. She wasn't wearing a bra, her nipples revealed through the thin fabric. She blew him a kiss and shook her raven-black hair out of the headband she was wearing, making her melonlike breasts bounce.

Stop it, he mouthed. He said into the phone, "Don't forget to have the helicopter at Ezeiza landing pad on Wednesday. I don't want to be hanging around the Buenos Aires International Airport waiting for transportation."

He listened again and responded, "Yes, Mrs. Esquedas will be accompanying me. And, speaking of my lovely wife, here she is looking stunning in her afternoon gown." He closed his cell phone as Vanessa Esquedas came out of the suite's dressing room.

"I hope we're not overdressed, Louis," Vanessa said. She turned to look at her profile in the mirror. The open armoire door screened the wingtip chair and the fact that Carlotta was sitting in the room.

Louis Esquedas gathered his wife in his arms and told her, "You look beautiful, my love. We have a few minutes if you'd like." He motioned toward the bed.

She was a gorgeous ex-model. He felt aroused inhaling her smells. That she was the daughter of the Mexican ambassador to the U.S. gave him inexplicable feelings of power.

She accepted the nuzzling of her neck and then pushed him away. "No. Don't mess up my hair, Louis. Why do you do that?"

"Do what? Nuzzle your neck? I do it because I love you, and I love being around you."

"You know what I mean. I enjoy your attentions, but whenever you're talking on the phone, you hang up when I come near and then try to divert my attention. It's like you're hiding something. What am I missing?"

"You're missing more than you will ever know," Esquedas's daughter said abruptly. She stood and started to walk out of the room.

"Carlotta, I'm so sorry," Vanessa said. "I didn't realize you were here."

"Right. Well ... I'm not going to sit in the room with you fucking. Try not to be too loud. It was embarrassing last night." She slammed the bedroom door behind her.

Vanessa looked at Esquedas. "What? What's that all about? That's crude and rude!"

"Try to ignore her, my love," Esquedas answered, pulling his wife close. "She's not used to having to share me yet. She's still not over her mom's death."

"Well, it's inexcusable. She's not a little girl. She's twenty-five. Please talk to her. And tell her to wear some clothes. She shouldn't be strutting around you dressed like that. And you're still avoiding my first question." She pushed herself away to look into his eyes.

"Vanessa, please ... please don't be cross with me. It's a Cuban custom not to trouble a wife in matters of business. That's all. I apologize. I was discussing acquiring some merchandise. It's that simple."

He put his arms around his wife once more and said, "Please don't be angry with me on this special day, sweetheart. I will do better."

He'd realized long before that Vanessa de la Renza Montverde Esquedas was more than a beautiful trophy wife. She was a hugely successful opera singer, with frequent appearances at the Lincoln Center, Metropolitan Opera and the Kennedy Center. Educated at the prestigious Julliard School, she owned and operated her own Children's Academy for the Performing Arts in New York City. She'd met and then married him in a whirlwind engagement.

She was inexperienced in matters of the heart, and he knew he'd swept her up in what was a fairytale courtship. She was enamored with a handsome, rich bachelor who was on a first-name basis with world leaders.

He detected recent doubts. She was losing patience with his travels and absences. His trips to strange places with little notice seemed perfectly normal to him, but not her. *I'm going to have to make some changes if this one is to stay around for a while ... and my lovely Carlotta ... we need a better understanding.*

"I can hardly wait for this hoopla to be over," Esquedas said, holding the room door open for her to head to the elevator. "I want to return to Argentina."

"I think you enjoy all the attention. But I'm looking forward to a vacation myself. Maybe we can finally spend some quality time together."

"Of course we can, my love," he answered. Climbing into their limousine, he added, "I look forward to a nice getaway. The Gutierrez estancia is the perfect place."

Ten minutes later they entered the White House grounds. They were ushered into the Roosevelt Room, and Esquedas noted that a photographer was already set up. The President and First Lady entered.

"Louis. Vanessa. It's great seeing you," said President Fisher. "I'm so happy you could be here."

"Mr. President, I am deeply honored," answered Esquedas. "Mrs. Fisher, you look lovely as usual."

"You're a scoundrel, Louis," answered the First Lady. "And please call me Betty." She then exclaimed, "Vanessa ... ohhh, my beautiful friend! How are you?" She gave her a hug.

After a polite interval to allow the friends to reconnect, the President asked his Chief of Staff if he was ready.

"Yes, Mr. President," answered Augusta. He handed the President a medallion on a blue ribbon pendant.

"Good. Come on over here, Louis." The President pointed to a spot on the red carpet. "We'll do the honors right here."

Draping the medallion, the President said, "Mr. Esquedas, it gives me great pleasure to recognize you for all you do for women worldwide. You are a tribute to mankind." Camera lights flashed.

"Mr. President, I am humbled. Thank you. I accept this on behalf of the thousands of people who volunteer their time and money. They are the real heroes."

"Well said, Louis," answered Fisher. "Now if you'll excuse me, I need to get back to running this place." A Secret Service agent opened the door for the President at the moment when two men were walking down the corridor.

"General Penfant, Director Tavares," the President called to the two men. "Come in here a minute. I want you to meet someone." He ushered the men in.

"Louis, this is unplanned, but it occurred to me that there might be some synergism between what you do and some issues that international law enforcement is dealing with. Let me introduce the CENTCOM commander, George Penfant. And with him is the North American INTERPOL Director Juan Tavares.

"General Penfant, Director Tavares, this is Louis Esquedas, the Chairman of Women's Resources International. You both know the First Lady. And the woman standing beside Louis is Vanessa Esquedas, his lovely bride."

When the handshaking and pleasantries were finished, the President asked, "Gentlemen, what do you think about establishing a working relationship?"

Before they could answer, the President added, "Louis, your organization is renowned for helping desperate women get back on their feet. Coincidentally, George and Juan are meeting with me about coordinating operations against human trafficking.

"As you know, human trafficking is a multibillion dollar cash cow for crime syndicates and terrorists. I'd like to suggest you three look for common areas."

"It would be my pleasure, Mr. President," Esquedas quickly answered.

"I look forward to hearing your thoughts, Mr. Esquedas," Tavares remarked. "Perhaps we can also compare notes on old times in Cuba. I heard you're an ex-patriot. I lived there until I was twelve."

"Uhh, yeah ... uhh, I would love to," Esquedas said. "I look forward to it. Uhh, Mr. President, you'll have to excuse me. My schedule is pressing. Thank you again for your thoughtfulness." Esquedas took his wife's elbow and quickly led her out of the room.

☆☆☆

Jenny O'Shane was waiting for Penfant in a glass partitioned interior room outside the Oval Office. She felt awed. It was her first visit to one of the most famous symbols of America. *This is so cool.*

In the midst of laughing at a joke by one of the Secret Service agents, a wave of coldness engulfed her. She felt goosebumps, and the hair on the back of her neck prickled.

Mystified, she glanced around. She locked eyes with the man who'd almost attacked her in the airport. He was hurrying down an adjacent corridor.

Chapter Thirteen

President Fisher looked at his wife, who was staring open-mouthed. They had just been given the brush-off by the guest of honor. The First Lady was blushing. It'd been her suggestion that Esquedas be recognized.

Fisher tried to make light of the moment. "Well, maybe cooperation with Mr. Esquedas isn't such a good idea after all." Everyone joined in a polite chuckle. He shrugged and switched the conversation to business, ushering his wife to the door.

"Fellas, even if Esquedas has some bone to pick with the military or law enforcement, he still may be worth pursuing. He knows a lot of people who may be able to help us."

"I agree, Mr. President. We'll make contact again," Penfant said. Tavares murmured his agreement.

He waved everyone to seats. "I think we agree that kidnappings have become pandemic worldwide. Juan, as an INTERPOL regional director made up of one hundred and ninety member nations, you have an established network to lead an investigation to find out who's responsible. George, you have the world's best intelligence assets at your fingertips as the commander of Central Command. I've directed every intelligence agency to respond to your requests as a first priority for your campaign against terrorism. In this new mission against human trafficking, whatever Juan needs, you can provide. Let me know if anyone gives you any crap."

"Yes, sir. Juan told me earlier that he's going to set up an office in Tampa. I'll assign a top officer to provide local liaison."

"I'll need someone with the moxie to take on the big dogs," Tavares said.

"I understand," Penfant answered. "Let me run my thoughts by some folks back at my headquarters. I think you'll be happy with who I have in mind. Mr. President, you might ask the Secretary of Defense about one of my officers by the name of Jennifer O'Shane. He knows her personally."

"Is she that Army officer who took down those terrorists at the Secretary's residence a couple of years ago?" the President asked. "Didn't she break open the weapons theft conspiracy?"

"Yes, sir. She got a Silver Star for that. As you know that's very rare off the battlefield. She got another one in Korea. And, quite frankly, I think she saved my ass last week. I sent you a write-up on that little episode. The Saudis gave her a nice award, and I'm going to do something. She's dynamite."

"I remember reading the after-action report. I'd like to meet that woman."

"I'll make it happen, Mr. President."

"She sounds like she might be the ticket," Tavares said. "Whichever way it works out, Mr. President, I appreciate your willingness to assist the investigation with the U.S. intelligence assets."

"No sweat," he said. He rubbed his jaw for a couple of seconds, then added, "Gentlemen, I think we should keep this a top-secret black operation. Some members of INTERPOL wouldn't agree with our investigative plans. And some of them don't need access to this kind of raw intelligence. Also, agencies inside the U.S. might take exception to this special treatment and cause us heartburn."

Everyone nodded assent. He shook each of their hands and added, "Augusta will ensure the Congressional Intelligence Oversight Committee is briefed. Thanks for coming."

Chapter Fourteen

Three days after her visit to the White House, Jenny was strolling down The Pier in St. Petersburg, Florida, with her fiancé, Gary Patten. It was a beautiful day: bright blue skies, warm sun and a crisp, cooling breeze. In spite of the ambience, she was feeling unsettled.

"That guy was scary," she said, her skin crawling at the memory. "I've never seen anything like it. I wish I'd remembered to get his name." She'd described her encounters with her nemesis at the airport and the White House. "The security tapes will probably be erased before I get back … probably already are."

"Try to forget about it," Gary said. "You can check with the White House later. They'll have his name and what he does."

Jenny looked up at his California surfer-boy profile: big muscles, blond and blue eyed. Just like a guy. Dismissive of a woman's worries. *But I still love him.*

She remembered meeting him when she visited the Osan Air Base in Korea where he was an F-15 fighter pilot. She'd felt an immediate attraction and the relationship blossomed to the point that he'd arranged for a job at MacDill to be with her when she was assigned to Central Command. She knew it was a major sacrifice for a professional military pilot to volunteer for a non-flying assignment. She looked down at the big rock that sparkled on her finger. *Engaged three months already. Wow!*

"The chances are good that you'll never see him again," Gary added.

He took her hand. "Come on. Admiral Bryan was right about you taking some downtime. Let's try to think of something else we can do to keep your mind off of business. I know you liked the fish tanks."

"The Pier Aquarium has some cool exhibits, but I can only take so much of looking at jellyfish swimming in a glass tank."

"Oh, bull! You were the one who didn't want to leave the stingrays. The docent was giving you dirty looks for pushing that little kid out of the way."

"Ha! I didn't push him. It was a nudge. All the big rays were coming up to him."

"Whatever. What do you want to do now? Our dinner reservations aren't for two hours."

"Well," she said, stroking his bare arm, "what I want to do we can't do in public."

"God, woman, you're wanton. You keep that up and the hell with the public!"

She continued rubbing his arm. "You wouldn't dare!"

Gary used one hand behind her neck and mashed his lips against hers. With the other hand he grabbed her butt.

Jenny pushed herself away, laughing. "You pervert! I'll quit already."

She looked around at the nearby boats. "Hey, I've got an idea. How about we rent a boat for an overnight sail?"

He grabbed her hand again. "Great idea," he said. "That sounds like fun." He began pulling her toward the marina. Feeling the mood, she skipped like a teenager the three blocks to the piers. They were soon at a counter in the main office.

A ruddy-faced, pleasant-looking man greeted them. He had "Captain Bob" embroidered over his shirt pocket. "How can I help ya'll?" he asked.

She grinned at the deep Southern drawl. "We'd like to rent a sailboat for overnight."

"Well, all I got is that fifty-foot Catalina over there," answered Bob, pointing to a nearby slip. "She's got roller furling, A/C and a generator. Her name's Corky. She's expensive."

"Cost isn't a big issue," Gary responded. "Let's go take a look at her."

"We could," Bob answered. "But we only let that one out with groups of four or more. And at least two of them need to be certified. Like to help you but ..."

Jenny sighed, disappointed. She'd been certified in small boats as a kid, but hadn't kept up.

Gary persisted. "Hey, I'm American Sailor Association certified, and I have my one hundred-ton Coast Guard captain's license."

Jenny looked surprised. He answered her unasked question: "I would have told you. The subject never came up. It's no big deal. What do you say, Captain?"

"Well, you'd be qualified. And I'd love to rent that baby. But we still require a group. She's not single-handed. Sorry."

Following those words, Jenny heard a voice from a couple that had come into the marina.

"Excuse me," the man said. "I couldn't help but overhear. We came in looking to charter a sailboat too. We're both Coast Guard officers, and I also have a one hundred-ton license. What if we all four went together?"

"That'd be dandy. I'd have to see your tickets, but let's go look her over," Captain Bob answered with enthusiasm. Jenny guessed that he didn't often rent the big boat.

She checked out the "Coasties" while they walked to the boat. The man was good-looking and reminded her of Gary. The woman with him had striking green eyes. She cut a pert figure wearing short shorts and a tube top. Jenny sensed that they could become friends.

Soon, the charter was arranged, and the couples agreed on a seven a.m. departure, with "bring-your-own-food-and-drinks" as a plan. They got better acquainted after Bob's boat orientation.

"I'm Charlie Watson, and this is my wife, Brenda," the man said, offering a firm handshake. "I work at a boat construction firm in Tampa. I'm a contract manager for a new prototype Coast Guard deployable pursuit boat. Brenda's also a 'Coastie.'

She's assigned to the cutter *Resolute*."

"Gary and I are both military too," Jenny said, smiling at the coincidence. She added, "And the four of us could be twins—petite redheads with tall blonde guys. There's a small, minor difference—Gary's Air Force and I'm Army."

"We won't hold that against you," laughed Charlie.

Jenny briefly explained where she and Gary worked. She ended with, "Boy, I'd love to ride in that new pursuit boat. I hear it's hot. I've seen some of the communiqués at CENTCOM."

"The prototype is awesome," Charlie said. "It's thirty-eight feet, with state-of-the-art electronics, jet propulsion and a stealth profile. The controls and maneuverability in the water are similar to the new Russian jet fighter."

He looked Jenny over for a second and then added, "Careful what you ask for. I might be able to hook you up if you're serious. The Coast Guard is stretched thin with the illegal immigrant and drug interdiction programs, combined with new Homeland Security requirements. We're always looking for qualified volunteers to help on test runs."

"Wow. Count me in, man," Jenny said. "I'd love that."

"We can talk about it during our sail tomorrow," Charlie answered.

With brief goodbyes, the two couples parted company. Jenny and Gary headed toward the Columbia Restaurant for their dinner reservations.

"Boy, interdicting the illegal aliens must suck," observed Gary as they walked.

"Yeah. I can't imagine the misery. From what I've heard of the drug thing, it sounds even more brutal."

In spite of those brief thoughts clouding her mind, they had a relaxing dinner and soon returned to their weekender suite at the Pier Hotel.

She told Gary, "I'm going to try out the fancy shower. Why don't you set up the movie we picked."

"You got it."

She got the water temperature right and stepped into the see-through shower cubicle.

Three jets of water sprayed her from separate showerheads. She began to shampoo her hair. She chuckled when she heard the shower door open.

"I watched for a minute, but the glass fogged up," Gary said, pulling her against him, aroused. "What's that?" she said with a coy tone, pretending surprise.

They flopped onto the bed, soaking wet, in a fast frenzy of uncontrolled passion. Then they made love, cherishing every touch.

Afterward, intertwined as only lovers do, they lay in bed and watched through the terrace windows as the sun slipped beneath the horizon.

Dozing in the afterglow of their lovemaking, Jenny heard a scratching sound, as if someone was trying to unlatch the room's door lock.

She slipped into Gary's button-down shirt and peeked out the peephole. She could see two men crouched in the hallway.

She jerked open the door. "Hey, what the hell are you guys doing?"

The men were surprised by her aggressiveness. They backed away. One of the men said something that sounded Arabic, and they began to sprint down the hall.

"Wait a minute," she shouted, and took off after them.

She almost caught up with one of them when he pulled a maid's service cart into her path. She crashed headlong into the cart, sprawling to the floor. She lay stunned for a few seconds. It was enough time for the culprits to disappear. *Dammit!*

Gary came running up. "Jenny, what's going on?"

She scrambled out from the midst of cleaning supplies and toilet paper and pulled the shirt down to cover her butt. She summed up what happened, and then said, "Thieves, I'd guess. They probably thought the room was empty."

She and Gary righted the cart and started restocking it as best they could.

"Chasing those two goons alone was nuts," Gary said. "What were you thinking?"

"I, uhhh—"

"Right ... don't bother explaining. You scared the hell out of me."

Jenny put her arm through his arm, tiptoed and kissed him on the cheek. "I'll be more careful. Promise."

"I don't believe it for a second. But thanks." He gave her a return kiss on top of her head. "Let's go back to our room and call security."

When she closed their room door, her cell phone rang. "This is Major O'Shane," she answered. *Nobody's supposed to have this number, business only. Something's up.*

"Praise be to Allah," she recognized the voice of Minister Kaliq. "You're safe," he said.

"Your Excellency, how did you get this number? What's wrong?"

Gary put his arm around her waist, his hand moving under the shirt. He asked, "Who is it?"

"Shhh. Stop it," she whispered, pushing his hand away.

"Pardon me, Princess. Is that a man with you?" asked Kaliq.

"Uhhh ... no, of course not, Excellency. You were saying?"

"I called to warn you that you are in great danger. It's about the dagger. Unfortunately, the gift has had repercussions among a religious sect."

"I'll return it immediately. I had no idea."

"Of course you didn't know. We were only recently made aware. But you'll not return the dagger. It would bring dishonor to the Crown Prince. However, according to these zealots, the dagger should never have left the Kingdom. The sect's ayatollah instructed his followers to get it back at any cost. We've put you in serious harm's way. Mohammed warned me before he committed suicide."

"Mohammed did what?"

"It's true. He committed suicide. He was my nephew and trusted assistant. Our family is in deep mourning. It was so sudden and unexpected. We'd heard of disgruntlement among his wives, beatings and the like, but we had no idea. The unrest seems to have also involved purchasing young girls." He paused briefly. "That's another subject, Princess. The reason for my call is to tell you to be careful."

"I'll be fine, Excellency. I'm so sorry about Mohammed."

"Thank you. It is a sad affair. But, more importantly, don't underestimate these fanatics. They're dangerous. We suspect that they may be connected to an Al Qaeda cell, but have no proof. I was afraid we might have been too late."

"Well, we did have two visitors a few minutes ago," she said.

"That's unfortunate. They moved fast. You're all right, I presume. I hope your visitors were not harmed."

"They got away."

"Good. And the authorities ... it would be best not to involve them."

"I was about to call hotel security. Why is it good not to catch a couple of thieves?"

"It's delicate. We would prefer not to embarrass the Ayatollah if possible. It seems that the Crown Prince negotiated a compromise." He paused. There was a lengthy silence.

"This compromise involves me, doesn't it?"

"Ahem," Kaliq cleared his throat. "Well, it seems that the Ayatollah dispatched two subordinates to verify your worthiness as guardian of the holy dagger. His Highness asks that you host them and to please be on your best behavior."

"Minister Kaliq, I know little of your traditions. This could be a disaster."

"I assured the Crown Prince that you would manage. The mullahs will arrive via the Crown Prince's personal plane at noon on Monday at the Tampa airport. Thank you, Princess."

Jenny heard a dial tone. *Oh my God!*

Chapter Fifteen

Louis Esquedas had a self-satisfied twinkle in his eye. "Welcome to the mile-high club, Vanessa," he said, pulling up his trousers and buttoning his shirt. They were flying from the Buenos Aires airport to Francisco Gutierrez's estancia in a light-blue executive helicopter. The Women's Resources International (WRI) logo was emblazoned across the outside fuselage.

"I never expected to do it in a helicopter," his wife answered. She retrieved her panties from one of the six seats in the cabin. Still breathing heavily, she added, "Keeping up with you is impossible."

He smiled at her reference to his stamina and insatiable sexual appetite. He took pride in satisfying women to the point of exhaustion. He loved the sense of control. He'd counted four orgasms for her on the flight before he allowed himself release. And it was the second time that they'd had sex that day.

"You're going to wear it out," she said.

"Well, I certainly hope not," he answered. His hand moved up her thigh.

"No. Please, Louis. No. I'm done. Please ..." She squirmed, pushing him away.

"Oh, all right," he said in feigned exasperation. "Let's have a glass of wine, and we'll see how you feel later. We have another hour to the estancia. I'll make a few phone calls to let you catch your breath."

He donned a headset and spoke on the radio through an attached microphone. Although the Sikorsky had VIP acoustics, the twin aerial engines drowned out Esquedas's conversation.

"May I speak freely, señor?" asked Francisco.

"Sí. We are on the encrypted radio link, and the noise blocks most sound. I've also switched off her headset so that my lovely wife can't possibly hear us," answered Esquedas.

"Excellente. That new model aircraft is superior, but engine noise has advantages."

"Yes. Now tell me why you left me a voice mail."

"Sí, señor. I was passed an urgent message for you from someone claiming to be an undercover operative with a code name of Stopper. The message was two words: identity secure."

"Ahhh. I understand. My concern about my White House meeting was unwarranted."

"I hope the source is reliable, señor. You had a close call. It could have been a disaster. Your fake Cuban persona was difficult to arrange even with Raul Castro's aid. Who is this Stopper person? I thought I knew every operative."

"No you don't, my friend. The fact is that I don't even know the person's identity. But the information has always been reliable. It comes through a source in Cuba."

Esquedas paused for a moment and then said, "Well, given that my Cuban credentials seem to be intact, the Women's Resources International continues. Good. Let's make sure I stay at arm's length from Tavares. What else? Did you alert the European leaders about my concerns?"

"I'd planned to do so today. I also wanted to update you on our immigrant operations. You were right again. There's—"

Esquedas interrupted his comments. "Wait. I see what you're doing. You're hoping I'd forget about my special project. You must have bad news. Tell me!"

"Of course, señor. I wasn't being evasive—"

"Bullshit. Speak!"

"Señor, as you know, I contracted with an Al Qaeda cell in Florida for the second operation. We were still in the planning stage. But it appears that their leader went loco. I have no other explanation."

"What are you talking about?"

"Initial information is that he was close to being caught during a burglary. My sources report that he was after some religious symbol. That's seems unlikely, but communication with this deep-cover group has been disrupted. I'll need time to find out what's going on. That's all I know at this moment, señor."

Esquedas paused to allow his anger to subside and to consider what he'd heard. Then he said in a voice cold with fury. "Francisco, I've decided that you're not at fault for this fiasco. It seems that both you and our target lead a charmed life. Offer a bounty or something for our primary target. Do anything! I'm too upset to hear more. Call me tomorrow."

He disconnected, trying to think of a diversion to help him calm down. He took off his headphones, smiled and said, "Vanessa, my love. How are you feeling now? Better?"

At the remote Argentinean estancia, Gutierrez listened to the radio static after El Toro disconnected and wondered for the hundredth time at his own sanity for working for the man. Pushing an intercom button, he said, "Vladimir, come in here."

The outer office door opened, and Gutierrez watched his chief deputy come into the study. Vladimir D'Alexandreapov was the ex-KGB chief for South America.

His hound dog features hid a keen intellect and an exceptional administrative acumen. His face was pockmarked by acne, and punctuated by deep-set eyes—one blue, one brown. A thin scar pulled his face into a permanent scowl.

Gutierrez felt like he'd struck gold since the demise of the USSR and the Cold War. Senior members of the KGB and other connected agencies had suddenly become unemployed and available. Vladimir was a perfect example. His abrupt "retirement" had proven invaluable in providing Gutierrez worldwide contacts that would have otherwise been impossible to obtain.

"Sorry to be sweaty," Vladimir said, wiping his forehead with a towel draped on his shoulders. "I was working out with some staff."

Gutierrez silently congratulated himself for choosing Vladimir. He was more than a talented administrator; he was a world-class kickboxer—lightning reflexes were the secret to his success. *Unmatched bodyguard*, Gutierrez reflected. *His presence among staff has bolstered estancia security tenfold.*

"I hope you didn't kill anyone," he said. He was joking, but his comment served only to deepen his deputy's scowl. Too late, Gutierrez recalled that Vladimir didn't like to be reminded that he was barred from international competition because he'd killed two men in tournaments.

Vladimir let the comment pass. Instead he said, "You should exercise with me to relieve the stress of working for that man."

"I've worked for El Toro for nearly twenty years. He leaves me little time for pleasure. Speaking of work, inform our sector leader in Europe to move more slowly. He's getting too anxious. Also, put out that we are offering a two million dollar bounty on our special target. That should get some attention."

"I'll get the word out about the bounty," Vladimir answered. "Good idea. Regarding our sector leader, I'll phone him tonight. His problem is training. Ex-KGB and Stassi agents are accustomed to more freedom of action. Kidnapping is not a big deal for them. And they've never seen so much money. However, he'll understand the situation better after my call. I also heard some rumblings about Stack, our supervisor in New Orleans, that I'll deal with."

"Excellente. Now tell me. Have you heard from our Coast Guard contact?"

Chapter Sixteen

In the luxurious Pier Hotel in St. Petersburg, Jenny and Gary stopped by the catering service to pick up a picnic basket that they'd ordered for their sailing excursion. There were several uniformed police in the lobby. Jenny heard some hotel staff talking about a missing maid named Isabella. She idly mentioned it to Gary, wondering aloud if there might be a slave-trade connection.

"You need to clear your mind for a few days, Jenny. You're obsessing on this slave thing. I wanted this overnight sail to be without any worries."

She hugged his arm. She loved it when he was sensitive to her feelings. "Thanks. I know I get a little—"

"Anal? Just a little?"

"OK, OK. I'll try not to bring it up again."

"I'll believe it when I see it," Gary said, laughing. "Hey, I heard you tell one of the security staff about the two goons last night. I thought Kaliq asked you to drop it."

"I don't care what he asked. It's not right that people break and enter without paying for it. If those two felt OK about breaking into our room, what else are they involved in? I don't like it. They could be involved with the missing maid for all we know."

"Good point," Gary said. "But it doesn't look like the police will be able to find much. The security guy said that the camera system was broken yesterday."

Jenny mulled the situation as they walked in companionable silence to the docks. "Let's forget about it for now," she offered. "Why don't you go get a weather check at the marina office, and I'll find Corky."

"Sounds like a plan."

"And I'll stop fretting. Promise." She stood on tiptoes and gave him a peck on the cheek. Then she headed down the slips.

Within a minute, Jenny heard Brenda's voice: "Get that picnic basket from her, Charlie. It looks heavy."

"Sure. Got it." He took the basket out of Jenny's arms, lifting it into Corky's cockpit. "Man this is heavy."

"Yeah, the Pier kinda overdid it. I love the service at that place."

"It's a first-rate hotel. It looks like we'll have plenty to eat," Charlie responded. "I think Brenda brought the entire kitchen from our house. Where's Gary?"

"He's checking the marine forecast." Stepping onto the boat, she could feel engine vibration. "Well, you got her started. That's a good indicator."

"The boat seems to be in great shape," Charlie reported. "We got here early to go through the equipment checklist. The heads are both operational, the GPS system and generator work, and the A/C's on. I'll do a radio check, and we should be ready to cast off."

"Fantastic. I'll go into the galley and put some of this stuff away," she said, starting down the cabin stairs.

"Let me give you a hand," Brenda said. "We went ahead and set up in the front berth. I hope that's OK?"

"No sweat," Jenny answered. "I think we got the better end of that deal. The rear berth is much larger. Are you sure that's OK with you guys?"

"Sure. We love wave motion for sleeping and the bow rocks more under anchor. It's a good trade for us. Besides, it's only one night."

"It sounds fine to me. Gary has our bedding in his bags. We'll set up the berth after we're underway."

Charlie came into the cabin and began fiddling with the microphone connection on the navigation panel. Simultaneously, they heard a hail from dockside.

"Ahoy, Corky. Where is everybody?" Gary called.

"We're down here," Jenny answered.

"Hi, everybody," Gary greeted, climbing down the gangway stairs. "The weather forecast looks great. I also got a local area chart if we need it."

"Super," Charlie responded. "I checked out the GPS equipment and electronic plotter. Everything's up and running. Let's untie this tub and get out of here."

When the dock lines were cast off, Jenny suggested that they make for a beach near Casey Key. "It's deep water but within easy swimming distance from offshore."

"Isn't Donna Bay nearby?" Charlie asked.

"Yep. That's it. It's called Nokomis Beach. We can overnight in Donna Bay if weather comes up. What do you think?"

"I think that sounds perfect. We should be there in about ten hours in this breeze. Let's kick back and relax." Charlie took the helm and steered them away from the dock and into the channel.

"You look natural there, Charlie," Jenny offered. "You and Brenda both have the most recent sea time. Why don't you guys do the captain and mate bit. Gary and I will crew."

Charlie and Brenda shared a glance and a shrug. Charlie answered, "Sure. Let's go that route today. Maybe tomorrow we'll switch off."

Before long they were cruising under full sail, with both the main and jib set. They hadn't even cleared the Skyway Bridge and the rail was nearly in the water.

"Man, would you believe we're making eight knots?" yelled Charlie. "This old girl can sail!"

"I'm sure glad I took Dramamine this morning," Jenny said, bracing against the heel of the boat. Her stomach did a flip, and she felt the onset of a nausea headache. "This is bumpier than I thought it'd be."

"I'm feeling queasy too," Brenda offered. "Hopefully it'll smooth out after we turn south into open water. Tampa Bay is always rough from boat traffic and currents."

A derelict fishing trawler accelerating across their bow punctuated Brenda's comments. Its wash caused a cascade of seawater.

"Boy, that was rude," Jenny remarked, ducking to avoid the splash that came over Corky's gunwale. She glanced at the name on the stern of the trawler: *Gotta Girl* of Acme Trans Fisheries. "Let's look him up when we get back," she added.

The seas mellowed and Jenny soon forgot about the trawler fisherman. Charlie set the autopilot and the boat practically sailed itself. The only noise was water sluicing under the hull and a tiny whine of the autopilot adjusting the rudder.

Conversation ebbed and flowed over drinks and snacks. Charlie was animated talking about the new pursuit boats and was excited when Jenny agreed to crew for a week on an upcoming test run.

"I can hardly wait. It'll be a blast," she said.

Chapter Seventeen

Crystal awoke with a start when the trawler thumped against the dock. She smelled the fetid, brackish, oily odor of harbor water. She heard feet crossing the deck above her head. Trying to sit up, she groaned, stiff after being in a confined space for an extended period.

Although there was limited headroom, Crystal managed to sit on the edge of her bunk. She had to pee.

She felt Isabella stir. In the dim light provided by a red bulb attached to a bulkhead, she saw tears streaming down her face.

"Don't cry, Isabella. I'm scared too, but we're going to get through this. I know it." Crystal patted Isabella's leg reassuringly. "My grandpa escaped from a Viet Cong POW camp. He told me that he kept alive by telling himself over and over, 'Never give up.' That's got to be us. All right?"

Isabella nodded, "Sí, señorita."

"Good. Right now let's get in line for the bathroom." She padded barefoot to the tiny head. Isabella followed. They stood behind two others.

Within minutes, Frankel came down the companionway. "OK, girls. Welcome to New Orleans. Time to get your asses in gear. Upstairs. Now." He began to herd the girls to the deck above, his stun gun at the ready.

Crystal stumbled up the gangway into a gathering twilight. Assembling with the others on deck, she heard the man she knew as Sims speaking to someone. "Sure glad that trip's over. That was some rough water."

A voice Crystal didn't recognize responded with a heavy accent and a sarcastic tone. She looked toward the voice and saw a man who looked Asian.

"You no see Gulf when ugly," he said with a bitter laugh. "Should see storms in South China Sea. Those little waves last night nothing. You think I no handle boat good?" he asked.

Sims backed away from the Asian. "Hey, sorry I mentioned it."

"Tranh, take it easy," Frankel's familiar voice piped in. "Sims didn't mean anything. Let's get the merchandise off-loaded, and you can get back out on the water."

"Hmm," Tranh answered. In the brightening morning light, Crystal could see the man called Tranh fingering a fish fillet knife strapped to his side. "You watch it," he said.

"Sure. No sweat," Sims responded.

"Very well. I do need go fishing. I go to wheelhouse."

"Yeah, and keep that fake nurse you brought away from us," Frankel added.

"You should be more respect," Tranh answered. "Mary lost license through accident. Not her fault. She qualified nurse. Take good care of girls. They sleep whole trip. No piss her off."

"Tranh, do I look like I give a flying fuck about that woman's feelings? You drive the boat and she's the nurse. Fine. Now get your yellow ass out of the way so we can do our jobs."

Crystal could feel a menace in the air—a confrontation looming.

"Hey, goddammit," Frankel said when Tranh hesitated. "Move it! We need to get this boat out of here."

All the girls were now up on the deck watching and listening. Crystal sensed an unexplained anger from Tranh, but he turned on his heel. He called out, "Mary, need go wheelhouse."

"Easy, Frankel," Sims said when the Asian man walked away. "We need Tranh, his boat and the nurse. He's squirrelly, but we're making good money using them."

"Oh, fuck off. I've heard the stories about him losing his wife and kid trying to get into the U.S. They suffocated in a cargo container. Tough shit. Don't blame me. I'm sick to death of his glares. He gives me the creeps."

There was a short pause when he realized he had an audience. "What are you looking at?" he asked the group of young women. "Get your butts down the gangplank."

Crystal was the first in line. "Where are we?" she asked, heading down the gangway.

"Shut up," Frankel responded.

"Can't you at least tell us where?"

A sharp pain seared her arm and drove her to her knees. "Owww! That hurt!" She grabbed the boat railing to keep from falling into the water. She quivered.

"I told you to shut the fuck up," Frankel said. "That was on the lowest amp. Next time I'll turn it up. You do what you're told. Immediately. No questions."

Glaring with hate-filled eyes, her pain slowly subsiding, Crystal led the girls onto the dock.

"We're going into that warehouse," Frankel instructed. "Open the door and go in."

A decrepit air filled the building. It leaned to one side with broken windows. The door Frankel pointed to hung from one hinge. The abandoned warehouse was strewn with discarded boxes and cobwebs. The wooden flooring was wet with the slime of age and neglect. A few bare low-watt bulbs hanging from the ceiling lit the interior.

Looking more closely, Crystal detected that the appearance was a façade. The floor didn't sag as one would expect, and the walls were supported by new bracing. *They're hiding something. This is a big place.*

A large black man stood in the center of the floor, feet spread wide and hands resting on narrow hips. A grin creased a tattooed face. Crystal saw seven tears inked on his cheek. She remembered high school Social Studies classes that discussed similar markings. The tears were linked to a Voodoo religious group and prison gangs. They represented kills of rivals.

"Welcome, ladies," he sneered. "Hope you had a nice trip."

Bulging muscles on a bare, heavily tattooed upper torso rippled. "I'm called Stack," the man said. "From this point forward, you'll do exactly what I tell you when I tell you. Understood?"

Not waiting for an answer, he pushed a button on a device he was carrying. A section of the warehouse floor shifted to reveal stairs. The opening blended into the wooden floor, invisible to a casual observer.

"Follow me," Stack instructed, leading them down the stairs and into a narrow corridor. On one side of the corridor were doors. "These doors lead to rooms where you'll stay," the giant man told them.

He pointed to Crystal. "You're assigned to room four. When I push this remote, the door will open." Pointing to Isabella, he said, "You, go into room five."

He assigned each of the women a room and then said, "Drop your shifts on the floor."

Crystal watched him take a stun gun out of a side pocket. She'd had all of that she needed. She quickly brought the shift over her head and dropped it, standing in her bra and panties before the three men.

Isabella didn't understand the rapid instructions, her English failing. Her brief hesitation was enough. In a swift motion Stack brought up his gun, placed it against her breast and pulled the trigger.

A look of intense pain crossed Isabella's face. Her body convulsed, and her eyes rolled back in their sockets. She collapsed in a heap on the floor.

"Don't mark 'em, Stack," Sims said. He reached out to restrain him.

Stack whirled and grabbed Sims's wrist. He bent it roughly, twisting. Sims fell to his knees and groaned.

"Shut the fuck up," Stack said. "I'm short guards because I got rid of others who didn't follow my directions. You don't want to go there," he said in a menacing voice.

Crystal found she was holding her breath. She recalled hearing about steroids. Roid rage. Perfect example. *Guy's a time bomb.*

Stack let go of Sims and turned a pair of bloodshot eyes back to the girls. "I'm only going to tell you bitches to do something once." He reached down and ripped Isabella's shift off. Then he grabbed her ankles and dragged her into the open door of room five.

Crystal didn't need another demonstration. When the door to room four opened, she didn't hesitate. She stepped across the threshold, shuddering when the door slammed shut behind her and a latch engaged.

In a daze of disbelief, she registered what was before her. It was a prison cell—a narrow room with a metal sink and toilet and a bed attached to the wall. There was a thin mattress lying on the bed frame. No blanket and no pillow. A tray of food was on a small stool.

She heard voices in the corridor outside her cell. It was Stack bragging about his domain.

"This is a perfect setup," he said. "The stairs work from this remote. They recess into the ceiling for added security. No one gets out of here unless we want them to. The floor above folds down perfectly to cover them. It's almost invisible in the warehouse and no one on the dock could tell that there are stairs or rooms down here.

"We use another warehouse as our office and dormitory and an abandoned utility tunnel to get back and forth. We're so isolated out here, no one can hear if the girls start yelling.

"Ships often anchor nearby when the harbor is congested, so when our ships come in, nobody pays any attention. It's hiding in plain sight."

Stack continued, "We built a special exercise room down the hall. All prisoners work out daily to stay in shape. It's not optional. There's also a shower. That's also not optional."

His voice took on a different tone. "Here's the deal. You two will help provide security until the ship shows up next month. Watch the corridor, see that the girls get their exercise, and oversee chow.

"You can divide the shifts up anyway you want with another team you'll meet in a minute. But, when I come down, one of you had better be here. Lastly, don't play with the merchandise. That's off-limits, a big no-no.

"You'll eat and sleep in the other warehouse. I'll take you over there now, and you can stow your gear."

Crystal heard their voices receding down the corridor. She sat on her tiny bed and tears welled up into her eyes. She tried to focus on her grandpa's motto, "Never give up." But she couldn't help the sobs that racked her body.

Chapter Eighteen

In Tampa, Florida, Jenny O'Shane met with the Central Command staff psychologist at the MacDill Base Exchange ten days after her sailing trip. They sat in a small booth in the rear of the cafeteria drinking coffee. The eight a.m. meeting was nothing like she'd imagined.

"Where's the couch, huh?" Dr. Ernie Pabst asked. "And you're expecting questions about the abuse from your dad, or why you hated your mom and how many times you had sex last week. Right?"

Jenny choked on her drink. "I guess that's close," she finally managed through her coughing.

"I usually get that reaction. No one appreciates being told they have to see me, and everyone expects to be asked about the juiciest parts of their private life."

He had a melodious, pleasant voice. "I'll bet you thought I'd have heavy, dark-rimmed glasses and smoke a pipe. Disappointed?"

"No, not really," Jenny smiled, her reservations about the meeting evaporating. "Pleasantly surprised, I guess."

She sized him up as she spoke. He was a nice-looking man

who spoke with what she guessed was a New Jersey accent. He wore a Navy uniform with the rank of commander. He struck her as being a man from a big Ivy League school, who played squash and was divorced.

"Good. Let's dispense with the questions that I always get asked. That'll help clear your mind of all the trivia. We're here to talk about you.

"So, answers to your questions about me—New Jersey, Notre Dame, boxing scholarship, married, and three kids. OK?"

Jenny smiled and nodded her head. He spoke in a rapid-fire, staccato fashion, and was reading her mind with a disconcerting accuracy.

"Reading minds is a part of my job," he continued. "A surprising number of my clients have difficulty expressing their feelings. They often leave out important information, or they plain lie. I'm paid to help get to the truth about their behavior. I'm good at it."

He paused for a beat and then added, "Also, so you know, I like to initially meet clients in this kind of setting. I get a better sense of them in a relaxed atmosphere.

"Usually my patients have a short relationship with me or they have a lengthy one. Hopefully, you'll get the short version."

He let his comments sink in. "I'll decide about you here. Today. Right now. This is it. Are you comfortable with that?"

"Sure. What do you want to know?" Jenny answered. She felt relaxed with his manner, and her concerns about seeing a "shrink" had disappeared.

"Well, I've seen your file, and I have to be honest. It doesn't look good."

A scowl darkened his face. "After all, records show that you've killed five men in the last two years. There was one at Reagan National, two at the home of the Secretary of Defense, and now two in Riyadh. And, although undocumented, you probably killed a couple more men in Korea.

"Didn't you have some alternative? Haven't you been taught that killing is wrong? Do you enjoy it? Where's the remorse? What are you, some kind of self-appointed judge and jury—a vigilante?"

Jenny felt a flush move up her neck. *This asshole doesn't*

have a clue.

"Listen, buster," she said. "If you bothered checking you'd know that my life was on the line in each of those situations. The guy at Reagan was torturing me. He planned to rape and then kill both me and a friend."

She found herself leaning forward in her seat, sitting on its edge, her finger pointing in Pabst's face. At the same time, tears welled up.

"If you think that someone will be allowed to shoot at me or my soldiers without paying a price, you can forget it. They better be ready to die. The same goes for anyone assaulting me. I won't hesitate to use deadly force to defend myself.

"As for remorse, of course it bothers me. I usually throw up, or pee in fright, or both. That's a stupid question. Killing would bother anybody.

"But I figure it's either me or them. So is guilt a long-term problem for me? No. At least not for long." *Need to get out of here before I hurt him.*

"Are we done here? I have things to do." She started to get up.

"Sit down, Major," Pabst ordered. A friendly smile reappeared. The jovial man from New Jersey was back.

Pabst had played her. Her eyes flashed, and her temper erupted again with the realization.

"Relax, Jenny." He put a calming hand on her arm. "Trust me. If you hadn't displayed any emotion when I challenged you, we'd have a problem.

"Emotion evokes emotion with normal people. So, I showed you emotion. I got the reaction I needed. Do you want some more coffee?"

Thirty minutes later, Jenny was sitting in her small office at CENTCOM headquarters at MacDill, talking to Gary on the phone. She described her meeting with Pabst. "It was over that quick. Can you believe that guy?"

"Sounds like a real pro to me," Gary answered. "He had your number."

Chapter Nineteen

Jenny stood outside a small hangar on the fringes of the Tampa International Airport, waiting for her guests. Brenda agreed to accompany her as chaperone to offset the Muslim issue of a woman being with men, unescorted. Jenny wore her Army Camouflage Uniform, and Brenda wore the Navy equivalent.

"Thanks for doing this for me, Brenda. I hope it's not too painful."

"I don't mind. It's pleasant not being on the ship for a few hours and doing something different. I'll stay in the background and watch."

"Well, I owe you dinner. This part should be simple. We'll drop them off at the hotel and get back to work." The Saudis were traveling under diplomatic passports, so Jenny arranged for customs and TSA staff to greet and clear them at the hangar. As she spoke, a C-17 jumbo jet with Saudi identifiers slowly taxied toward them.

Men dressed in dishdasha robes and embroidered vests exited the aircraft. At the bottom of the stairway, customs stamped their passports, gave their carry-on bags a once-over, and waved them through.

One of the men was bent with age and grey of beard. Gnarled hands held a worn cane. But age had not dimmed the bright eyes.

The other cleric was about Jenny's age. A short wisp of a beard was his only notable facial feature. A sneer curled his upper lip.

When Jenny approached, the young man was whispering into the ear of the older cleric.

"Marharba Sheik Abdu Baktar and Sheik Mustaliq, welcome to the United States and my home. Ismy Jenny. Tashannafna," she said, and then introduced Brenda.

The older gentleman gripped Jenny's hands with both of his, completely ignoring the customs of his land. He looked her directly in the eyes, seeming to pierce her soul.

He said in English in a gentle tone, "I am Abdu Baktar. Thank you for a considerate greeting. It's a pleasure meeting such beautiful women. We—"

The younger cleric interrupted, "Don't speak your broken Arabic to us, little woman. We are well educated and speak excellent English.

"For you both to meet us in a soldier's battle uniform is rude. As I expected, you are impertinent and insulting. Do you have the dagger? Give it to me!"

Sheik Baktar said something in a quiet, melodic undertone in a language that Jenny didn't understand. The effect was astonishing. Mustaliq bowed his head and stepped aside as if he'd been given an instant tranquilizer.

"Please excuse my impetuous young associate," said Baktar. "He has much to learn. I apologize for his behavior."

"That's OK. I meant no offense," replied Jenny.

"Of course not. Come," Baktar said, taking her arm. "We've much to discuss. We've heard many stories about you. I look forward to becoming acquainted. Thank you for meeting us."

"It's my pleasure. I have a car waiting to take you to your hotel for the evening. I'm sure you're tired from your travels and would like to freshen up."

"We are honored by your thoughtfulness. However, we rested on the Crown Prince's airplane and would prefer spending time with you. Would that be convenient?"

"Uhhh, sure. I'll need to make a few phone calls. But I'm at your service."

"Excellent. Minister Kaliq assured me that we would enjoy your hospitality. I can see we will not be disappointed. However, I need to ask, do you have the dagger with you?"

"Yes, sir. It's in a special sheath." Jenny patted the back of her neck. "Would you like to see it?"

Sheik Baktar smiled and held up his hand. "No. That won't be necessary. We can examine it in the privacy of our hotel room. After we check in, perhaps we could visit your workplace and residence? We would also like to host you to dinner at a restaurant of your choice. Our plane leaves tomorrow at ten a.m., so I'm afraid we have little time."

"I'll make the arrangements," she responded. She rolled her eyes when the clerics weren't looking. She hadn't expected the visit to be so compressed. She glanced at Brenda, who returned her look with a grin. "I guess our plans for tonight are off," she whispered.

To the clerics, Jenny asked, "Do you need to pick up anything at baggage claim?"

Mustaliq spoke for the first time since being silenced by his companion. "We've brought what we need as carry-on. Please take us to our rooms without delay."

He strode down the corridor of the terminal toward the parking lot and began whispering into Baktar's ear again. He pointed at the bars and restaurants that lined the corridor and at the women in short skirts and tank tops.

Jenny activated her cell phone. She called Gary to ask him to make dinner reservations and gave him some names and phone numbers of guests she wanted to invite. She also called Admiral Bryan's office to see if he had a few minutes to spare.

After a short drive to their hotel, the clerics inspected Jenny's dagger in the privacy of their hotel suite. She was glad she'd had the presence of mind to ask Brenda to accompany her.

Mustaliq gave the dagger back to Jenny with his characteristic scowl. "I will see that this is returned to its rightful owners," he told her. Baktar made no comment.

They then drove to Central Command headquarters in tension-filled silence.

Chapter Twenty

In the remote estancia in Argentina, Louis Esquedas was having a tense encounter of a different nature. "Vanessa, please come to bed with me," he said. "We're separated so often, let's not waste the opportunity."

"Louis, I want to make love, but you made me so angry, I couldn't respond right now. It's the same issue. There's something going on. You're hiding something, closing me out of part of your life. Why did you turn off my microphone when you were talking in the helicopter? That was rude."

"I'm sorry, love," Esquedas responded. "It's business. You need to understand."

"I don't understand," Vanessa said. "You haven't explained. For example, you never did tell me why you felt compelled to rush out of the White House yesterday. Those were my friends. And who was that woman you were staring at?"

"Vanessa," he answered, starting to get annoyed at her questions. "The woman was someone I thought I recognized. And your friends weren't offended. I told you, it was something that needed my immediate attention. It was important. I was ..." He paused.

"You don't even remember," Vanessa said, raising her voice. Esquedas was not accustomed to being confronted by women. He started to raise his hand.

"What? Now you're going to hit me? Louis, I don't even know you." She started out of their bedroom, shouting. "I'm having the maid pack my bags now. New York never sounded so good!"

Esquedas stood and blocked the doorway.

"Let me out of this room this instant," Vanessa insisted, stamping her foot in anger.

"You are being unreasonable, Vanessa," Esquedas answered, his voice a soft, dangerous purr that his enemies knew to their misfortune.

"It's customary in Argentina that when a husband asks his wife for favors of the bedroom, he is not refused." He dropped his robe on the floor. He was naked and aroused.

"You bastard," Vanessa said. "Don't you dare touch me!" She pulled the throat of her own robe tighter.

"Get in bed, Vanessa."

"Stop it, Louis. I'm not getting in bed with you right now. That's final. Now put some clothes on."

His slap to her face was lightning fast. She stumbled from the blow. He hit her again with his open palm. She fell to her knees. He pushed her to the floor, yanked open her robe and ripped off her panties.

"Louis. Please, not like this. You're hurting me ..."

Minutes later, Esquedas rose from the floor and said, "The next time I say to come to bed with me, dearest, you will do so."

Vanessa stood, sobbing silently, and put her robe back on. "I would like to return to the U.S." Her voice quavered. "Please make arrangements." She stalked from the room.

Esquedas sat on the edge of the bed, his body trembling. He felt gratified both sexually and on a sadistic level.

Vanessa's prompt return to the U.S. could bring unwanted and embarrassing attention. It wouldn't do. He recalled that his first wife had also been something of a problem before her "accident."

Chapter Twenty-One

At MacDill, the stares from coworkers were the hardest part when Jenny O'Shane escorted the clerics through CENTCOM headquarters. Work stopped and chatter died down. You'd think they'd never seen a Muslim cleric before.

She thought Admiral Bryan's assistant, a Navy chief petty officer, was the only cool one. He stood up from his desk when they arrived in the outer office, unruffled by the clerics' presence or appearance.

He welcomed them in Arabic as if he'd been speaking in their native tongue on a daily basis. They conversed at length before he turned to Jenny. "Sorry, ma'am," he told her. "I haven't had a chance to exercise my language skills for some time. That was fun."

"You're a real surprise. I didn't know you knew the language."

"Yes, ma'am. I was a translator on a Navy SEAL team. Those in high places decided Admiral Bryan needed an Arabic linguist, so—"

"I appreciate your welcoming them like that. Thanks. But you talked enough. What was that about?"

"Well," he said with an embarrassed look, glancing at the

clerics, "they were asking about you."

"The petty officer is correct, Princess O'Shane. I asked a few questions about you," responded Sheik Baktar. "After all, finding out about you is why we are here. And it's been my experience with your military forces that if one wants reliable information about an officer, one asks an enlisted person."

"Oh, great. And you said?" Jenny asked.

"Ma'am, I told the truth. You are—"

"It's minor in nature, Princess," interrupted Baktar. "Could we see Admiral Bryan? I want to spend time with him. I've heard some interesting things."

"Of course, sir," answered the assistant over Jenny's withering stare. "He has an opening on his calendar right now. If you'll excuse me, I'll let him know you're here."

They were soon seated with the Chief. Hot tea was served in the Arab custom.

After the barest of pleasantries, Mustaliq asked in an impatient tone, "What is this O'Shane woman supposed to do? We were told she is in the Military Police of the U.S. Army. Why is she not doing police work?"

Admiral Bryan explained Jenny's security responsibilities, and how they fit within the scope of Military Police duties. "She was handpicked for this job and is performing in a superb manner," he concluded.

Bryan's explanations seemed to provide the necessary information. Baktar stood as if to conclude the meeting. Before turning to leave, he made a request.

"Admiral, may I have a private moment with you?"

"Of course, sir," answered Bryan. He nodded to Jenny. She got the message and started out of the office. When she stood, Baktar said something in Arabic to Mustaliq. He nodded and followed Jenny.

Less than five minutes later, Baktar rejoined them in the outer office with another enigmatic smile. Jenny wondered at what he was thinking. She figured it would be pointless to ask.

Instead, she said, "Sheik Baktar, why don't we go over to my quarters now, and I can show you my apartment and the community where I live."

"That would be excellent," responded Baktar. "It's exactly

what I had in mind. Then perhaps we can visit a local eating establishment. I'm famished."

When Jenny was walking out the headquarters building with her charges, two junior officers approached. Both were sharp in appearance and deferential to Jenny. One of them asked, "Ma'am, have you got a minute?"

"Sure, Captain," answered Jenny. To the clerics she asked, "Do you mind if I take care of some business? These are two of my commanders."

"We don't have—," Mustaliq began.

"What's up, guys?" she asked, ignoring Mustaliq.

"Major, we need your help with the CG's aide," answered the captain. "Colonel Everett has this thing about tasking us. He's not following any chain of command."

"Ma'am," continued the other officer, "he damn near took my head off this morning when I tried to ask him about tasking one of my sergeants. It was a job for the local Air Police squadron, not the security team."

The captain interjected, "The sergeant was finishing a twenty-four-hour shift. The Colonel seems to think that if a soldier has an MP brassard on, he or she is available for any tasking."

"OK, guys. Calm down. I got it," answered Jenny. "Don't you two get crossways with Everett. I'll get it squared away. Anything else?"

"No, ma'am," answered the captain. "Do you want us to hang around?" He nodded toward the oddly dressed clerics.

"That's nice of you. Thanks. I got this. They aren't as bad as they look. You two get some work done. I'll be back tomorrow."

Jenny rejoined the clerics. "Sorry for the delay."

"It's not a problem, Princess," responded Baktar. "Who are those soldiers?"

"They both work for me on the security detail for General Penfant."

"Those men work for you?" asked Mustaliq, disbelief tingeing his voice.

"Yes. Among one hundred and fifty-five others."

Mustaliq almost looked impressed, raising his eyebrow and slowly nodding. They climbed into Jenny's car, where Brenda was awaiting. Jenny gave her a look that silently communicated "I appreciate this." Brenda nodded her understanding.

They were nearing Jenny's apartment when her cell phone rang. She punched the hands-free button on her windshield visor and answered, "Major O'Shane."

"Major," they all heard the Southern drawl of Admiral Bryan, "What have you got going with General Penfant?"

"Sir," Jenny answered, "I haven't seen him since D.C."

"Yeah, I thought so. But he called me a few minutes ago and invited you for lunch in his office tomorrow. I wondered if you knew what was happening."

"Sir, you know as much as I do."

"Well, apparently he likes you. Don't get a big head. See you at noon tomorrow."

"Roger that, sir."

After Jenny disconnected, Sheik Baktar asked, "Do you have frequent contact with General Penfant, Princess?"

"I guess," she responded. "Wherever he goes, I'm usually there.

"Harrumph!" Jenny heard from Mustaliq again. She glanced in the rearview mirror and made eye contact. He had a quizzical look.

They had a short tour of her apartment where she changed to civilian clothes. She introduced Nikki, her cat, who hissed at Mustaliq's attempt at a greeting.

It wasn't long before they parked at one of her favorite restaurants. Named The Cairo, the restaurant specialized in exotic dishes of the Middle East. Brenda took the car and promised to pick them up in two hours.

Walking into the entrance, they were greeted by a tall, wide-shouldered black man dressed as a maître d'. "Miss Jenny, look at you! Where have you been?" He gave her a big hug, lifting her off the ground.

"Uhhh, it's good seeing you too, Big John," Jenny mumbled against his lapel. "Put me down, you big lug!"

"Just happy seeing you, missy." He let her down and looked over her guests. "You must be the visitors I heard about. Welcome." Shaking hands, he paused for the barest of seconds with Mustaliq.

"This is a special friend," he added, nodding toward Jenny, a protective glint in his look.

"John—"

"It's OK, Princess," interrupted Sheik Baktar. "We understand."

To Big John, he said, "You look familiar. Aren't you on professional wrestling's world champion tag team?"

"That's right," John answered. "How did you know?"

"We have the Wrestling Channel on TV in my home. They have reruns of your matches every week. You're famous in Saudi Arabia."

"Well, isn't that special," Big John responded. "Wait till I tell Bubba." He put an arm around the old man's stooped shoulders. "Come on in. Now you're my special friend. Missy never calls anyway. I've got a table for you." He guided Baktar into the restaurant, leaving Mustaliq and Jenny to follow in their wake.

Jenny had invited other officers from CENTCOM headquarters to join them for dinner. After Big John led the clerics to the table, she introduced her guests who were already seated.

"These are military liaison officers from Egypt, Jordan and Turkey," she said to the clerics. "They heard of your visit and insisted on meeting you. I hope you don't mind."

"Of course not, Princess," answered Baktar. As hands were shaken and everyone was reseated, Jenny couldn't help but notice another grin on Baktar's face.

Mustaliq asked Jenny, "You work with these officers?"

"Yes, these are my first points of contact when General Penfant schedules a visit to their countries. They sometimes accompany us on the trips."

"Major O'Shane is a pleasure to work with," the group chorused.

"Whoa, guys. Don't embarrass me. My new friends are going to think I set you up," Jenny said.

"No, no. We are speaking the truth," started the Jordanese.

He was interrupted by a loud voice that boomed from the restaurant kitchen doorway.

"Jennifer O'Shane, why didn't you tell me you were coming." A massive man approached the table and lifted Jenny out of her chair. He gave her a wet kiss on each cheek. "You're a sight for sore eyes, you beautiful creature," the man continued.

"Put me down, you slobbering fool," Jenny spluttered, laughing. "Maybe I'll introduce you to a couple of friends from Saudi Arabia. I was hoping to maintain some dignity, but you've taken care of that."

She did the introductions after being deposited back in her seat. She then added, "Bubba is the owner and the chef of the restaurant. He claims lineage from the Middle East, but he's a wannabe."

"Shhh, Jennifer," Bubba responded, chuckling. "Not so loud. It's bad for business. Play nice."

He shook hands with the guests, saying, "Any friend of this young lady is a friend of mine. Has she told you the story about saving Big John's life?"

Catching a glare from Jenny, he continued, "Well, that's for another time. However, let me tell you what I prepared for your enjoyment tonight.

"We have pit-baked goat, served over lemon-dusted vegetables and wild rice, overlaid with mushroom gravy made with semi-sweet goat milk."

"Wow, that sounds delicious," Jenny exclaimed. Soon they were enjoying an excellent meal and a lively discussion.

Afterward, Jenny and Brenda walked the clerics from her car to their hotel entrance. Sheik Baktar invited them upstairs. "We need a few more minutes of your time."

On the elevator, Baktar asked about Big John. "I'm assuming the story Bubba was referring to involved the terrorist attack on the residence of the Secretary of Defense?"

"You're well-informed, sir," Jenny responded.

"Yes ... we hear things. And the Intelligence Services of our governments share important information. Elimination of a drug cartel, capture of terrorist leaders and recovery of stolen secret weapons would rise to that level."

"There were others involved in those operations besides me," Jenny said.

Her comment was rewarded with another smile. They walked in silence until arriving at the cleric's suite. Baktar laid two scrolls on the coffee table.

He said, "Princess O'Shane, our ayatollah gave us authority to allow you either to keep the dagger or to ask that you return it. Each of those scrolls details one option.

"Our decision was to be based on your prowess as a warrior, the position of authority you command and the respect you have achieved among your contemporaries. You excel in each of these categories."

He paused for a moment and then added, "However, it is mandated that you keep the dagger with you at all times. Unfortunately, when you dressed for the evening, it appears that you left the dagger. I'm sorry to have to tell you—" He didn't finish the sentence.

Jenny reached behind her neck and flicked her wrist. The room lights glinted off the blue steel of the blade when the dagger was tossed toward the suite's vaulted ceilings.

She caught it by the hilt and then flipped the end around so that she presented the jeweled dagger handle.

"I keep it in a sheath I had made for a back harness," she said. "I always carry this dagger, even when I wear civilian clothes."

Baktar smiled his mysterious smile once more. He looked toward Mustaliq, who reluctantly nodded his head. "Well, I am pleased to present you with this official scroll from our ayatollah. Please guard our holy dagger. May Allah be with you."

"Thank you, sir. It's an honor to be accorded this privilege. I'll never abuse your trust."

Chapter Twenty-Two

The latch clicked on Crystal's cell door. It was Isabella. Stack had made her his personal assistant. Isabella's duties included serving meals on food trays.

A week had gone by and the prison routine never varied: Breakfast, run on the treadmill, shower, lunch, weight machines, shower, dinner, and lights out—approximately two hours between activities.

Crystal had timed events by counting seconds and minutes, which helped relieve the boredom. She also used the time to plot her escape.

"Never give up" her grandfather had coached. She remembered his counsel as if it were yesterday. "It took me three times, but I finally got it right," he'd said of his POW camp experience after his F-4 was shot down in South Vietnam. Little could he have known that she would relive his experience as a captive; she also was determined to relive his experience as an escapee.

Isabella interrupted her thoughts. "You know the drill," she said. "Please stand in the corner."

Crystal got up from the hard bed and walked over to the

farthest corner of the cell. She was supposed to face the wall. Instead she remained facing the doorway.

"Isabella, what's going on?" Crystal asked.

"Don't talk," Isabella answered, her eyes rolling in panic. "He will hurt both of us." She held her finger to her lips.

She raised the shift she was wearing. There were burn marks and raised welts on her stomach from the tongs of a stun gun. She pulled the top down and exposed other marks on her shoulder and breast. "Stack," was all she said.

"My God! We've got to get out of here," Crystal mouthed.

"No way," was the quiet response. "He will kill us."

They heard the latch release. Stack filled the doorway. "You're done here, Izzy. Get out. I'll deal with you later."

Terrified, Isabella scuttled out the door.

"It's not her fault," Crystal offered.

Stack moved to within inches of her face, his spittle spraying. "I know whose fault it is, bitch. What did I tell you to do when someone came into the room?" His stun gun was in his hands.

"Please, don't. I'm sorry. It won't …" She'd turned to face the corner and didn't see Stack's movement.

He placed the stun gun on her shoulder. The jolt caused her to convulse. Crystal felt every muscle spasm.

Losing control, she urinated and fell to the floor in the puddle. She heard Stack speak through what sounded like a long tunnel: "Now clean this mess up."

Crystal trembled on the floor. He slammed out of the cell. She dragged herself over to the bed and collapsed in tears.

Soon the door unlatched again and a bucket and mop were placed inside the threshold. The door was closed and latched.

Pulling herself upright, Crystal began mopping, residual tremors rocking her body. She was feeling more and more desperate. She wasn't sure how much longer she could hang on. Fighting depression, she tried to refocus. "Never give up."

At the estancia, Francisco Gutierrez was reviewing his human trafficking operation with El Toro. It had become a monthly routine.

"The Women's Resources International staff is our most reliable resource. Protecting that information base is our top priority," Gutierrez stated. "Contacts in drug clinics, homeless shelters and other service agencies refer at-risk women and children. The WRI staff generates a worldwide central database of those receiving support. We hack into their server from here and select the most vulnerable. Sector leaders are given their kidnap targets from the data we provide. It's too easy."

"That's why we have to be so careful," El Toro said. "When it's too easy, people become careless. There's been no major variation detected?"

"I haven't identified any. Not among the operational groups. The snatch teams are making more money than ever. Security seems intact. Has there been any suspicion from WRI staff?"

"I video conference with the executive directors every month and they've expressed no concerns. If we remain slow and methodical, there should be no alarms. Is the immigration side continuing successfully?"

"Sí, señor. The last ship launched is called the *Intrepid*. It will make our southern run and drop off in New Orleans and Houston. That makes six in the Acme Trans fleet. With our small fleet of fishing trawlers to shift our guests between collection points, we are fully functional."

"It's good to hear that all the ships are in operation. Did the drop off of immigrants go well in London?"

"Sí, señor. Perfect. And in both U.S. ports. Each ship disembarked their cargo in small groups. Every immigrant was given authentic looking photo ID cards with Social Security numbers. The IDs are flawless."

"Excellente. And it appears that the communications link from our operations center here is working."

"Sí, señor. Buying into that Chinese satellite was brilliant. We are keeping up-to-the-minute track of the ships and the collection points."

"Bien. What of our Homeland Security contact? We don't need our ships intercepted."

"The informant has been effective. He or she remains anonymous and cash to a P.O. box is working."

As Gutierrez spoke, Carlotta came into the room and sat on

the couch. El Toro had begun to include his daughter in their conferences. Gutierrez didn't like her. Her body language and constant criticisms conveyed that she wasn't fond of him either.

"It doesn't matter how you do it as long as it works," Carlotta said with a nasty tone.

There was a lull in the conversation and they had a staring match. He knew El Toro would choose her in any disagreement, so he broke eye contact first. She smirked at him. He wondered how soon he could dispose of her. Not soon enough.

El Toro interrupted his thoughts. "What did I hear about the New Orleans collection and drop-off point?"

"There's a minor problem with the man who runs the collection point. Reports are that he's too quick with the stun gun. He also killed two of the guards. We don't yet know if the killings were necessary. "

"You need to keep better control of those people. We can't allow some freak to compromise the site," Carlotta said. There was another brief locking of eyes.

"We understand, Carlotta. Thank you, but I think Francisco has taken necessary steps," El Toro responded.

"Sí, señor," Gutierrez answered, pleased with the response.

Carlotta took one of El Toro's hands in hers and gently caressed it. "Of course, Papa."

El Toro smiled at her, a glaze forming over his eyes. He turned to Gutierrez. "You may leave us now. But before I forget, INTERPOL is sending a representative here to speak to me about my ideas on shutting down human trafficking. They think my work with WRI might provide insights I can share."

"That is priceless, Señor," Gutierrez laughed. "Do we know the name of our visitor?"

"Not yet. It may be more than one person. We should know the names soon, and I'll make sure it's not Tavares himself."

Chapter Twenty-Three

General Penfant did introductions in his office at MacDill. "Director Tavares, this is Major Jennifer O'Shane. She's the young officer I was telling you about."

After shaking hands and exchanging greetings, Tavares said, "I've heard a lot about you, O'Shane. Reports are that you single-handedly took down a terrorist cell in Saudi."

"Sir, that's exaggerated," answered Jenny. "I had a security team.

"Don't let her kid you, Juan," interrupted Penfant. "You had to see it to believe it. However, that's not why we're here. Let's have a bite to eat while we talk. I'm hungry." Through mouthfuls of sandwich, Penfant explained his plan.

After only two spoonfuls from the Yoplait fat-free yogurt she'd brought, Jenny sat the container on the coffee table, unable to eat more.

"O'Shane, we believe that human trafficking has evolved into a worldwide network that is now funneling money to support terrorists. As you know, counterterrorism is part of the CENTCOM mission. INTERPOL is mounting an operation to ferret out and eliminate the network. CENTCOM has been given the mission to assist. I'm assigning you as the military lead.

"Frankly, you're on a fast track for promotion. You've been here for over a year, and you've done outstanding work. However, all of us move on, especially those being promoted early." He gave her a hard look.

He's telling me without telling me what he's not supposed to tell me. I'm on the next promotion list; two years early.

She tried to keep a straight face and took a bite of yogurt to cover the silly grin that wouldn't go away. She felt like jumping up and high-fiving everyone, but saw Penfant's face remain passive. *Be cool*, his eyes said.

He continued, "You'll work as my personal representative to INTERPOL. Your primary task will be to coordinate access to all intelligence assets under CENTCOM control to help INTERPOL in their mission. In a secondary role you'll assist Director Tavares in the investigation. Here are your written orders." He handed her a sheaf of papers. "If anyone gives you flak, call me. Any questions?"

"No, sir. Not right now. Thanks, I think."

"Well, keep me posted. Good luck."

Jenny walked out of Penfant's office with Tavares. She didn't know whether to be elated about the prospects of an early promotion or worried about involvement in something way over her head.

Tavares didn't help. "O'Shane, I have to be honest with you," he said, walking down the corridor. "This isn't my idea. In fact, I think it's a mistake. Even though your personnel file reflects uncommon accomplishment, I'm not convinced that this is the job for you."

Jenny's mind went into overdrive. Her reservations about the job redoubled.

"The bottom line is that I agreed to your attachment to my staff because I want access to the intelligence assets. You will be my conduit. However, that will be the extent of your responsibilities. I'll find you an office."

She stopped walking. Her patience with macho male condescending attitudes had run dry. So much for an early promotion.

Tavares noticed she'd fallen back. He turned and said, "Come on, young lady. I have a lot to do."

She stayed put. "I'm sure you do, sir. But I think it's going to be without me." It was OK for her to have self-doubts, but she wouldn't work with a supervisor who clearly doubted her qualifications and abilities. Besides, his condescending manner was out of line.

"What? You have your orders," he said.

"Director, those orders can be changed, and the sooner the better as far as I'm concerned."

After pausing for effect, she said, "Sir, I'm a trained police investigator. Because my background doesn't include your international perspective doesn't mean I'm not qualified to assist. If you're not going to use my talents, then we need to go our separate ways. Either I'm on the team, or I'm not."

"Major, I'm unaccustomed to subordinates speaking to me in this manner," Tavares said with pique and a haughty tone in his voice. "However, this is a rather unique situation, so I'm prepared to overlook your impertinence." He paused and gave her what she imagined was his hardest look.

She stared right back. She knew he needed her, and she wanted the job, but she wasn't willing to start out on the wrong foot.

He broke eye contact first. "OK. OK. I accept your position," he said, smiling for the first time. "Damn, you're a hard nut. I may have underestimated you. We'll talk more when you report in after your leave next week. Admiral Bryan said something about you doing a test run for the Coast Guard?"

Jenny briefly explained her plan to help Charlie with his pursuit boat project.

"All right, but keep it short," he said, following her cryptic explanation. "You can report to my Tampa office afterward." He rubbed his chin for a moment. "You might be a lot more help than I initially thought."

He looked at her some more. She thought she could see his mind working. "Think about bringing some of your own people to round out a team," he continued. "INTERPOL doesn't have many boots on the ground in this area."

He then nodded his head as if he'd made a decision. "I have funding for four temporary personnel. I've used temporary resources before. They have to be vetted for security, but usually they provide a nice balance and some fresh eyes." He smiled at her again. "This is going to be interesting."

He shook her hand, turned on his heel and walked out of the headquarters building. Jenny breathed a sigh of relief and pumped her fist. *Yes!*

Chapter Twenty-Four

Crystal awoke to the clatter of footsteps outside her cell in New Orleans. She heard Stack's distinctive voice. She'd been napping to conserve energy.

Doors slammed. She thought she heard someone crying. It was lunchtime and new girls had arrived. The guards would be distracted.

She had a general plan in mind, but she needed luck. The last few times Crystal had been out for exercise, she'd seen the remote for the stairway lying on a table in the hall.

Also, Isabella carried a door remote for the cell in the right-hand pocket of her shift. Crystal had seen her put it there.

Lastly, it helped that Isabella was completely trusting of Crystal. She'd begun to back into the room, using her butt to push open the door, her hands full with a food tray.

More importantly, the two guards had stopped monitoring the meal service. They were getting complacent. It was time.

Crystal decided she would wait inside the cell door so that when it opened, she would be behind Isabella for a second. There'd be a brief opportunity.

The door latch clicked. She moved to her chosen spot, her

bare feet soundless.

For an instant Isabella had her back to Crystal. "Hey, I brought you an extra apple." The door closed and latched.

Isabella turned. "What?"

"Sorry, Izz" Crystal said. She struck as hard as she could with an upward blow using the heel of her hand. She hit the base of Isabella's skull. Her blow was instinctive. *Hope this does it.* It did. Isabella dropped, out cold.

Crystal lunged, grabbing at the food tray, trying to keep it from falling. "Stop. No. Wait ...," she whispered. The plasticware clattered to the floor.

Panic stricken, she held her breath, trembling, waiting and listening. No one came. "Whew!" she said out loud.

Moving with renewed determination, she stripped the shift off Isabella and slipped it over her own head.

She pushed the door remote button. "Here we go," she murmured.

Pulling the door open, she peeked around the doorframe.

Frankel was sitting in a chair down the hallway. It was tilted against the wall. He was sleeping.

She looked at the desk. The stair remote was there. "Yes!" she whispered again. She picked it up and pushed the button.

The stairs began a noiseless descent. Frankel didn't move. *Come on. A couple of seconds more.*

The light in the cell hallway brightened when the opening in the ceiling widened as the stairway descended. Frankel awoke, startled. "Hey, what the fuck?" He jumped to his feet.

His stun gun fell out of his pocket. "Shit!" he said. He stooped to pick it up.

Crystal used the precious seconds to leap for the first step. Even though the stairs hadn't fully descended, she took a chance and jumped.

It was too far. She didn't make it. She landed chest first against the stairway edge.

"Never give up."

She grabbed the edges of the stairs and pulled herself up and scrambled to the top of the stairway, scraping shins, knees and elbows.

She heard Frankel's footsteps in the corridor behind her.

"Come back here, you bitch. You'll never get away. I'll track you to the end of the earth."

She pushed the remote button again. The stairs began to raise back into their recess.

Still on the last stair into the main warehouse, Crystal felt the stairs raising and then a pronounced jerk. She looked back. Frankel had somehow grabbed the stairway before it fully closed *Dammit!*

She ran toward the warehouse exit. She could hear Frankel's grunts of exertion.

Crashing through the warped door, she saw a docked trawler identical to the one that she'd been on. The bow was painted with the name "*Gotta Girl.*" It was the same boat that she had been on. The Asian man was standing on the wharf. Crystal started running.

In seconds, splinters from the dilapidated wooden dock pierced her bare feet.

Hobbled, Crystal's pace slowed to a fast walk. Every step was agony. Her feet left smears of blood.

Fifty feet down the dock she heard Frankel call out, "Give it up, Crystal. Don't make me chase you. You don't have a chance."

Frankel trotted up beside her. "Stop, dammit. It'll be lots worse if I have to carry you back." He pulled out his stun gun.

Crystal braced herself for the shock. She kept walking.

Instead of the expected shock, Crystal heard a subhuman keening in her ear. Turning, she saw the Asian man standing behind Frankel, holding his hair with one hand and pressing something into his back with the other.

Frankel collapsed on the dock, writhing. His legs moved as if to run away.

The Asian man stood with a bloody knife in his hand. "You sit," he commanded Crystal.

Feeling the pall of failure, Crystal obeyed.

He hurried onto the trawler and soon returned with a woman Crystal didn't recognize.

The man told Crystal, "Hold up feet." Bracing herself, she lifted a foot.

He told the woman, "Pull splinters."

"Wait a minute," the woman said. "I don't want any part

of—" She stopped talking when she looked at Frankel. A pool of blood was spreading under him. "Tranh, what have you done? Are you crazy?"

"Fix feet," Tranh responded, gesturing toward Crystal.

Hesitating only briefly, the woman bent to her work. She methodically pulled the splinters, using a set of tweezers she carried in a belly pack. She applied an ointment and then asked, "Can I leave now?"

"Get back on boat," Tranh answered. "We leave soon. Go Houston. They no see again." He then handed Crystal a set of tennis shoes. "Take these," he said. "Belong other girl. Go now. Hurry!"

Surprised, Crystal hesitated. She looked over at Frankel, who was still softly moaning, blood bubbling from his nose and mouth. Tranh pushed her to her feet and gave a small shove. "Go! Must hurry."

In another movement, as casual as gutting a fish, Tranh reached over to Frankel and sliced his throat. Blood sprayed over Crystal's legs. "He no hurt little girls again," he said. He spit on Frankel's still form.

Crystal didn't understand the reasons for the Asian's actions. She didn't need to. She ran down the dock into an afternoon mist that was building off the water.

Chapter Twenty-Five

At Francisco Gutierrez's estancia in Argentina, El Toro was practicing putting on an indoor green in the main house study. He'd missed three putts in a row listening to Gutierrez describe communication problems. He could feel his anger build.

"Don't tell me about sun spots. I want to know the status of our ships," El Toro said. He felt the vein on his forehead throb.

"Señor, we are doing our best," Gutierrez answered. "It's the Chinese. In their haste to put a commercial satellite into orbit, their lead scientists failed to protect against the fourteen-year-cycle of solar activity. They tell us it will be a few days to reset their instrumentation. Some encryption devices were destroyed."

"You're an idiot to rely on those Third World cretins. I should have never listened to you. What are you doing for communications in the interim?"

"We're using a combination of cell phones and landlines to receive updates. Relays, cut outs and phone cards keep calls untraceable."

"Stop those calls, you stupid man. Every incoming call terminates in our operations center. A pattern could be detected.

You're not thinking!"

"But, señor," Gutierrez said. "You wanted information. And INTERPOL is the only organization seriously looking at organized human trafficking. They don't have access to equipment sophisticated enough to intercept—"

El Toro exploded. "Where is your mind? This is more than slavery. It's immigration, national security and terrorists. What do you think they were discussing at the White House—the Rose Garden? It doesn't take a genius to figure that out. They now have access to the most sophisticated intelligence equipment in the world, and you can bet their satellites are shielded from sun spots. Am I going to have to replace you? Stop the fucking calls!"

He missed another putt and smashed his putter against Gutierrez's oak desk. Dents covering the face of the furniture reflected earlier outbursts. "I'm sure you didn't interrupt my putting practice without having more of an update," El Toro continued, his voice becoming a silken purr.

"It's the ship *Intrepid*. She's having difficulty with her power train," Gutierrez blurted out.

"What does that mean? We rebuilt the power train in Rosario."

"Sí, señor, we, uhh, we only completed the one engine. In the interest of getting the ship out of port and becoming productive, I elected to finish the second engine with the ship underway. It worked well on two other ships, and I saw no reason it wouldn't be successful for the *Intrepid*."

"Hmm. I see. What's the ship's status?"

"She's still under power, but only making steerageway. We need some parts that were supposed to be delivered in Port-au Prince, Haiti. Our parts and cargo were to be pre-positioned there. However, not everything arrived by the time the ship departed. Nueva Gerona, on the Isla de la Juventud of Cuba is the next port. We will have the parts meet them there."

"You determined this all by cell phones?" El Toro asked, his voice now hypnotic in its gentle tone.

"Uhh, not entirely, señor. As I said, we—"

"You didn't recognize the serious risks of your decisions? Operational security, the delays, the costs?"

"Sí, señor. The decisions seemed reasonable at the time."

El Toro didn't miss his fifth putting stroke. He hit Gutierrez squarely in his eye socket. The end of the putter blade penetrated three inches into his skull. Dead before hitting the ground, Gutierrez collapsed, folding as if an accordion.

El Toro dialed a number on the desk phone. "Vladimir, please come to the study," he said.

Within minutes, Gutierrez's assistant appeared. He gave his boss's body only a casual glance. El Toro cleaned off the putter blade on Gutierrez's shirt.

"Clean up this mess and set up secure communications," El Toro said. "Also arrange for WRI to purchase the estancia from Gutierrez's estate. I'm beginning to like this place, and it has the operation center at hand.

"Additionally, get me the current status of the *Intrepid*, and I don't want the world listening. While you're at it, get a status report on the New Orleans collection point."

El Toro stalked out of the room and bumped into Vanessa in an adjoining hall.

"Dearest, how nice to see you up and around," he said with a belying calmness and tried to embrace her.

Vanessa pushed him away, saying, "Don't touch me you pig. Do you think you can rape me and then have everything back to normal? Not even."

With a look of loathing, she added, "Louis, I was serious. I want to go back to New York. I need to cool down and then talk about our divorce."

"Vanessa, I explained to you already. It would be unseemly for you to leave so quickly. I cannot allow it. A divorce at this stage is out of the question. What can I expect you to say to our friends?"

"I would never say anything, Louis. Never! I'm too embarrassed and ashamed."

Esquedas stared at his wife for a considerable time. Saying nothing more, he turned on his heel and walked away.

Chapter Twenty-Six

Jenny arrived at the MacDill command helicopter pad early. She knew that Penfant would be miffed if she were even one minute late. She'd been alerted to her unscheduled trip by a call from Admiral Bryan.

"Sorry to call so late," he'd said without preamble. It was ten-thirty p.m. "The boss wants you to meet someone tomorrow. Dress casual."

"Roger that, sir," she'd responded. "What's up?"

"Your guess is as good as mine. Be at the chopper pad at 0600."

She'd planned on an early morning ocean swim with Brenda, but had to beg off.

The helicopter blades were already turning when she arrived at the pad. She hadn't had a lot of time to plan a wardrobe and hoped her charcoal grey slacks and blue blazer over a pearl-white blouse were adequate. She liked the way the blouse highlighted her red hair. The crew chief greeted Jenny with a salute. "Morning, Major," he said. "Lookin' sharp this morning."

"Thanks, Sergeant. I hope so," Jenny said, feeling validated. Still not fully awake, she yawned. "Why is the CG's plane at

Tampa? I thought he kept it at MacDill"

"SOCOM is having a big ceremony honoring the SEAL team lost in Afghan last week. The CG had his plane moved to free up some parking on the VIP ramp," the sergeant answered as she helped buckle Jenny in.

Penfant was punctual as usual. He was also in civilian clothes. Climbing into his seat, he said into the microphone, "Nice to see that flush to your cheeks, Major. That fiancé of yours must be keeping you happy."

"General Penfant! Some would call that sexual harassment, sir. But I guess I should expect that from an old man."

Penfant chuckled. "Ha! Cute. Bryan said you had a smart mouth." He turned to the pilot. "You going to get this bucket moving, son?"

The helicopter lifted off within seconds of his words. It was a short hop to Tampa International where the CENTCOM command Gulfstream sat waiting.

The airplane started its roll as soon as Penfant was seated. Jenny felt compelled to ask the obvious. "Where are we going, sir?"

"Myrtle Beach," he answered succinctly. "Some people have a private compound there. We're going to pay them a visit." Changing the subject, he said, "By the way, Bryan mentioned that you volunteered for a trial run on the prototype Coast Guard pursuit boat."

"Yes, sir. The first leg starts tomorrow."

"In the Caribbean, right?"

"Yes, sir."

He gave her an assessing look, as if trying to read her mind to determine if she had ulterior motives. He gave an almost imperceptible nod, and then said, "Well, have fun. Let me know how it goes. Stay out of trouble and stay the hell away from Cuba." He then changed subjects again. "Did you read that stuff that Tavares sent you?"

"Yes, sir. Admiral Bryan had shown me something similar. It's scary business, those women vanishing."

"No kidding. Any thoughts?"

"A couple of things come to mind, sir. First, the number of reports is increasing. My guess is that there's an organization involved and that it's becoming more and more sophisticated."

"Yeah, there has been a substantial increase in numbers. That and the publicity over the girl in Aruba are what got everyone's attention. There's been talk about a syndicate, but nothing's been substantiated. What made you think that?"

"First of all, one of the reports refers to mysterious transfers of funds to bank accounts for known terrorist groups. The inference is that there's a connection between terrorists and the slavery market. It'd require a high-powered, well-recognized organization to make that kind of financial interface."

"Good point. Interesting. What else caught your eye?" he asked.

"Did you notice that many of the women were reported missing from coastal locations?"

"That's not true. Women are reported missing from all over the U.S. and Europe."

"Yes, sir. Their homes are from all over, but they're not disappearing from their homes—a majority go missing near heavily populated centers on coastlines. Additionally, my guess is that the organization includes some type of transportation system to get kidnap victims to collection points at central coastal locations."

"Hmm. Central coastal areas ... I haven't heard anyone say that before. Be sure to ask Tavares if he noticed the connection."

"I'm sure he has," Jenny answered with a dismissive wave of her hand. But warming to the subject, she added, "I was also curious about the source of reports of the missing women."

"Sorry," Penfant responded. "You lost me."

"A lot of the reports are from help agencies. You know—drug clinics, runaway counselors. My understanding is that many of those agencies offer anonymity to clients to entice them to seek help. But the standard protocol is that once the clients are officially enrolled in the system, missing appointments at the agencies breaks their contract. If there isn't a good reason for not being at the appointment, an automatic report to the police is generated."

"I hear you. But all of the reports I saw included parental input. I think you're reaching on that one."

"Yes, sir. Parental input after the fact—after the initial

report."

He paused and gave her an amused look. "Hmm. That's a good take in a short time. I've heard you were clever that way. Nonetheless, make sure that the coordination of intelligence resources remains your focus. It's essential Tavares has all the access he needs."

"I'll keep my eye on the ball, General."

"Right. I've also heard you are something of a maverick. Don't take my direction lightly, O'Shane. When I tell someone to do something, I mean for it to happen."

"You don't have to worry about me, sir."

"Then why am I worried?" He held up his hand to indicate his question was rhetorical. "Never mind. When will you be back from the Coast Guard test run?"

"Wednesday, sir," Jenny answered.

"OK. Be sure Tavares knows." He opened his briefcase, indicating that the conversation was over.

Squirming in her seat, and biting at a thumbnail, she tried to communicate through body language that she had more to say.

"Biting your nails is a bad habit," he said. "What else has got you wired up?" His tone and look communicated his own message that he was losing interest.

"General, I know this is out of left field, but I have a gut feeling that illegal immigration is involved in this somehow. My thinking is that a majority of recent illegal immigrants coming into this country find themselves used as virtual slaves in U.S. businesses."

"What are you basing that on?"

"Well, for one thing, updates from the Coast Guard and Border Patrol report significant reductions in the influx of illegal aliens through Mexico and Florida."

It was Penfant's turn to wave a dismissive hand. "What's that have to do with anything? We've been successful in shutting down the flow. That's all. It was expected."

He continued, "Look, I don't want to be rude, and clearly you have good instincts. But I have a lot of work to do, and I don't want you chasing down every rabbit trail. Keep focused on the overall mission. I'm serious about that." He gave her another steely-eyed look, reaching into his briefcase.

They rode in silence for the next hour of the flight. Jenny bit her tongue, struggling with whether to mention that she'd also read that the number of illegals had quadrupled in major port cities. She decided not to push her luck.

The plane began to descend and decelerate. Penfant closed his briefcase and said, "Tavares mentioned that he'd authorized you to form your own team for investigative purposes. Where are you with that?"

"I contacted some friends in the private sector that I've worked with before."

"Would I know them?"

"You might know one of them. He's retired Army and my godfather. He's an ex-Command sergeant major named Jim Cavanaugh. He helped me bust that terrorist plot." She mentally crossed her fingers. She'd already briefed Cavanaugh over the phone and had asked him to speak to the others.

"Was that the operation when your dad was killed?"

"Yes, sir. That was it. Jim Cavanaugh was nearly killed himself."

"That was a terrible business. I'm sorry. Didn't I hear something about Cavanaugh also helping you break up a drug cartel in South Korea?"

"That's him, General. He's a great guy."

"Sounds like a good choice. Who else you got?"

"Two others, sir. I may need some help convincing the Director about them."

"So, I'm not going to like this, right?"

"Sir, I can explain—"

"I've heard about your explanations, O'Shane."

"General, these are great guys to have in a pinch. They're both smart and quick on their feet. They're currently licensed private investigators and they own a popular restaurant."

Penfant began to frown, but Jenny pressed on. "They've had a checkered past—a tiny bit of criminal history when they were young. However, Cavanaugh and I would've both been killed if these two hadn't helped. The Secretary of Defense met one of them at his residence in that shootout you heard about."

"Mmm. Your role in that little episode is partly why you're here. What are their names?"

"They're the Hunter brothers—Big John and Bubba."

"My God, O'Shane. The names alone sound screwy."

"General Penfant, I wouldn't steer you wrong. These are top-drawer people. They just have strange names."

"OK. OK, in for a penny, etcetera. I'll say something to Tavares. It'll be his call."

Changing the subject, he said, "Now, listen carefully. You're about to meet some important people. Speak only when spoken to. Are we clear on this?"

"Of course, sir. I wouldn't embarrass you."

"Right. And leave your pistol, holster and cell phone on the plane; also that fancy throwing knife the Prince gave you. These guys are trigger-happy."

She gave him a long look and then took the knife from her back scabbard. "Jesus, General. Who're we meeting—the Mafia?"

"Not even close. Behave yourself."

☆☆☆

Jenny's helicopter ride coincided with Brenda leaving Jenny's apartment. She'd spent the night because of their swim plans. Brenda decided to go on a run after she found out Jenny couldn't go swimming. She borrowed one of Jenny's West Point sweatshirts and started out at a slow jog down the street. There was hardly any traffic at six a.m.

A block away, a pick-up truck idled. Vladimir sat in the driver's seat. He'd come to the U.S. to deal with Stack in New Orleans, but couldn't resist an opportunity to put eyes on the quarry his boss had been hunting. And there she was—it had to be. Right height, size, red hair, West Point shirt—too good to pass up. He gunned the engine and gave chase.

Chapter Twenty-Seven

Penfant led Jenny down the stairs of his command jet onto a sunbaked empty airfield cut through clumps of palmettos and sand dunes. They were at the end of its single, narrow runway. She could see a short, military-looking command tower in the distance. She also thought she detected camouflaged equipment. Ocean waves broke faintly in the distance and the air felt salty.

A shiny black suburban with darkly tinted windows waited for them near the bottom of the stairs. Two men wearing sunglasses were holding the doors open.

One of the men shook hands with Penfant with familiarity. Then he introduced himself to Jenny. "Morning, Major. I'm Alan Palmer, chief of security. Hop in the car and we'll go up to the main house."

The ride was short. When the car stopped, Jenny could see that they were facing a gated entry extending through a line of sand dunes leading into a fenced compound. It was hot and the wind was whipping up the sand in gritty gusts. Other dark suburbans were parked nearby. Two serious looking, well-built young men in sport coats approached the vehicle.

One opened Jenny's side door. *That bulge under his jacket*

isn't muscle...

She watched his eyes give her a quick scan. *Not being fresh. Making sure my bulges are in the right places.*

She noticed a camouflaged Army Humvee in the distance that was equipped with the Avenger, one of the latest short-range surface-to-air missile systems. *That must be what was camouflaged at the airfield too. What is this place?* Now she could hear the surf pounding close but unseen.

She followed Penfant as the two men led them through the gate. She heard a small beeping sound. She realized that they'd passed through a hidden metal detector.

They were escorted up a long walkway that led to a house with a view of beach and ocean. Two men were sitting on a chair on the veranda. One she instantly recognized.

"Secretary Doakes!" she exclaimed. "It's a pleasure seeing you again, sir."

The Secretary of Defense stood and hugged her. "The pleasure's mine, Jenny. If it wasn't for you I'd be dead—"

"Mr. Secretary, you know that I had a lot of help." The unexpected attention made her feel uncomfortable, and she quickly turned to introduce herself to the other man who also stood. He looked familiar.

The Secretary didn't give her a chance. "Mr. President, this is the officer we've been talking about. Major Jennifer O'Shane ... your Commander-in-Chief."

Jenny was tongue-tied in surprise. She only managed to stutter, "M-my pleasure, Mr. President."

"Mr. President, this is the first time I've ever seen O'Shane at a loss for words," Penfant said. Jenny felt herself blush.

"Have a seat, O'Shane," President Fisher said. "Time is short. Let's get right to business. Major, I asked General Penfant to bring you here so that I could meet the person behind all the stories. I also wanted to personally explain my motive in having you assigned to INTERPOL."

"Sir, I thought I was—"

The President interrupted her. "I'm sure you've been thoroughly briefed as to the operational aspects. But, there's more ..."

He went on to explain his certainty that INTERPOL

operations had been infiltrated at a high level. Criminal organizations and drug cartels were being forewarned of planned counter operations. The leaks were affecting international police actions.

"Our nation alone is investing millions in operations that see less and less benefit," he said. "Other nations are reporting similar experiences."

Jenny's mind reeled at the implications. "Good men possibly killed ... for nothing. Was the DEA ambush in Mexico an example?"

"Nice guess," Fisher responded. "We suspect you're right. Two good men were killed. However, we've formulated a plan with the Brits and Russians to help ferret out the leaks. The international benefits are enormous, and they far outweigh political differences. Without INTERPOL leaks, the Brits think they can clean up IRA remnants, and the Russians believe they will get a better handle on the Chechens."

Jenny's mind leaped ahead. "So, you want a U.S. operative inserted into the INTERPOL organization?" When she saw his head nod, she added, "Mr. President, I feel way over my head—"

"Nonsense," the President said. "General Penfant tells me that you're his first choice to find out what's going on. From what I've seen of your record, I agree."

"I do too," chimed in the Secretary of Defense. "Don't forget, I've personally seen you in action. You have great investigative instincts."

"Major ...," Penfant said when she started to object again. His lips thinned. She got the message—the words "Shut up and listen," were left unsaid.

The President continued his explanation. "At this point, the Brits and Russians are sharing some intelligence findings. In due course, they'll assign operatives you'll work with."

At his next statement, a glint came into his eyes. "Obviously, other nations don't know of our tri-country operation. They would be offended or less than cooperative."

Her mind jumped ahead again. "You want this to be super-secret."

"You got it. All of the operation is top-secret, but the INTERPOL part is a black operation that is 'Eyes Only' for those on this porch."

The Secretary of Defense then took the lead to explain what the black designation meant for the operation. "Because of the international sensitivity, the President has to maintain reasonable deniability. Therefore, if push comes to shove, you're on your own. We won't publicly acknowledge this operation or your assignment. I'll personally brief the House and Senate Intelligence Committee chairs for political cover, but that's all who'll know on our end."

President Fisher summed up, "When you finish the job, I'll handle the public release of information. That's it. Any questions?"

She was certain that there was a ton of things she should ask, but the situation dulled her senses. She could only repeat, "Sir, I feel out of my league. I'm just an Army major—"

"Soon to be a lieutenant colonel, I believe," the President said before she completed the sentence.

Jenny tried to speak, but her mouth felt like cotton—no sound came out. She finally was able to mumble, "I'll do my best, Mr. President."

"I know you will. One more thing. The code word for this operation is Griffin, as in Greek mythology. If there's an emergency, contact my office using that name. The White House operator on the secure line will know how to reach me. Here's a letter giving you my authority to use any U.S. assets to accomplish your mission. Use it wisely and only if all other options fail." He gave Jenny a thin sheet of bond paper signed and embossed with the seal of the President.

"Naturally, we'll claim it's a forgery if it gets in the wrong hands," Secretary Doakes added.

Chapter Twenty-Eight

Intrepid engineering officer Angie Stephens braced against the ship's roll, holding to a railing in the engine room. At five-ten, she'd landed an athletic scholarship as the varsity setter on the volleyball team at the Merchant Marine Academy. She loved playing the net almost as much as learning ship operations.

On her third cruise since graduation, she knew she was doing what she was meant to do. However, even her experienced seaman's legs had to have the extra support in the rough sea. The Acme Trans ship was one hundred and forty miles southeast of the Isla de la Juventud, Cuba, and was getting pounded by an approaching storm. Without power, the ship wallowed in steep wave troughs, unable to respond to steerage commands.

"Goddamn those idiots at Hyundai," ranted the ship's first officer, Jorge Nazarios. "There's no reason they couldn't have had the engine parts at Port-au-Prince on time. This is ridiculous!"

Stephens looked over the first officer. He was a ruddy-faced, overweight Argentinean of medium height. He was an experienced commercial sailor, but the scuttlebutt was that he'd been fired from his last ship for being drunk on duty.

She smelled the liquor on his breath and guessed the rumors

to be true. She was getting fed up with his bitching.

"Look, mate," she said, her own voice rising in volume. "I explained to you and to the Captain yesterday, by some freak of nature it seems that our propeller hit some debris. Probably one of our containers broke loose off the bow and was sucked under the ship. It's rare, but it happens. If we continue to use the power train, the damaged propeller will destroy the bearings and the shaft. You felt the ship shaking. Call an ocean tug and get us a tow."

"But the engine was running perfectly until yesterday," Nazarios said stubbornly.

"God!" exclaimed Stephens. "Listen to me ...," she started. Then she took a deep breath and tried to calm herself. She'd long since decided that Nazarios was clueless.

Stephens was lured to the Acme Trans job by a high salary and the promise of a future management position in the new shipping company.

Captain Popov Slovinski was another reason Stephens decided to take the job. She'd done research on him. She'd found that, although born in Poland, he'd also graduated from the U.S. Merchant Marine Academy through a student exchange program. The *Intrepid* was his sixth ship command. She viewed him as a role model and great boss—level-headed as they came. She thought he might be a big reason she'd been picked for the *Intrepid* engineer job.

Her rapid rise to department lead was rare. She felt Nazarios's simmering jealousy in every exchange. Tonight was no exception. "You need to watch your mouth, Stephens. You might be the Cap'n's pet, but that don't mean nothing to me. Understand?"

"Yeah, right, Jorge. I got it. Now can I get back to work?"

"Sure, just don't forget who's in charge."

As soon as he closed the compartment hatch, Stephens was on the phone to Slovinski.

"Cap'n, you're gonna have to do something about Nazarios. He was down here again tonight. He might know ship operations, but—"

"Calm down, Angie," Captain Slovinski interrupted in his accented English. "I'll have another talk with him."

"Talking isn't going to do it," she answered. "Please keep him out of my engine room."

"I'll do what I can. You know that management wasn't being picky. He came in at the same time they brought in the team to help with our special cargo."

"I'm out of the loop on any special cargo," Stephens said. "As you know, I've been stuck in the engine room since I came on board."

"You're right. I'd forgotten you aren't briefed up. Keep in mind that my hands are tied regarding some aspects of this ship's operation. I'll explain in time."

He paused to let those instructions percolate, and then added, "On another subject, are you certain we can't engage engine number one?"

"Cap'n, there's no way without further damaging the drive shaft. The propeller is off balance, and the bearings are burnt. You felt the vibrations.

"If we engage the engine, and the shaft turns on those worn bearings, there will be permanent damage. The shaft may have to be replaced in dry dock. In the meantime, the vibration could shake this old boat to pieces. But if you want me to engage the engine—?"

"No, no. Come on, Angie. You know I go with your recommendation. But you should also know that there's a storm approaching. We might have to take the risk until the tug gets here. OK? We'll talk more later."

"Roger, sir. Thanks for listening. I'll keep the engine in standby."

☆☆☆

In the *Intrepid's* wheelhouse, after hanging up the phone, Captain Slovinski spoke to his communications officer. "Radio our updated location to Acme headquarters, and let them know we're awaiting a tow to the Isla de la Juventud."

"Roger that, sir."

Slovinski was bending over the navigation table when Carlos Pasqual and Sergei Velstinevitch entered the wheelhouse, led by First Officer Nazarios.

"Cap'n, these men wanted to talk with you," Nazarios said.

"Hey, shorty," the Captain greeted the small, rail-thin Pasqual. "What are you doing in here? I thought I asked you to call if you needed to talk to me."

"Captain Slovinski, my name is Carlos Pasqual, as you well know. I represent the senior management of this shipping company. Please do me the courtesy of using my name." The Captain watched Pasqual's eyes glance over the chart table, at the helmsman and at Nazarios.

"Sure. Sure, Señor Carlos," the Captain responded, putting a sarcastic emphasis to the name. "I haven't had much time to learn names. Nor have I fully inspected the ship. Nazarios and I have been twelve-on and twelve-off since I got here. Getting her from point 'A' to point 'B' has been a grind."

"Quit complaining. You knew the challenges when you signed on. You were fired from your last ship, so count your blessings."

"That's bullshit, and you know it. It was trumped up charges so the company could get out of paying my retirement. Don't give me that 'fired' crap."

"It doesn't make any difference, Captain. You were unemployed and couldn't find work. You have a son in college and a family to feed.

"It doesn't matter, and I'm not here to argue with you. And don't bother inspecting the forward superstructure. That's not your business.

"What is your business is that I notice that we aren't under power. I've been informed that you decided to await a tug rather than risk damage to the ship's equipment. Please engage the engine. We're falling too far behind in our schedule."

"Say what? Who the fuck—?" Slovinski said. Pasqual moved incredibly fast. A pistol appeared in his hand in a blur.

"I will not repeat my instructions, Captain. I said that I'm not here to argue."

"Whoa, amigo. Easy does it." Nazarios backed away.

The Captain remained stoic. It wasn't the first time he'd been threatened with a gun or by some thug.

"What? You going to shoot me?" he challenged. "We're already short-handed."

"Of course I'm not going to shoot you, Captain," Pasqual answered.

Despite the reassurance, the gun discharged. Slovinski felt hot gases burn his cheek. The gunfire reverberated in the small space.

Slovinski closed his eyes, half-expecting that he was dying. But he felt nothing. No pain.

He opened his eyes. Pasqual was standing in front of him with a thin smile on his face. "Perhaps now we can begin to communicate," he said, looking over the captain's shoulder.

Slovinski turned to see where Pasqual was looking. Nazarios was sitting on the deck; a small hole was in the center of his forehead. A trail of blood trickled down the steel bulkhead behind him.

Chapter Twenty-Nine

Slovinski stared at the sight of Nazarios slumped against the bulkhead. "Are you out of your mind?!" he shouted at Pasqual. "You killed our most qualified deck officer."

"Settle down, Captain," Pasqual said. "He was a worthless drunk. We'll replace him in Cuba. In the meantime, you'll have to manage. Now get us underway."

"You have no idea what you're asking," said Slovinski.

"I think I do, Captain. Underway. Now." Pasqual pointed his pistol toward the helmsman.

Slovinski picked up the ship phone and dialed the engine room. Stephens answered. "What's up, Cap'n? I have diesel fuel all over my hands."

"Engage the engine."

"Cap'n, you can't mean it. Sir, with respect, you know that'll screw up the drive—"

"Do it, Stephens. No argument. Engage the engine. Put in the log that I gave you the order. Date and time the entry. I'll sign it later."

"Sure, Cap'n. Sure. Whatever you say."

☆☆☆

Stephens hung up the phone in the *Intrepid* engine room, puzzled by the captain's abruptness.

She wiped her hands off with a rag and reached up to the switches to begin the cycling of engine engagement with the drive train.

"Whoa, ma'am," Rocky, her second in command said. "Don't we have enough problems?"

"I can't explain it. The Captain told me to get underway right now. He said it was an order."

"That doesn't sound like him."

"I know. Something strange is going on. You continue sequencing. I'm going up to find out. I'll be back."

"You got it," Rocky answered.

Stephens climbed the ladders to the bridge. Two men she didn't recognize squeezed by her carrying a large rolled bundle of canvas.

"What's up, guys?" Stephens asked them. They mumbled an unintelligible reply and kept moving.

When she entered the bridge, Stephens saw another unfamiliar crewman washing what looked like ketchup off the far bulkhead, and still another strange man was conferring with Slovinski over the navigation chart table.

Slovinski looked up when she came in. He asked, "Stephens, what are you doing up here?"

"I came up to check in, Cap'n. I meant no disrespect about your orders, sir."

"No sweat. Go on back down to engineering." The Captain was doing something strange with his eyes, rolling them and canting his head.

Stephens wasn't satisfied, but she got the message that he wanted her off the bridge. She turned to go.

"First Engineer Angela Stephens, is it not?" the stranger with Slovinski asked. "I'm Pablo Pasqual, vice president of Acme Trans." Pasqual put his hand out for a handshake. "The captain's manners are suffering from the stress of the moment, I think."

Shaking Pasqual's hand, Stephens sensed something amiss.

"And this is Sergei, my assistant," Pasqual continued,

pointing to Velstinevitch.

Stephens said, "Nice meeting you, gentlemen. If you'll excuse me, I need to get back to my engines. Good night."

Stephens closed the wheelhouse door behind her and wiped her hands on her overalls.

"She's a beautiful woman," Pasqual said to the captain. "A close friend, I take it?"

"She's someone I've heard good reports on, and she's doing well for us," the Captain answered.

"Oh, come on. I'd bet you've been fucking her."

"Not even!" the Captain said with a sneer. "We're professional on my crew."

Pasqual shoved the muzzle of the pistol against Slovinski's throat. "You address me with respect, Captain, or your worst imagining can't contrive of what I'll do to your girlfriend."

Slovinski glared at him.

"It appears I've got your attention. But I think a demonstration would be appropriate. Call her back."

"That's not necessary."

"Call her back." He pointed his pistol at the helmsman. "Now."

"All right, already." Slovinski leaned out the hatch and yelled for Stephens.

"What's up Cap'n?" she asked, back in a blink.

"Stephens," said Pasqual, "The Captain and I have a bet. He said I couldn't get you out of your clothes. I think he's wrong."

Stephens looked at him in a disdainful way. "You wasted your money." She started to leave.

"Wait, señorita. I can be very persuasive."

She turned. Once again, Pasqual had his pistol in his hand.

"You're not going to force me into anything with that," she said. "Go ahead and shoot. I figure that's a lot better than what you have in mind."

"You're very brave. But I won't shoot you." Despite the reassurance, a gunshot rang out, deafening in their small confines. The helmsman yelped in pain. He folded on the floor, moaning. He was shot in the foot.

"Now, I can do this for hours without killing him," Pasqual said. "You can make his life painful, or you can be embarrassed.

But you will obey my orders. Now remove your clothes!"

"You're a bastard!" She began unfastening her uniform. Soon she was down to a thin bra and panties.

"I meant all of them. Take everything off," Pasqual said.

Stephens stared at him with a look of hate in her eyes. She unfastened her bra and stepped out of her panties.

"There. Satisfied?" She stood tall, with a defiant air.

"Oh, yes. You're very beautiful. Your breasts are perfect and I love your nipples. Now, you may dress and go back to work. Remember. I'm in charge. You'll do as I say. Do you understand?"

"<u>Fine</u>!" she said, zipping up her coveralls without putting on her underwear. Her look provided a combination of contempt and loathing.

"Go back to your engines, señorita. Get this ship moving."

"Yes, sir," Stephens responded. She yanked open the hatch and stormed out of the wheelhouse.

"You're a real shit, Pasqual," Slovinski said, kneeling to help the wounded helmsman.

"Don't push me," Pasqual responded. To Velstinevitch he said, "Follow Stephens. Make sure she doesn't cause us a problem."

"Got it," Velstinevitch said, hustling off the bridge.

"I hope Stephens has the sense to do her job," Pasqual said to Slovinski.

"You so much as touch a hair on her head, I'll kill you, asshole."

"Tut, tut, Captain. Calm yourself. Do as you're told and no one else gets hurt. You have my word. Why don't you send for a doctor for our young sailor?"

"We don't have doctors, Pasqual. This is not a cruise ship."

"Well, do whatever you need to with him. Have someone up here to steer this thing in the next few minutes."

Slovinski spoke into the ship phone, and soon a replacement arrived for the helmsman. A nurse also arrived and attended to the wounded man.

☆☆☆

"Hey, how'd it go?" Rocky asked when Stephens returned

to the engine room. Tears streamed down her cheeks as she described what happened.

"That bastard," Rocky said. "I'm going to go up there and kick his ass." He picked up the nearest wrench and started out the compartment.

"No, wait," Stephens said, holding his arm. "I'll be all right. If you go up there, he'll kill you. Or he'll kill a crewman. The man's certifiable, Rocky. Besides, I'd bet he's got his henchmen watching our every move."

She continued, "Rocky, as weird as it sounds, I think we've been hijacked." She explained what she'd seen.

"Why would anyone want to hijack a container ship in the middle of the Caribbean? That doesn't make any sense."

"I know. I can't explain it."

Stephens could feel the ship begin to make steerageway. Two bells sounded from the bridge, directing the engineers to set the engine for medium speed.

The ship started vibrating when the drive shaft began to spin.

Stephens envisioned the drive shaft rotating within damaged bearings. She pictured the shaft wrenching off the aft bulkhead.

"I'm going topside to get some fresh air," Stephens told Rocky. "I can't stand this."

On deck Stephens noticed a signal lamp attached near the rail. In the distance was the vague outline of a ship.

Chapter Thirty

Vladimir watched El Toro having another temper tantrum. "I can't believe that one ship can cause so many problems. You've got to get this under control." Vladimir had heard about El Toro's explosive temper, but didn't flinch.

Vladimir's calm made El Toro even more furious. He threw a penholder against the wall.

"Señor, I'm sorry," Vladimir said. "Pasqual is one of our most reliable men. The circumstances on the ship are out of his control."

El Toro began to sputter another response. But before he said more, a shadow moved into the room from the estancia's veranda. A small voice asked, "Louis, why are you yelling? What ship are you talking about?" Vanessa Esquedas walked toward the two men.

"Why did you sneak up on me?" El Toro exploded. "This is business. Leave us!"

"But, I—" Vanessa started, and hesitated only for a fraction of a second. With a looping swing, El Toro hit his wife full in the face with a closed fist. She spun and collapsed like a rag doll, splayed on the floor, moaning.

Spittle sprayed from El Toro's mouth. "You will do as I say, when I say. Never, ever question me."

"Get her out of my sight," he commanded Vladimir. "Lock her up ... in fact, sell her like the common trash she is."

"Do you want her to disappear or offered for sale?" Vladimir asked without emotion.

"Sell her," he said, chuckling sadistically. "She will make an excellent concubine in a harem in Libya."

"As you wish, señor." Just then, a green light on his satellite phone lit.

"Wait, El Toro," he said. "I think we may be reconnected to the *Intrepid*."

Into the phone receiver, he said, "Pasqual, can you hear me?"

"Sí, señor," Pasqual answered. "I'll speak quickly before we drop the link again." He then told of his efforts to get the ship moving again.

"Get into Cuban waters before you're intercepted by the U.S. Coast Guard curious about the ship's strange behavior. You're a perfect target!" El Toro yelled. He grabbed the phone just as the red light illuminated again.

"Dammit! This is impossible." He started to throw the phone. Vladimir grasped his wrist.

"No, señor. It's all we have." They glared at one another. Not intimidated, Vladimir removed the phone from El Toro's hand and stepped back. "I'm sorry, señor," he said. "We must remain calm."

"You remain calm," El Toro sputtered. "But don't dare touch me again. And never challenge me. Are we clear?"

Vladimir gave a faint smile and inclined his head. "Sí, señor. I apologize."

He pointed to his wife, still weeping on the floor. "Get rid of this trash," he said, and stormed out of the room.

Vladimir touched speed dial on his cell phone. "Eduardo, I need your help," he said to the foreman of the ranch's gauchos.

Vanessa Esquedas was soon imprisoned in one of twenty cells located in a nearby outbuilding. Vladimir had supervised the building's construction. Disguised as a horse stable, it was also a prison built to house women and children who were kidnapped in South America. The victims were either ransomed back to families or sold on the international slave market.

Those kidnapped were usually from major coastal cities—Rio de Janeiro, Buenos Aires, Santiago and Montevideo. The syndicate was selective, spacing activity to minimize undue alarm among South American authorities and communities. Their ransom fetched a fortune. One child alone could bring as much as a million dollars.

"The van will be here to pick up and drop off some merchandise next Tuesday," Eduardo informed Vladimir. The two men were walking back to the main house.

"That's good. We'll plan on sending the Esquedas woman to Africa as soon as possible. I'll arrange a customer. We'll be having special visitors in the next few weeks, and her presence may be an unnecessary risk."

"Sí, señor," answered Eduardo. "It will be done." He paused for a moment and added, "Señor, did you notice the weather forecast?"

"I saw that a storm is moving inland from the Caribbean. Rain shouldn't interrupt our plans. It'll dissipate before getting here."

"Sí, señor."

Chapter Thirty-One

At INTERPOL offices in Tampa, Jenny and Jim Cavanaugh were spitting mad at the receptionist in the lobby. They'd just come from the funeral for Brenda, who was killed by a hit-and-run driver while Jenny was in Myrtle Beach. In a dark frame of mind to start with, Jenny had no patience for petty bureaucrats. The receptionist gave Cavanaugh's private investigator business card a disapproving look and said, "I'm sorry. You and your lady friends cannot see Director Tavares now. You'll need an appointment. Please leave before I call security."

"Ma'am," Jenny tried, "I'm a major in the U.S. Army. Here's my ID." She showed her military ID card and MP badge. "At least call the Director. Please. Tell him that Major Jennifer O'Shane is here. I'm supposed to report for duty on Monday. But I have information the Director needs to be aware of now."

"Your names are not on my roster. And I certainly don't intend to interrupt the Director. We have rules here, and I'm paid to help enforce them." She waved to the security guards.

"You're making a big mistake, lady," Cavanaugh said. "Come on, Crystal," he spoke to a young Hispanic girl who was with them. "We'll have to figure something else out."

Docile and mute, the Hispanic girl clung to Jenny's arm. Tears streamed down her cheeks.

"Don't cry, honey. I told you we'd get help and we will. You can stay with the Cavanaughs. Ginger will take good care of you." Jenny opened her cell phone and speed dialed a number after they got into Cavanaugh's car. "Hi, Big John," she said into the phone. "As you predicted, we didn't get in. We didn't even get past the receptionist."

"Yep," John responded. "Bureaucrats live in a different world. They have rules that help justify their jobs. There's no getting around it. Has Crystal opened up anymore?"

"No. Not another word. She still appears scared to death. I'm surprised we got her first name."

"Whoever had her captive must've been rough."

"No doubt and I think that's only part of her story. Her being found at a port, minimal clothes, no ID, shackle marks on her ankles ... my gut tells me she's linked to this sex-slave thing. I'd hoped INTERPOL would be more interested. I think they have access to professionals who could help get her to talk. At any rate, would you and Bubba keep an eye on the Cavanaugh house for the time being? Whoever's scared her like this might come after her."

"No sweat, Miss Jenny. We've got great staff to cover us at the restaurant."

"Thanks, we're headed home now."

After hanging up, Jenny said to Crystal, "Well, it looks like we go into a holding pattern for the weekend. Let's get you back over to the house. Momma will wonder where you're at."

"Momma's nice," Crystal responded.

"Ha! Don't tell her that," Cavanaugh said, referring to his live-in mother-in-law. "She still thinks she has us fooled."

His response elicited a hesitant smile that Jenny noticed. She thought it might be a good time to push for more information. "You feel like telling us about New Orleans yet?"

"No!" Crystal wailed and pressed herself against Jenny's side, gripping her blouse with both fists. Tears started rolling down her cheeks again.

"That's OK, Crystal. Calm down. We'll talk when you feel up to it." She wrapped both arms around the sobbing girl.

Cavanaugh reached over to pat her leg.

Crystal recoiled, her eyes as big as saucers. "Jesus," Cavanaugh said under his breath. "What the hell happened to you?"

It was fifteen minutes into the drive before Jenny could feel Crystal's body slowly relax. Her fists uncurled and her breathing settled. "You poor thing," Jenny said, holding her tight.

To Cavanaugh she said, "There's no doubt in my mind that this is connected to the INTERPOL thing. It's key, I'm certain of it."

"Your instincts are usually good, but there's a lot of missing pieces to get from here to that conclusion. How are you connecting the dots?"

"I wish I knew. It's just a hunch. If the Humphreys had—" She didn't finish the thought.

"Now, don't go blaming them," Cavanaugh said. "They were just as surprised as we were." They were referring to Vernon and Georgina Humphrey, who had shown up unexpectedly at the Cavanaugh's house Thursday night. Jenny and Gary were there having dinner with the Cavanaugh family.

Vernon Humphrey had been Jenny's driver when she was assigned to Korea. She and Cavanaugh had kept in touch with him as he and his wife, Georgina, moved from station to station during an Army career.

Like Cavanaugh, Vernon was also retired. The Humphreys had a retirement job driving eighteen-wheelers as a husband and wife team.

Thin and pale, Crystal had been hanging on the arm of Georgina as the couple stood in the entryway.

After the general greeting typical of friends who hadn't seen each other for a while, Crystal was introduced. She remained mute and looked away when Jenny tried to make eye contact. The young girl appeared to be in a daze.

It was with huge relief when Momma asserted her emergency room nurse training. "Aren't you a pretty little thing," she'd cooed to Crystal. She'd gently smoothed Crystal's hair. "Come into the kitchen, honey. We'll find you some chocolate chip cookies and warm milk." She, Ginger and Georgina led the girl into the back of the house.

"It's been a while, Vernon," Jenny had said. "What's going on?" Her mind did an instant of flashback to when she and Humphrey had taken on North Korean infiltrators in a firefight. She'd earned a rare peacetime Silver Star, and he'd been awarded a Bronze Star for valor.

They reminisced about Korea for a few minutes.

"Those were some great times," Humphrey had said. "Jim, I remember you helping Jenny bust up the drug ring and deal with that asshole MP Battalion Commander."

"Well, a godfather's got to be good for something." They'd chuckled at the shared memories.

Humphrey had continued, "Scuttlebutt has it that you helped solve the murder of Jenny's dad too."

Cavanaugh nodded, avoiding a direct response. Jenny knew that some aspects of that operation were still classified. Changing subjects, she'd said, "That was a couple of years ago. Why don't you quit stalling? Tell us what's up with the girl."

Humphrey had turned serious. "Sorry to drop this on you, Cap'n. We heard that Jim had turned PI since retiring, and we remembered that you were assigned to this area."

"Jenny's a major now, on the promotion list to lieutenant colonel," Cavanaugh corrected.

"Wow! I knew you'd be on the fast track, ma'am. Congratulations. Maybe we can set up a celebration next time we come through."

"Humphrey," Cavanaugh had interrupted. "Why are you here—the girl?"

Humphrey had taken a deep breath. "Well, after we delivered a ship container in New Orleans two days ago, we took a wrong turn getting off the waterfront. Trying to find our way out, we passed Crystal aimlessly wandering down the middle of the road in an abandoned section of the dockyard. Since Katrina, there are a lot of those empty spaces."

He'd told them about her not having ID, the burn marks on her shoulder and bruises on her ankles. She was incoherent. "Georgina nursed her in the cabin of our truck. We were worried that, without identification, the girl might end up in an immigration detention center, or worse. Georgina wouldn't even consider leaving her at the dockyard. We knew the Cap'n, uhhh,

Major O'Shane, would be better at helping her out. We couldn't figure out what else to do. Sorry."

"I don't know what you expect from us," Cavanaugh said. "Crystal's most likely an illegal immigrant. If that's the case, my hands are tied."

Chapter Thirty-Two

Admiral Bryant sat in his CENTCOM office at MacDill and stared at Jenny, open-mouthed. "You want me to call who?"

"Admiral, I know it sounds like a big deal, but it's really simple," she responded.

"Don't give me that crap. Deploying one of the Navy's special weapons systems is not simple. I don't even know if they have an operable Advanced SEAL Delivery System. That program was publicly canceled years ago."

He shook his head. "Let me get this straight. You want me to contact the Special Ops commander and ask him to let you use a secret weapons system, assuming he has what you want. Your request to use his equipment is based on copies of intercepts of cell phone calls that the Intel weenies gave you. Does that sum it up?"

"Sir, I don't think—"

"On top of that, you want me to obtain authorization for you, a U.S. military officer, to board a neutral ship in international waters. O'Shane, get real! What does Tavares say about all this?"

"The security at his office turned Jim Cavanaugh and me away yesterday. We weren't on their 'list' yet." She waved pages of transcribed intercepts in the air. "This is just the stuff he was wanting." She'd asked her staff to see what they could find when she'd been at Central Command headquarters with the Muslim clerics.

"Perhaps," Bryant answered. "But I think you're getting way ahead of yourself. Anyway, Tavares's people were just doing their job. They have certain security protocols like we all do. You were two days early."

As he talked, he got a thoughtful look on his face. "You thought Tavares might have someone who could get the 'Crystal' girl to unload?" She had already explained the situation with Crystal.

"Yes, sir. It sounded plausible to me."

"Well, for your information, INTERPOL isn't staffed like that. They have a small support staff organization, especially in a temporary office. Why don't you try Dr. Pabst, the staff psychologist here at headquarters? By the way, have you seen him yet?"

"Yes, sir. We talked. He's some weird dude," she said.

"Don't be too quick to judge. He's an expert on treating post traumatic stress disorders. He's no slouch."

"Is he authorized to take on civilians?" she asked.

"I'll give him a call. I'm sure he can make an exception. But you're still reaching about the girl. I have to agree with Cavanaugh. She's probably an illegal trying every angle to keep from being deported. Just because she was found in New Orleans, and this ship thing ..." He paused to refer to papers she'd given him. "Just because the *Intrepid* is headed to New Orleans and is involved in some questionable phone messages doesn't necessarily connect the two."

"Sir, I think it's—"

He put his hand up to interrupt her again, pinching the bridge of his nose with his other hand. "Look. I'll tell you what. Go over and talk to the J-3 staff at SOCOM Headquarters." Jenny knew he meant the operations staff at U.S. Special Operations Command that was also based at MacDill. "I'll call and tell them you're coming. If you can convince them to use some of their Star Wars gear based on this story, I'll try to get our legal staff to find justification to board the ship. And I'll talk to Pabst to arrange for him to meet the Crystal girl. You get SOCOM on board, and we'll see. That's the best I can do." He waved her out of the office.

"Thank you, sir," Jenny responded, trying to sound appreciative. However, her thoughts were less than positive.

☆☆☆

Thirty minutes after her meeting with Admiral Bryant, Jenny stood outside the SOCOM headquarters building. A Marine lieutenant walked toward her. He sported a high-and-tight haircut, bright intelligent eyes and wide shoulders. Jenny thought he exemplified the Marine-poster-boy look for recruiters.

A crisp salute was followed by a straight-to-business introduction. "Afternoon, Major," he said. "We're expecting you. I'm Lieutenant Culver, aide to General Simpson. He's asked me to bring you directly to him. Follow me, ma'am."

Several corridors and stairways later, Jenny was led to a small conference room. Its walls were replete with pictures and banners of those that she believed were America's finest warriors. They served at the tip of the country's military spear—Delta Teams, SEALS, Rangers, and Army, Marine and Air Force Special Forces.

At the head of a table in the center of the room sat a grizzled Army major general. He wore an ACU that was adorned with every badge and insignia awarded for Army special force training. His bulldog face was set in a scowl.

He was flanked on one side by a man wearing the uniform and rank of a Navy master chief petty officer and on the other by a man wearing what she thought was a British combat uniform with the rank of captain on it and no nametag. The General didn't waste time on introductions.

"Don't stand there at attention, Major," he told her. "Relax. My name's Simpson. SOCOM J-3." He spoke in clipped, no-nonsense, abbreviated sentences. He gave a vague wave that served as a return of the salute she rendered upon entering the room. "You wouldn't be here if Bryant and I weren't friends. He asked me to listen. You've got five minutes. I'll introduce my two associates after we hear what you have to say." Almost as an afterthought, he added, "We don't get many MPs here. Certainly no women."

"Thank you, sir. I think—"

"Don't thank me yet. Your time's already started."

Jenny got his meaning. Simpson was the senior Staff Director of all U.S. Special Operations. If she didn't sell her idea to him, and do it quickly, her plan would be stillborn. She wondered if the general's mind was already made up; just extending a courtesy to Bryant.

Nothing to lose. She outlined her findings—the *Intrepid's* erratic course, the phone intercepts, and the girl named Crystal. She'd brought copies of transcribed phone intercepts, the satellite location of the ship, the reports showing dramatic increases in illegals in coastal cities, a report from INTERPOL agents observing the ship being loaded with hundreds of passengers at one of its ports of call, and a copy of the manifest registered with the International Maritime Authority by the *Intrepid* that showed New Orleans as a destination.

She kept eye contact with Simpson during the entire time she talked. He scanned the pages she laid on the table and then looked away briefly when she finished. She guessed he'd decided.

He surprised her by asking the man in the Navy uniform, "What do you think, Master Chief Cullis?"

"Sir, I think it's pretty farfetched," he answered. "She's just guessing about the girl involved in a human trafficking operation in New Orleans. That's just a hunch. And the ship's behavior, there could be a lot of reasons for that. I don't want to risk my SEAL Delivery System on this sketchy information, and I sure as hell don't want to get it close to Cuban waters."

"Major. I think you just got your answer," Simpson said.

She sighed in resignation and began to pick up her papers. Just before she stood to take her leave, she remembered the President's orders.

She handed Simpson a thin piece of paper from her wallet. "Sir, you might want to take a look at this before you decide."

He unfolded the paper and read the few lines. "I don't believe it. Is this supposed to be the President's signature? Where'd you get this?" He handed the paper to Cullis.

Jenny answered, "Sir, you'll notice that any and all U.S. military assets are to be made available to me. I apologize if this is inconvenient."

"Inconvenient, my ass," Simpson sputtered.

"General, may I suggest you call the Secretary of Defense for confirmation. I believe he'll clear up any misunderstanding."

"You can bet on it. Wait in the hall," he snarled. Jenny watched him pick up a phone on the conference room table as she closed the door behind her. Two minutes later, Lieutenant Culver opened the door and motioned her back into the room. A ruddy-faced Simpson was holding the phone receiver out toward her.

"Secretary Doakes would like a few words with you."

"Major O'Shane, sir," Jenny said into the receiver.

"You have a real knack for winning friends, Jenny," she heard Secretary Doakes say, chuckling into her ear.

"Sorry about that, sir. I feel like I'm running out of options."

"OK, I'm assuming Director Tavares wasn't very helpful."

"No, sir. His staff wouldn't even let me in the building the other day. And I got the distinct impression he wasn't too keen with the idea of my helping. Besides, I think we may be short on time. If that ship docks in New Orleans, evidence could disappear in hours."

"Well, I agree with Simpson. This is really thin stuff." Jenny's heart sank.

"I know this is a secure line," Doakes continued. "Has the phone got a speaker option?"

"Yes, sir," Jenny answered, feeling somewhat foolish. She pressed a button on the phone console.

"General Simpson, can you hear me?" The voice of Secretary Doakes sounded loud in the small conference room.

"Yes, Mr. Secretary. I hear you fine."

"Good. I know this is against your better judgment, but the President was pretty clear as to what he wanted, so I'm authorizing you to give Major O'Shane the assistance she requires. Do you need that in writing?"

"No, sir. Not if this is a black op. I got it. Thanks for your time." There was a distinct click as the Secretary hung up his phone without further comment.

Simpson glared at Jenny as he handed back her thin sheet of paper. She stood trying to keep a smirk off her face.

"Well, I hope this doesn't turn into a fiasco, Major. I see an embarrassment to the President unfolding," he said.

"Sir, I think we're going to be just fine," the British officer piped up.

"What are you talking about, Captain Reimers?" General Simpson asked the Brit.

"Sir, some of my SAS chaps are at Eglin Air Force Base for training. It includes an orientation on the ASDS. This may be a perfect opportunity."

"Bullshit. I wondered why the British Special Air Squadron liaison officer wanted me to include you on this little chat. Don't tell me you already knew about this, Reimers?"

"Not at all, sir. Not the slightest clue. Nonetheless, I think Major O'Shane is onto something, and she and I will have a jolly griffin time sorting it out."

Jenny's mouth dropped open when she heard the code word. She stared at Reimers. *Holy cow! My Brit counterpart.*

Chapter Thirty-Three

Captain Reimers and Jenny left SOCOM headquarters together. She felt somewhat shocked by the rapid turn of events: the almost unexpected permission to use the Navy SEALS top-secret ASDS min-sub. "Let's walk and get some air while I get my head around this," she said.

They started walking toward MacDill's ceremonial park. "How did you know I'd be there and what I was going to request?" she asked.

"We heard you were coming over," the Brit said. "We knew the subject, and we just put two and two together."

"Great. It's still unsettling to be so transparent."

"If it makes you feel any better, you should know I won several quid on a bet that you'd get the support you wanted."

"There was a bet? Great! So much for the classified mission."

"No worries. It was just my chaps. They're pretty tight-lipped.

"I had a little inside information. My brief on you from MI6 gave you high marks. You have quite a reputation."

"How so?"

Reimers didn't answer and Jenny changed subjects. "How

do you figure it'll go with the ASDS? That Master Chief isn't going to be easy to work with."

"I'll have my chaps work on him a bit. SEALs and SAS types get on well. It'll be easier than you might think. We have an exercise scheduled in the Dry Tortugas. It's just a hop-skip-and-jump to where the *Intrepid* should be in a few days. That'll give us plenty of time to get oriented on the ASDS."

"I hope you're right. I've wanted to see how the ASDS operated ever since I heard about the system." She thought for a minute. "There has to be a submarine in this somewhere. Do you know which one is scheduled to support your training exercise?"

"We wouldn't have needed the sub for our training. This new twist of yours is kind of spur-of-the-moment. The sub will have to be configured to carry the ASDS. To my knowledge, that's either the USS *Charlotte* or *Greenville*. However, I don't think you'll be going, ma'am. Sorry. The ships aren't built for women passengers. Besides, my chaps can do the recon."

"I guess you don't know as much about me as you think you do, Reimers. This is my op. I'm going. It's nonnegotiable. They're going to have to make accommodations."

Reimers made eye contact. They had a staring match. He must have detected her steely resolve. "Our MI6 file on you was pretty accurate. This may make it a little tougher sell."

"What file?"

Again, Reimers didn't answer. Instead he said, "I think we need to make transport arrangements to the Key West Naval Air Station."

That night Reimers and Jenny walked down a remote, low-lying dock at Fleming Key, just north of Key West. It was the home of the Army Special Forces Underwater Operations School. They were carrying duffel bags packed with their personal items. They were wearing wet suits, and had swim fins, masks and snorkels slung over their shoulders.

The only sound was the nearly silent slap of waves against the dock pylons. Visibility was limited to small red lights edging the dock and a narrow gangplank.

Jenny's nose wrinkled at the stench from oil, gasoline, dead fish, rotting seaweed and affluent from drainage systems. She fought back a gag reflex as her dinner churned in her stomach. To get her mind off the smell, she focused on what was floating next to the dock that began to take shape as they approached.

It looked prehistoric. Protuberances from every surface— long tubes, antennas and knobs pointing every which way. There were only two large windows in the front and a small open hatch on the top. It lay low in the water, as if it would sink at any moment. She realized that she was looking at an Advanced SEAL Delivery System. *Hope that thing stays afloat*, she thought as she surveyed the awkward looking contraption.

She nudged Reimers with her elbow. "That doesn't look too stable to me."

"Don't be so quick to judge, Major. The ASDS is advertised to carry sixteen SEALs with all their equipment for over two hundred miles."

"Judas Priest, you could've fooled me."

A man also dressed in a wet suit met them at the top of the gangplank that led to the hatch of the ASDS. It was Master Chief Cullis from SOCOM.

"Good morning, ma'am," he said. "Welcome to the *Angel*. She's a lot more than she looks floating in the water. If you'll follow me, I'll orient you on the system. Captain Reimers, your SAS team is already on board."

"Excellent," Reimers answered.

"Yes, sir. Let's get aboard. We only have an hour until moonrise, and we want to be underwater before then. We're rendezvousing with our host submarine in three hours."

"That's fine, but why all the secrecy? Arriving in the wee hours. Blackout conditions. What's going on?" Jenny asked.

"Ma'am, more explanations will be provided after we rendezvous with the *Greenville*," he said, casting off the lines holding the boat to the dock.

She followed the Master Chief down a ladder into the mini-sub. The interior was battleship grey. Strictly business.

Toward the bow she saw two seats amid a myriad of control devices, dials and levers. Toward the stern were benches on which six men were already seated. Farther back was what looked like a storage area where she could see gear stowed. The rest of the interior was made of steel struts and bracing.

Reimers introduced her to each of the six men. They were members of his SAS team. Jenny knew that the British Special Air Squadron team was an elite special operations force similar to the Navy's SEALs. She waved them down as they tried to stand in the cramped quarters.

"Relax, guys. I'm just here for the ride," she told them, hoping to assuage what she was sure would be discomfort with a woman in their midst.

She sat on one of the bench seats. Despite her reassurances, there were throats cleared and avoidance of eye contact. It didn't help that she looked sexy in the tight wet suit.

Reimers cut off errant thoughts. "Chaps," he said in a voice that communicated authority, "it's unusual having a woman with us, but she's earned her stripes, and she's a senior officer. You'll accord her the appropriate respect."

"Aye, sir," was the instant response from each team member. Jenny thought she heard a snap as eyes and heads turned almost simultaneously, looking straight ahead.

"Welcome to the Navy's SEAL Delivery System," Cullis said. His tone was anything but friendly. He squatted on deck space between the benches. "I have a short orientation as we get underway."

The sub tilted downward and Jenny made a conscious effort to push away feelings of claustrophobia. Her mouth went dry as she watched water drip in a steady stream from the seal of the hatch that Cullis had just closed.

He appeared unaffected by the drip or the creaks of the sub's bulkhead as they descended. "There are onboard safety features for all of you swimmers," he said in a calming, confident voice. "There are face masks under your seats that will provide you air from an alternate source if we take on water or the air becomes foul for some reason. The 'foul' air signal is this small yellow light." He pointed to a bulb mounted on the bulkhead.

He gave everyone time to spot the light and then continued. "Above and behind your seats are small portable air tanks if we have to do an emergency evacuation."

"Has that ever happened?" one of the SAS swimmers asked.

"I won't lie to you. There were some problems with the original ASDS prototype during testing, and that's a big reason this baby was in for refurbishment. The air tanks are an added feature."

Jenny's heart rate bumped up. *That's just what I needed to hear.* The ASDS program had been widely panned as a failure. The mini-sub, which attached to a larger host submarine, was reported to be unstable and plagued with cost overruns. The program had allegedly been scrapped, but obviously a few of the secret vessels remained in operation.

"No worries," Cullis assured them, eyeing Jenny's pale face. "We've not had any problems with this boat. We do have all passengers in wet suits for that eventuality, but there's little chance. I'll tell you to access the air tanks if we need to. There's ten minutes of air in each tank, which should be more than enough for us to swim to the surface."

"We stay in shallow water, I take it?" the same swimmer asked.

"Correct. We don't take the *Angel* down more than one hundred feet with passengers in it. We stay snug in the mother ship until she reaches a depth safe for swimmers to enter the water and for them to surface without decompression if necessary."

He waited for a few seconds to see if there were more questions. No one asked anything else, so he continued. "There's only one more item on the safety brief. You need to fasten your safety belts. We don't want you bouncing off the bulkheads if we bump the mother ship while docking." He laughed.

Oh, you're a riot, Jenny couldn't help but think.

"Our mother ship, the USS *Greenville*, is waiting for us approximately twenty miles west of the harbor. We should be there in about two hours. Sit back, get a little nap and enjoy the ride." With that, Cullis gave a thumbs-up and headed toward the bow of the boat.

Jenny leaned her head against the steel bulkhead. *Sleep? In these confines. Nothing but a steel headrest. Man's crazy.*

She tried to clear her mind and started to doze off. In what seemed like seconds, she awoke to metal clanging, air hissing, water gurgling and latches shutting. The strange sounds were unnerving. She glanced around, frantic, looking for the source.

Her eyes caught those of Cullis standing over a hatch cover in the deck. "Relax," he said. "In a few more seconds we'll be mated with the mother ship." A green light came on over his head. With a short hiss of air, he unlatched the hatch cover. "Follow me, folks," he said, climbing down a ladder leading out of the bottom of the small sub.

Glad to be getting out of the confinement of the tiny sub, Jenny was close behind. Reimers and the other SAS team members quickly followed. She found the haste with which they moved gratifying. *I'm not the only one who didn't enjoy the ride.*

At the bottom of the ladder, she looked around and saw they'd entered another battleship grey area almost identical to the little sub. The same type struts and braces were interspersed with shelving and hooks for dive gear. She was surrounded by scuba tanks, air compressors and dive suits.

Before she had much more time for thought, a man wearing a Navy blue jumpsuit with lieutenant pips on his color points walked up. She recognized the submariner's utility uniform.

"Morning, ma'am," he said. "I'm Lieutenant Hendricks. If you'll follow me, we have an area for you to change, and then the Cap'n would like a word with you in the officer's wardroom."

"Sounds fine, Lieutenant," she answered with as much enthusiasm as she could muster. The bigger sub did little to ease the claustrophobia.

Hendricks led her to a latrine/locker room adjacent to the dive bay. "Ma'am, I've put a set of submariner utilities on the bench in the shower area," he said. "I'll close this hatch and you can pull the curtain across one of the personal showers. I've cleared the shower bay before your arrival, and I'll keep the area clear from this side of the hatch. It's a little primitive, but I'm sure you know that we're not set up for females, ma'am."

"No sweat, Hendricks. This is perfect. Tell everyone I said thanks for the effort." Jenny knew she was inconveniencing a lot of the sailors. She figured she was probably the first female to set foot inside the sub. She hurried so that the area would be available as soon as possible.

As promised, Hendricks was waiting on the other side of the hatch when she twisted it open. She felt a sense of awe following

Hendricks down a companionway. In its nearly three hundred feet of length, the *Greenville* carried an incredible array of weaponry—missiles, torpedoes and mines—that made it one of the U.S. Navy's most potent platforms of destruction. The ability to transport the ASDS with multiple SEAL teams transformed the submarine, adding a formidable force projection system.

Reimers had also changed clothes. He joined them as they proceeded down two sets of ladders and then through a narrow corridor just wide enough for one person to transit. They passed through three separate hatches. A brief glimpse of the control rooms revealed a maze of valves, gauges, dials, control devices and miscellaneous equipment, much of which was covered with canvas and signs saying Authorized Personnel Only. White, red, yellow, and green knobs and levers lined the bulkheads. She wondered how long it would take to learn their function.

Continuing into the sub's interior, she was amazed at how clean all the surfaces appeared. There was a low-level whir of machinery, and the air she felt blowing from vents was dry.

After passing through some berthing spaces, Hendricks announced, "Here we are." He opened a hatch from the passageway that had a sign on it: Officer's Wardroom. They stepped into a well-lighted small area that Jenny thought could fit in her bedroom. There was a relatively large table in the center and an open pass-through window on one wall that she could see led to the galley. She had trouble envisioning how the thirteen officers she knew to be assigned to the *Greenville* could fit inside for a meal.

"Major O'Shane and Captain Reimers, sir," Hendricks announced to three men seated in the room.

"Thanks, Lieutenant. That'll be all," one of the men on the bench seats said while licking an ice cream cone. He was wearing the rank of commander on the collar points of his blue jumpsuit.

"Aye, aye, Cap'n," Hendricks responded, closing the hatch behind him.

"Welcome aboard the *Greenville*, Major O'Shane and Captain Reimers. I'm Chuck Thomas." Finishing his cone in one bite, and wiping his hands on a napkin, the commander stood. Thomas looked them both in the eye and shook hands.

Jenny liked his easygoing carriage and was taken by his

piercing green eyes behind rimless glasses. A cowlick of black hair covered his forehead.

"I hope this isn't too inconvenient, Cap'n," Jenny said.

"We'd be lying if we told you otherwise," another officer sitting at the table responded. His voice dripped with sarcasm.

"Play nice, Mac," Thomas said. "Folks, this mellow fellow is my executive officer, Lieutenant Commander Bill MacManawiea. Mac is our token Hawaiian and a graduate of the Navy's charm school in Annapolis."

Catching a disapproving look that he got from his subordinate, he added, "He objects to my referring to his heritage, but it isn't every day you can warn people of the presence of an Annapolis grad." There were polite chuckles at the humorous chiding.

"Don't be fooled by his pleasant demeanor. He's also the best XO in the Navy." There was another man sitting at the table that hadn't been introduced as yet. His back was to Jenny when they came in. Thomas said, "You know the Master Chief I believe. He's just arrived as my new Chief of Boat. He'll see to your orientation on procedures and accommodations. Also, he'll familiarize you with the ASDS."

The Master Chief from SOCOM stood to shake their hands. A huge hand engulfed Jenny's. She got an inexplicable negative vibe from the big man. She decided to confront him immediately. She knew his resistance could jeopardize the entire mission.

"Master Chief, we seem to have gotten off on the wrong foot when we met at SOCOM. Let's clear the air. Obviously, we need your help to have any chance of success for what is already a difficult operation."

"Difficult doesn't even begin to describe this lark, ma'am," he responded in a disparaging tone. "Impossible may be more like it. May I speak frankly, Major?"

"Yes, please. Let's get this over with," Jenny answered. She tried to ignore the fact that the man towered over her. She was determined not to be intimidated by his size and gruff demeanor. They all took a seat.

"Well, you have to know I'm not here by choice," the Master Chief said. "I'm assigned to the *Greenville* because General Simpson and the Secretary of the Navy ordered me here. The reasoning is that I'm a SEAL, and one of very few personnel certified on the newly renovated Advanced SEAL Delivery System, plus I have my submarine ticket as a Chief of Boat. Simpson wants trusted eyes on this operation."

Jenny stared at the Master Chief after his brief comment. She wasn't going to offer anymore of an explanation of her mission at this point.

"There're only a few people in the Special Ops world that know that we even have an active SEAL Delivery System," the Master Chief finally continued. "As far as the public knows, the whole project was scrubbed due to an accident on the prototype version and the subsequent loss of funding. You've got everyone at SOCOM going crazy trying to find out how this leaked."

"I read about the ASDS as a plebe at West Point," Jenny answered. "Groton Ship Building bid against Newport News Shipyards on building the follow-on versions of the prototype. It was in *The New York Times*. That paper was required reading for plebes. For some reason the factoid stuck in my mind, and when I needed a way to get on the *Intrepid*, I remembered what I'd read. It seemed like the idea could work. I didn't know anymore than that until I spoke to General Simpson. When we talked, you both confirmed it existed."

"Well, ma'am," a degree of respect beginning to appear in his voice, "it was darn smart of you to smoke out the Delivery System story, but there is one more sticking point. The SOCOM staff wants to know why you don't just seize the vessel when it gets into U.S. waters."

She smiled at the question. "One of the first things they teach Military Police officers is that you have to have a basis for asking for a search warrant. The same goes for seizing a private vessel. At this point, there's no real evidence. There's not a judge in the world that'd issue a warrant to authorize me on that boat when it gets into U.S. water. The evidence I've got is sketchy at best. I need eyes on the target to confirm my suspicions. Some pictures will help."

The Master Chief paused for a bit more and then added, "I'm getting a might more comfortable with this, Cap'n. I need to get on your secure line to pull off Simpson. He's getting ready to launch a full-blown investigation to find out about the leak."

Jenny started to breathe easier, believing she'd convinced

him. She knew that things would be a lot simpler with him on her side. MacManawiea, the XO, interrupted her thoughts.

"I'm not so convinced about this little adventure," MacManawiea said.

"I beg your pardon?" Jenny responded.

MacManawiea didn't answer her. Instead he turned to Commander Thomas. "Sir, as you know, we were diverted on our way home to the Pacific Fleet after the retrofit at Newport News. We were ordered to come here under flank speed. We arrived to find an ASDS already here. All of this was done on the authority of this ... Army Major." He looked Jenny up and down, inferring her small size, rank and branch of service was a factor.

"More to the point," he continued, "if this is so important, why not send a SEAL team? I can't believe the President knows about this little scheme at all."

Jenny reached for her wallet. MacManawiea waved her off. "I heard about your little piece of paper. I don't believe it applies," he said to Jenny. "Don't bother getting it out."

He addressed the commander again. "Cap'n, this sounds too farfetched for me. We need to take the initiative and pull the plug before this gets even more out of hand." He stood as if to leave to give the necessary orders.

Commander Thomas's eyes flashed. "Sit down, Mac. Last time I checked, I'm still in charge of this tub." Jenny detected some of the mettle that identified Thomas as one of the Navy's top thoroughbreds chosen to command the lethal weapon system.

He then said to Jenny, "You know, Mac's got a point. I'm half-tempted to take his advice."

"Cap'n, that would be a serious mistake," Jenny responded.

"Prove it," MacManawiea said. Hesitating only briefly before she could say more, he added, "See what I mean, Cap'n. She can't."

Jenny paused for a second before asking, "Sir, is that phone secure?" She pointed to a phone next to their table.

"Of course. I don't know what you have in mind, but we've got secure communications around the globe," Thomas answered.

"Would you ask your communications folks to connect to Central Command?"

"Sir, this is a giant waste—," MacManawiea started.

"You asked me to prove it. Humor me," Jenny interrupted.

Thomas picked up the phone. "Con, take her up to sixty feet. Sparks, connect me with CENTCOM headquarters on a secure line." He pressed a button for speakerphone.

Less than five minutes later, over some static, they heard, "CENTCOM headquarters. How can I help you?"

She recognized the voice of the operator. She crossed her fingers that he'd recognize hers. "Evening, Sergeant Woodall. How are you?"

"I'm good, Major. You're up early this morning. Do you need me to find Admiral Bryan or General Penfant for you?"

Jenny breathed a sigh of relief at his recognition of her. "Neither right now, thanks. I need you to set up a connection to the secure communications operator at the White House."

"Sure thing, ma'am. It'll take me a minute."

"I'll hold."

There was another pause and more static. A recording then stated, "This is a secure government line. Please state your business."

"This is a Griffin call for the President," Jenny said.

There was another pause, and Jenny began to sweat. An operator came on the line. "Good evening, Major O'Shane. This is the White House. Sorry for the delay. Our voice recognition and security systems needed to verify your identity. Would you like me to connect you to the President?"

Thomas raised a hand to stop her. "That won't be necessary," he said.

Chapter Thirty-Four

A sudden downward tilt of the *Angel* gave Jenny's stomach a lurch. She swallowed hard to keep her breakfast down. Her reflux was caused by the Disneylike ride in the confines of the ASDS. Nerves concerning her plans to board the *Intrepid* were also causing flutters.

She'd watched the SAS team drop through the bottom hatch the day before to head for their training mission to the Dry Tortugas. They'd swum away on underwater scooters. It had taken all night for the *Greenville* to position for the team's release.

Afterward, the ASDS had reconnected to the *Greenville* for a ride toward a proximate location of the *Intrepid*. That had taken most of the day. Now it was time to find and board the suspect freighter.

"We'll get periodic updates by hoisting our antenna to the surface," the Master Chief explained after disconnecting from the *Greenville* and turning the small sub's heading toward the east. "Our satellites will monitor the ship's position and download the data to us."

"That should keep us on track," Jenny said.

"It's not quite that easy. Raising the antenna is a risk. We only have a short antenna, which means we have to almost surface. Being close to the surface makes us vulnerable to unfriendly overhead satellites that can detect our sub's heat. The antenna length is a problem that hasn't been addressed in this model of the ASDS."

"It seems to me that the only 'unfriendly' country with that kind of satellite capability would be the Russians," Jenny responded. "They're supposed to be on our side in this."

" 'Supposed to be' are the operative words," Cullis answered. "The senior U.S. Navy staff doesn't think all of the Intelligence agencies in the Russian hierarchy will know about the INTERPOL cooperation. That being the case, the people handling Russian satellite imagery may follow protocol and alert the Cubans. Projections show the *Intrepid* may be in Cuban territorial waters when we intercept. If the Cubans become suspicious and start hunting for us, it will get nasty."

"I'd guess that's why the *Greenville* is standing so far off?" Reimers chimed in.

"That's partly right. However, the Cubans have a detection system in the Straits of Florida that the Russians helped them install. It's designed to track submarine activity."

"Then they already know that the *Greenville* is in the Caribbean or Gulf of Mexico?"

"They know something is going on," Cullis answered. "I don't believe they identified the exact boat, even though the *Greenville* has a distinct underwater signature. We put other subs in proximity when she came through the Straits and had surface craft crisscrossing, churning the water."

"Wow," Jenny said. "I didn't realize this was such a big deal."

"We need the practice anyway. However, the Cuban detection devices are the main reason that this mission has potential for danger. When you have the fanaticism and paranoia that defines that country, you can expect that they'll believe whatever is going on is aimed at them in some manner."

"Great. The whole area will be swarming with patrol craft."

"It's not all bad. The Cuban naval maintenance sucks, so a lot of their sub-tracking ships are nonoperational. Besides, there's a storm in the area, and that'll keep their Navy in port."

"OK, then it's not so bad," Jenny said, unsure where the Master Chief was going.

"Yeah, but the downside is that with the sea conditions as they are, it'll be that much harder for you to board the *Intrepid*," the Master Chief responded. "I wish you'd let the SEALs handle this."

"I'll be fine," Jenny answered, grasping his intended concern. She knew boarding was going to be tough. It was irritating to keep being reminded.

Trying to keep her voice from sounding confrontational, she pointed to waterproof bags lying on the deck that had ropes, grappling hooks and wall ascenders packed inside. "Look ... we've been through this. I've done my share of rock climbing. All that equipment is familiar to me. Besides, Reimers will be there the whole time."

The chief shook his head, his lack of confidence in her ability showing.

"Well, sit back and relax," he said with a resigned tone. "The *Angel* only does six knots, so it'll take about three hours to cover the twenty miles to the last known location of the ship. I'll surface to get an update when we get close."

Jenny forced her mind into neutral and lay along the length of seats on one side of the ASDS. She didn't expect to get much rest, but she wanted to conserve her energy. She snacked on a PowerBar and closed her eyes.

It seemed like only seconds later that Reimers shook her shoulder. "Major, we need to get our gear on. I think we're as close as we'll go with the *Angel*."

He led her into the cockpit area. The Chief pointed to a computer screen built into the control console. "We don't have strong sonar, but it works from this range. This dot is the *Intrepid*. We're about one mile away."

"Let's get as close as possible," Jenny said. The look she got made her wish she'd not said anything. "Sorry ..."

"We're already inside the three-mile limit of Cuba's territorial waters," the Chief responded. "I'm going to drop you two off and then back away. I've got about twelve hours of battery left. That should give you eight hours to board, do your recon, and get back to me. The time remaining will give me plenty of battery to get back to the Greenville. If you're not here within eight hours, I've got to head to the mother ship for a recharge. I'll be back in twenty-four hours."

He handed them both a wristband with what looked like a watch attached. "These are GPS devices that are synced to my onboard computer. My computer is also calibrated with the GPS attached to your water scooter. We should have no trouble finding each other, but it's going to be increasingly more difficult to be precise the longer you're gone because of currents and wave conditions."

"I understand," Jenny said. She looked at Reimers. "We have every intention of making the eight-hour window." He nodded his agreement.

"We're at thirty feet of depth," the Chief continued. "Seas are steady at ten to twelve, with the wind gusting to sixty-five knots. Try not to get blown into the ship's hull. That'll hurt."

Jenny understood that Cullis was trying to add some levity. She shook his hand. "Thanks for your help, Master Chief. We'll be fine."

"I wish I had your confidence, ma'am. Good luck."

Jenny pulled her face mask down and followed Reimers out the bottom hatch. She gave Cullis a thumbs-up as she dropped into the water.

Fifteen minutes elapsed after they dropped through the ASDS hatch; during that time, Jenny and Reimers donned their air tanks, unlatched their dive scooter and started toward the *Intrepid*.

Jenny soon saw the outlines of the ship above. "That's got to be her," she said to Reimers over her Buddy underwater phone talker.

Reimers nodded his head. "The *Greenville* sonar showed no other ship in the vicinity. That's her all right. It looks as if she's dead in the water. The props aren't turning."

"That's a break. It'll make getting on board a lot easier."

"Let me anchor the scooter." He pulled a small anchor out of the forward storage compartment and dropped it. The line stopped paying out at the one-hundred-foot mark on the rope. "Nice and shallow," he said. "Just like the charts showed."

Then he pressed a button on the control panel. A red light came on. Jenny heard a tiny beep in her earphones.

"We should be able to find this thing blindfolded," he said. "The beep will continue for twenty-four hours. It gets louder as you get closer to the scooter."

He pulled the bag containing the climbing equipment out from a storage compartment. He also strapped on an M240 machine gun he'd put in the compartment. "Just in case we need some firepower," he added. "Let's get on the ship."

Jenny put her hand on his shoulder. "Reimers, there's a small change in plans."

"What's up, Major? We're wasting time."

"I know," she answered. "I've been wrestling with this decision from the start and just now made up my mind."

"Major, let's go. We have limited time to board, recon and get back. Tell me on the way," he said in a voice distorted by the waterborne talker. He started to swim away. Jenny grabbed his shoulder.

"No. Wait. We need to settle this now. It's going to be too chaotic when we surface in this storm. Look at me." He made eye contact, and even through his face mask, she could see the puzzled look.

"What?" he asked, impatience beginning to wear away a respectful tone.

"It's really not that big a deal. I've decided that I'm going to board the ship alone. You stay in the water nearby to help if I need you." Now she started to swim away, hoping to dismiss the subject without argument. It wasn't to be. He grabbed her harness this time.

"Major, that's bullocks." His look of puzzlement was replaced by an angry glint. "You've never boarded a ship in open water. Without my help, the chances of you getting on board are limited at best."

He looked at her for another second. She could see a look of disbelief appear on his face. "You bloody schemer. I'll bet you planned this from the outset so that the Master Chief and I would support your plan." He shook his head in disgust. "I'm going and that's that!"

He turned back toward the *Intrepid* and began to swim away. He couldn't see Jenny pull her knife from a sheath strapped to her calf. She reached out and cut the air line from his tank to his respirator. He dropped the carryall with the climbing gear and grasped at his air line. She grabbed the bag before it sank and swam ten feet away, treading water just out of reach.

"This is not even funny," he said. She thought the look he flashed her should have boiled the water between them.

"Relax, Reimers. Grab the spare tank in the scooter's storage area."

"You're nuts," Reimers said in a voice even more distorted by anger and the water filling his face mask.

"Listen. Two people on board doubles the chances of our being discovered. Besides, if we get caught, how are we going to explain a Brit and an American being together in those circumstances? We can't. Just cover my back so I can get up without being stopped. Let me do the rest. I can always claim I'm a stowaway." She didn't wait for an answer, and swam toward the *Intrepid*.

Chapter Thirty-Five

In the stormy Caribbean, on the starboard side of the *Intrepid*, Pablo Pasqual made his way down the exterior stairs leading to the lower decks. There were multiple landings, and he became disoriented.

The driving rain and high winds didn't help, nor did the numbering system on the old ship's hatches and decks. Room numbers were faded by age or were simply nonexistent.

"Where the hell is that damn blinking light?" he muttered to himself. He was certain he'd seen something flashing an SOS from the ship's side.

He leaned over the rail and looked toward the bow and the stern. No light. In fact, there was no bow wave.

The ship had slowed; no forward motion in the boiling seas. The only movement was the wallowing ship. He had to hold on to the railing to maintain his balance. He hated ships and even with Bonine and an anti-seasick patch, he was feeling nauseous and regretted ever taking the job.

He pushed his walkie-talkie autodial. "Velstinevitch, give me directions to the engine room." There was no answer. He tried again. He still got no answer. "What the hell is going on?" he said out loud. "I bet it's those damn engineers. They're up to something! They'll pay for this bullshit!" he muttered.

Giving up his search for the source of the blinking light, he began looking for the deck that had a throughway to the stern and the engine room.

Jenny treaded water, riding the waves about fifty feet away from the ship. The hull looked mountainous from the water. *Just an illusion*, she told herself.

The report she'd read on the ship described the sides as only forty feet. *Not that high ... you can do this.* She was shivering from the cold water. *Concentrate.*

She'd chosen the lee side to minimize the wind effect. Even so, the waves from the storm were fearsome at ten to fifteen feet. If she got close to the ship at the wrong moment, she'd be smashed into its hull like flotsam.

The wind, currents and proximity to the shoreline caused the waves to become choppy and erratic. She needed to pick one that she could ride parallel to the ship that would allow her to use her climbing equipment to grasp the metal sides. Her timing had to be precise.

She'd already ditched the grappling hook. She couldn't be sure of where it'd land on the ship even if she could aim the firing device while being tossed about by the waves. And who might be nearby wherever the hook did land? She decided it'd be less risky, and a little stealthier, if she used the ascenders given to her by Cullis.

They were a new device that had been developed especially for the SEALS in response to piracy in Somalia. Their purpose was to aid in the storming of ships on the high seas.

The devices were ultralightweight, but strong enough to offer a hand grip or a step for feet. Pressed against a flat surface, a small suction cup would activate and grip the surface. SEAL tactics for open sea boarding were normally not stealthy. They called for any noise of the ascenders to be offset by surprise, overwhelming numbers of boarders, and speed. In some cases, helicopter gunships and rappelling troops could be used to confuse and disorient.

Jenny didn't have any support, but she figured that the sounds of the storm would mask the noise. *Hope the bloody things work. Just need to get on board and get a couple of pictures. First get close to the ship without getting crushed against the hull.*

The wave patterns were too erratic, so she decided to start below the water line to minimize the sea's initial impact so that she could get a firm grip at the outset. She didn't know why the ship wasn't underway, but it made her task simpler.

She had thirty ascenders in the sea bag. Doing a mental calculation, she decided on using one ascender for every four feet. With thirty feet of hull to climb above the water line, she counted eight to ten spares. They would account for any malfunctions.

Jenny pushed the first device against the hull. There was a muffled thud. Water bubbles blew out both sides of the ascender. She tested the grip. It seemed secure enough. *Only a slight twist.*

Holding the grip of the ascender, she reached into her bag for a second device. Suddenly her arm felt as if it had jerked out of its socket. The pitch and roll of the ship pulled her upward, and then down. She lost her grip. She felt the ascender swish past her face as the ship did a downward roll.

Outside the *Intrepid's* engine room hatch, on the portside of the ship, Angie Stephens was staring off into the stormy sea. The ship she'd tried to signal with the light had disappeared into the blowing rain and spume from wave tops. A sense of failure engulfed her. Despondent, she leaned against the rail and looked down into the waves. It was then that she saw a person being buffeted by seas, climbing up the side of the ship. *Impossible!*

She squeezed her eyes shut, and then looked again to be sure she wasn't hallucinating. It was ... a person. "Hey! Up here," she yelled, waving her arms. The wind carried her words away. She continued to wave, screaming, bracing against the deck's gyrations.

Her yell was almost instantly followed by, "What are you

doing, señorita?"

She looked toward the voice. It was one of the men who'd been carrying the tarpaulin earlier. He was dark-skinned and wide-shouldered. He had a pistol pointed at her.

"No-nothing. Nothing at all," she said.

"It was something, señorita. Move away from the rail, or I will shoot." Dejected, Stephens slumped against the nearest bulkhead.

Into a walkie-talkie the man said, "Señor Pasqual, this is Guillermo. I have the engineer lady. We are on the portside next to the engineering hatch."

Stephens heard Pasqual's response: "Excellente. Keep her there."

It didn't take much longer for Pasqual to find his way. Approaching Stephens with a sneer, he said, "I warned you to keep the ship moving."

"There was a fire," she answered. "I can show you." She headed toward the engine room hatch, trying to divert his attention from the side of the ship.

"I'll bet I know who started the fire."

"Señor," Guillermo interrupted, "she was yelling over the side of the ship when I came up to her."

"She was what?" Pasqual glanced over the side. He recoiled away from the rail as if it was hot. "Impossible. Someone's climbing up the hull!"

Backing away, his elbow bumped into the signal light attached to the rail. He reached out with his hand and touched it. "This was the blinking light, you bitch!" He swung at her with his fist.

Overwhelmed with a burst of uncontrollable fury, Stephens lost it. She wasn't going to let Pasqual hit her without retaliating— Guillermo and his pistol be damned.

Pasqual swung wildly, clearly underestimating her response. She took full advantage.

She rolled away from his blow, his fist barely brushing her hair. She attacked with knees, elbows and fists.

Pasqual backed away, trying to block her blows. He tripped and fell on his back, dropping his pistol. She jumped on his chest and proceeded to pommel him.

A hand grasped her hair and pulled her upright. In spite of the pain, Stephens continued to kick and punch at Pasqual until the much bigger Guillermo pressed his pistol to her temple.

"Stop, señorita, or I will shoot." She felt the fight drain from her like she was a deflating balloon. She knew she couldn't fight them all alone.

"You want me to kill her, boss?" Guillermo asked.

"No. Not yet," answered Pasqual, wiping blood from his nose and picking up his pistol. "Let's let her new friend come up, and then we'll kill them both very slowly."

Stephens's lip curled in disgust. "You're a sick bastard."

During the confrontation between Stephens and Pasqual, Jenny clung to the *Intrepid's* side. Her muscles trembled, rebelling against the unremitting strain of her climb.

The ship rolled and twisted, crashing with the waves. The towering crests were relentless, smashing her into the side or trying to pull her away. Several times her grip slipped or her feet slid off the ascender steps. If she hadn't had a safety rope attached to snap links on the devices, she would have long since fallen. She'd dropped her air tank and diving gear minutes earlier. If she fell now, she knew chances of survival were slim.

Finally, she struggled clear of the water's pull against the hull. She began to make headway even with the wild twisting of the ship. She heard a woman scream and looked up. A man's face peered over the rail and then disappeared.

Above Jenny, outside the engine room compartment, Stephens was being held fast by Guillermo. "Bring her into the engine room," Pasqual said.

Entering the compartment, the sounds of the fire alarm still echoed. Stephens saw Velstinevitch bleeding on the deck and Rocky standing over him holding a bloody wrench. She quickly deduced that Rocky had begun to disengage the engines when the alarm sounded, and had fought with Velstinevitch, who probably objected.

"No, don't!" Stephens yelled, seeing Pasqual reach for his pistol.

She was too late. Pasqual drew and fired. The close range pistol shot pierced Rocky's skull. Blood and brain matter sprayed.

The bullet ricocheted off a handrail and punctured a steam line. Stephens's howl of anguish was lost in the shriek of escaping steam. She knelt beside her friend.

Pasqual jerked her to her feet. He yelled into her ear. "Get us moving!" He shoved her toward the engine controls.

She moved in a zombielike trance. Her eyes shifted between her friend's body, the jet of steam and Pasqual. She silently prayed that he would step in front of the vapor stream.

He didn't. Guillermo did.

Unfamiliar with the hazards, Guillermo started across the compartment to help Velstinevitch. The high-pressure steam cut into his side like a knife and knocked him sprawling into the far bulkhead.

His lungs exploded from the boiling heat of the vapor. Guillermo coughed two great gouts of blood and died in seconds.

Unfazed, Pasqual pointed his pistol at Stephens and mouthed, *Turn it off.*

Stephens spun a wheel nearby the escaping steam. The noise subsided.

Pasqual ignored the two bodies that lay on the deck before him. He kept his pistol pointed at Stephens.

"I should kill you now," he said, shaking. Stephens watched his finger tightening on the trigger. But then he said, "No. Not yet. That would be too easy. You'll fetch a fortune on the slave market. Restart the engines. Now."

Her reservoir of resistance was empty. In memorized, robotic motions, she set the switches. She prayed that the automatic fire retardant system had worked for the drive gears and that the engine would re-engage. They did.

When the vibrations from the shaft began, Pasqual told her, "Don't even think about leaving this compartment." To Velstinevitch, he said, "Come, Sergei. Let's see if the fool trying to board us has made any progress."

Chapter Thirty-Six

On the hull of the *Intrepid*, Jenny began to climb again when the man's face didn't reappear. She figured that his discovery of her wasn't good, but it could only get worse if she remained stationary. She kept glancing up as she climbed higher.

Suddenly, two men peered over the rail. Exposed and feeling very vulnerable, she waved, hoping they were friendly.

Not so. She saw muzzle flashes. Both men were shooting at her with pistols. She kicked out, away from the line of ascenders, flattening herself against the hull.

In the same second as she heard pistol shots, she also heard the unmistakable sound of the M240 machine gun.

She looked down. She saw Reimers surfing the waves, straddling the dive scooter like the surfboard she'd earlier envisioned. He was shooting up at the men, providing her covering fire. His chances of hitting anything were slim, but it made the men stop shooting. She heard a couple of Reimers's bullets ricochet off the railing above her.

With the scooter unguided, Reimers was being tossed about like driftwood. Twice it crunched against the hull of *Intrepid* and then the scooter's tiny bow plowed into a high wave.

Reimers didn't seem to have much chance. The scooter flipped, turning turtle. "Oh crap!" Jenny shouted into the wind.

Above her, outside the *Intrepid's* engine compartment, Pasqual and Velstinevitch both ducked behind the deck edge when they heard the M240 open fire. Bullets pinged off the steel bulkheads nearby.

"Ha! He can't hit anything with that flimsy water scooter bobbing around," Pasqual said. But he didn't take any chances. He stuck his pistol over the side, firing in the general direction of the little submersible. "Shoot back," he instructed Velstinevitch.

Hearing no response, Pasqual looked over to where his partner sat on the deck. "What're you doing, Sergei?" he asked.

Velstinevitch pulled his hand away from where he'd been holding his side. There was blood on his palm. "I think I caught one of the ricochets."

"Damn!" Pasqual exclaimed. He glanced at Velstinevitch's side. "It doesn't look bad. But the bullet also hit your cell phone. It's shattered."

Reaching for his own phone, he said, "I'll get some back up."

The next second, he said, "I'm cursed on this fucking ship. I must have dropped my phone in the engine room. I'll have to go get it."

He tried to turn the wheel to open the compartment, then kicked the bulkhead in frustration.

"That bitch locked the hatch. It won't budge!" he shouted.

He paused for a beat, and then said to Velstinevitch, "I'll be back."

He ran off down the companionway.

Jenny's head poked over the edge of the *Intrepid's* deck in time to see Pasqual's retreating feet. Every muscle groaned from the strain. Her hands were raw from a death grip she held on each of the ascenders.

Giving a final spasmodic thrust from aching legs, she reached over the signal light housing and grabbed the handrail. At that point she had to release her hold on her safety rope, and her feet lost purchase on the last ascender. She dangled from one hand on the rail.

"Oh crap!" she said to herself. Her fingers began to slip.

Just as her fingers lost their hold, a pair of strong hands gripped her wrist and underarm. She was jerked over the rail and dropped on the deck like a sack of flour.

"What the hell," she said.

"Are you alone?" a Slavic-featured man asked. He'd collapsed on the deck, leaning against the rail he'd pulled her over. Blood covered his side.

"Who are you?" Jenny wheezed, breathing hard from her climb.

"I'm called Velstinevitch. I'm a Russian, and I'm a Griffin." She gasped at his use of the code word.

"I thought so," he added when he noted her recognition. "They told me you'd come."

"Who're they?" she started. No answer. The man called Velstinevitch had passed out. "Now what?" she asked herself, gripping the rail for balance against the ship's roll.

She heard a hatch start to open behind her and whirled.

On the opposite side of the hatch to *Intrepid's* engine room, Angie Stephens felt unnerved by the gunfire in the companionway; her mind reeled from the surrounding stench of death—Rocky and then Guillermo.

Her need to escape the grisly confines of the compartment overcame her fear of the unknown. She started to unlock the hatch. Her foot slipped on a pool of blood. She gagged.

Swallowing back the bile, she forced herself to ignore the blood bath, open the hatch a sliver and peek out. "My God," she blurted.

Velstinevitch was propped against the railing, bleeding.

A woman, also covered in blood, was crouched in front of him. The woman spun, a look of feral determination etched on her face.

Stephens slammed the hatch shut and locked it. She curled into a fetal position and began sobbing.

☆☆☆

Jenny saw a face peer through the engine room hatch for an instant. Then it was gone. The hatch slammed shut. "Wait!" she called out.

"That was the ship's engineer," Velstinevitch offered, regaining consciousness again but his voice fading. He pointed to the signal lamp on the rail. "I think she was using that."

"Oh shit," Jenny said. "I need to talk to her." She banged on the hatch. "Please open up. Come back." No response. Starting to knock on the hatch again, she heard Velstinevitch's weak voice.

"Watch out!"

A weight struck Jenny's legs from behind. She was knocked face-first onto the deck. Someone landed on top of her, pinning her down. An arm wrapped around her neck.

Jenny couldn't breathe. Lights began to dim. Her peripheral vision narrowed. She squirmed and twisted, but she was held tight.

On the edge of consciousness, she heard a thunk. The pressure on her neck eased; the body above her sagged. She gasped for air. Someone pulled the dead weight off her back.

She heard a woman's plaintive voice. "Are you alive? Please don't die."

Jenny struggled to sit up. "I'll be OK," she rasped. She looked at the kneeling woman. She had a bloody wrench in her hand and a crazed look on her face. "Who are you?" Jenny asked.

"Angie. Angie Stephens. I'm the ship's engineering officer."

"Well, you saved my butt."

"I ... I heard the gunfire ... all the commotion ... I couldn't bear the thought of someone else dying ... I ..." Hysteria tinged her voice.

Jenny put her hand on Stephens's shoulder. "You did great. Calm down. We're OK now."

They were interrupted by a voice crackling over a walkie-talkie strapped to the waist of Jenny's assailant.

"José, did you find them?" the voice asked. "I found another phone and some help. We'll be there in less than a minute."

Velstinevitch stirred, pointing to the inert form of the man on the deck. "That's José. The voice on the walkie-talkie was Pasqual. He's the main bad guy on board. You've got to get out of here." His voice was now even thinner. "Go back into the engine room. Lock it. Try to call for help. I'll hold them off." He pulled a pistol from his jacket. His head lolled on his shoulders.

"You're in no shape to do much of anything," Jenny responded. "Let's all get—"

"I'm dying," he answered. "That ricochet must have hit something. I'll be in your way. Pasqual will kill you if you stay. Go ... please. You'll think of something."

He had no more than mentioned the name than they heard, "Hey, stop right there." Jenny saw a man with a pistol coming toward them from a forward passageway.

Velstinevitch fired at him. "That's Pasqual," he said and motioned to Jenny. "Go. Please."

"What are you doing, Sergei?" Pasqual called out. "Have you lost your mind?"

"There's been enough killing," Velstinevitch answered. He waved toward Jenny again. "Go," he insisted.

"Sergei, you heard El Toro's instructions. We've no choice," Pasqual said.

"I have a choice," Velstinevitch responded.

"Who's El Toro?" Jenny asked, her instincts sensing something of importance.

A bullet pinged off the rail next to her. She glimpsed a man who was leaning around a stern bulkhead. They were surrounded.

Velstinevitch fired in response. He was barely able to raise his pistol.

Jenny's last sight of Velstinevitch was of him firing his pistol toward Pasqual. And then his body jerked. He was hit by a shot to his side, then one in the jaw. Closing the hatch, she saw him slump to the deck.

Chapter Thirty-Seven

Jenny and Stephens dived into the *Intrepid's* engine room, slamming the hatch closed. The scene was gruesome: two dead bodies at her feet; blood and gore were splattered over every surface—dials, levers, rails and the floor grating.

"What happened?"

Stephens explained in a halting voice. "I couldn't stand being in here anymore," she said, trembling and pale.

Mind racing, Jenny watched Stephens's reaction. "I'm so sorry about your friend," she said, giving Stephens a hug, holding her tight. "Believe me ... I also just lost a good friend. Her name was Brenda. But you know that they'd want us to be strong. You have to hang on until we sort this out. Can you hold it together for now?"

She could feel the trembling slowly subside. Soon she felt an affirmative nod against her shoulder. She pulled away and helped wipe the tears off Stephens's cheeks.

"Do you know what's going on?" Jenny asked once Stephens had calmed.

"I'm mostly in the dark. As soon as I arrived on board, I began working to rebuild engine number two. We're shorthanded in the department, so I've been stuck here. Food was delivered ... we seldom left. Like any other container ship when we're in port, the crew loads and unloads cargo containers.

"Some of the seamen like Guillermo wear white shirts and act out of place. But that's true of any ship, and I figured they were apprentices. This is the first time I've seen any of them armed."

She looked away as if to gather her thoughts. "I got a late-night call offering this job. It was short notice. I'd just completed my contract with another ship and was looking for work. Acme Trans offered a ton of money. I was somewhat suspicious, but it sounded challenging. I thought that rebuilding an engine underway would look great on my resumé.

"When I came on the ship, I saw some work being done on the forward superstructure, but this area has been my world for five weeks." She pointed to engine parts and buckets of cleaning fluids sitting on the engine room deck spaces.

"What kind of work?"

"I'm not sure," Stephens answered. "They were renovating the forward areas and working on a few of the containers that were already on board. Most of it was screened off."

"I've got to get out of here to take a look at what's there. I have some ideas I need to verify."

"Who are you?" Stephens asked. "What are you doing here?"

"I am with the U.S. government. Just trust me for now, I'll explain later. But right now I have to go see what's in that forward area."

"No ... please," Stephens pleaded. "I can't be here alone again. Please."

"Calm down," Jenny told her. "I'll look around and come right back."

Jenny nodded toward the engine room hatch. "That hatch is probably guarded. Please tell me there's another way out of here."

"No ... well, yes. But you wouldn't want to use it," Stephens answered. "It's the fantail ladder outside the stern maintenance hatch. It's only for when we're docked. In this weather, it'd be next to suicide."

Jenny gave Stephens a look that stopped her cold.

Sighing in resignation, she gave directions. "Go through those sound curtains." She pointed to heavy plastic strips in an adjacent doorway. She handed Jenny a set of ear protectors. "You'll need these."

Taking another breath, Stephens continued, "That opening leads to the engines. Go down the stairs next to the engines." She paused again. "Just remember that the fantail ladder is extremely dangerous. Even in port at dockside, staff is required to use a safety rig.

"At the bottom of the engine room stairs there's a hatch on the right that leads into the spaces for the drive shaft. Follow the shaft toward the stern. Two small compartments to the rear of where the shaft enters the hull is the fantail hatch. Open the hatch and you're outside on a small platform that has a ladder next to it that goes to the upper decks."

Stephens put a hand on Jenny's arm. "Please don't."

Jenny shook off her hand and went through the sound curtains. She called out, "Take care."

Chapter Thirty-Eight

In the wheelhouse of the *Intrepid*, Pasqual was seething. "The hatch to the engine room is locked," he said to the captain. "Is there any other way out of there?"

"Not that I know of," Slovinski responded. Pasqual watched carefully, trying to detect if Slovinski was lying.

"That'd better be the truth, Captain," Pasqual responded. Then he asked, "What was that ungodly siren sound earlier?"

"It was the engine space fire alarm. The drive shaft bearings probably overheated like I warned you," Slovinski answered. "The fire suppressant system extinguished the fire, but the engines would have automatically begun to disengage."

"Well, I instructed Stephens to start them up again." Slovinski shook his head in disbelief.

Suddenly, a man wearing a U.S. Coast Guard camouflage uniform came onto the bridge. His nametag read "Watson."

"Hello, Charlie," Pasqual greeted the newcomer. "Did you deal with the pursuit boat?"

"Taken care of," Charlie answered. Then he whispered in Pasqual's ear.

"Interesting," Pasqual responded.

He pulled his walkie-talkie off his belt. "Have two men keep watch at the stern on deck three for someone coming up the fantail ladder. My informant tells me it may be a U.S. Army officer. Let me know."

To three thugs he had with him, Pasqual said, "Grab him." He pointed toward Slovinski.

In seconds, the three men had the Captain immobilized. "Put his hand flat on the navigation table," Pasqual instructed.

"What the fuck are you doing, you slimeball?" Slovinski said, struggling in their grasp.

With no further warning or hesitation, Pasqual pulled the emergency hatchet off the bulkhead, and in one smooth chop, cut off Slovinski's little finger. Blood spurted over the table. Slovinski howled in anguish.

With controlled casualness, Pasqual put the hatchet back in its clasp. He gave Slovinski a towel lying on the navigation table. "Use this and keep pressure on the stump," he said. "It'll stop bleeding soon."

Pasqual didn't bother looking at Slovinski, hunched over in agony when he added, "Never tell me a lie again, Captain. Now get us into port, dock us and don't even think about leaving this ship while we're there."

Chapter Thirty-Nine

In the *Intrepid's* shaft spaces, past the engines, Jenny's mind was numb from the hammering and vibration. Even with the ear protectors, the noise from the shaft was overpowering.

There was a smoke haze of burned oil and grease.

In the confined space, she had to bend at the waist to walk on the grating next to the spinning shaft. She'd brushed against the drive shaft. It was burning hot, the metal heated to a reddish pink in places. She could see movement inside the drive shaft support structure.

Low-watt bulbs spaced along the bulkhead lit the compartment. Each globe provided her an auroralike pool of light to see her way. They were covered with grime and dirt.

Jenny smelled the stench of bilge water that sloshed under the walkway. *That's got to be some toxic crap down there.*

As if prompted, the old, rusty grating under her feet gave way. One minute she was standing; the next she was submerged in a smelly, viscous substance.

She struggled to get her head clear and gulped a breath of air. She gagged. The odor at the surface of the bilge water was overpowering. She thrashed around in momentary panic.

Her feet touched bottom. She could stand upright. She told herself, "Stay calm."

The gooey mixture came up to her waist. It stuck to her clothes and skin in clumps.

Sickened by the stench, she vomited, heaving from deep in her gut.

When the nausea passed, she realized that her ear protectors had fallen off when she plummeted through the grate. The sound in the compartment was now deafening. Suppressing a constant gagging urge, she forced herself to focus. She tried jumping up to grab the grating above her, but the sludge held her down.

Try the sides. She soon found that climbing up the sloped sides of the hull was impossible. Scrabbling, slipping and sliding, she found the sides coated with the oily bilge substance; there was nothing to hold onto.

She waded toward the stern. Her movement broke up pockets of gas that hadn't been disturbed for years. Her eyes burned, her nose ran and her skin felt blistered.

Defeat was unacceptable. *Move!* She willed herself forward.

Unable to see, her hands found protrusions off the hull. A ladder.

She had to use all her strength to drag herself out of the slime, finally lying gasping on the grating.

She took a deep breath, struggled to her feet and took a visual inventory. She could see where the shaft disappeared into the bottom of the hull. She forced herself onward. *Almost there.*

On the aft bulkhead was another ladder that led to a small platform. Beside the platform was a hatch. "That's it!" she exclaimed out loud.

She scraped the biggest globs of bilge grunge off her clothes before climbing up. Already having had a bad experience with the ship's corroded surfaces, she clung to the sides of the ladder and tested each step.

The ladder was narrow and slippery from condensation. It took all her concentration to hold on as the stern of the ship rolled with the waves.

The platform at the top of the ladder next to the hatch was an oasis. For some reason it was intact, away from splashes and the corrosive effect of the bilge.

Jenny rested with her feet dangling over the edge for a full five minutes to catch her breath. She used the time to study the hatch.

It had a normal wheel-opening device, but she could also see a spring-loaded locking mechanism. In the closed position, the wheel automatically locked shut. She realized that it was a safety device to avoid water intrusion if crewmen became careless when they accessed the opening.

She released the lock and tried the wheel. It turned with minimal resistance. *Must have been used during overhaul.* She spun the wheel.

Then, with no warning, water pressure blew the hatch open, throwing Jenny backward into the railing of the inside platform.

Chapter Forty

Jenny discovered to her chagrin that the fantail hatch opening on the *Intrepid* was nearly at sea level. The ship's slow movement was allowing a following sea to push walls of water against the stern.

With the open hatch, each new wave brought floods of seawater into the drive shaft areas. She grabbed for the edge of the opening, fighting through the surges. *Have to close or will sink the ship.*

The rubberized edging gave her thin leverage. Gripping with fingertips, using brute force, she managed to wrestle herself onto the outside platform.

Then she tried to close the hatch. It seemed an impossible task given the seemingly constant, powerful water pressure.

Use legs. Wait for it. Gripping the hatch wheel, she planted both feet on each side of the hatch coaming. With all her might, she pulled on the handle with her arms and shoulders and pushed on the doorframe with her legs.

Finally, in a lull in the waves, the hatch slammed shut. "Yes!" Jenny shouted in exaltation to the open sea.

Realizing that there was no time to lose, she spun the wheel to hold the hatch door in place before the next set of rollers could crash against the stern.

She'd no more than twisted the device than a wave washed over the outside platform, crushing her into the mechanism. Simultaneously, the wheel lock engaged. She was committed. Jenny looked up the ladder attached to the stern. "Oh oh," she said out loud.

Little of the ladder remained. Several rungs were rusted away and many of the bolts holding the framework to the stern were missing. The platform she stood on shifted under her feet, groaning with a precarious list. Her weight was breaking it apart. Bare threads of rusted metal held it in place. The railing above was thirty feet away.

Even with her light weight, she felt the ladder begin to buckle when she grabbed the frame.

She scrambled upward as fast as she could, keeping her feet on the edges of any rungs and sharing her weight by clinging to the ladder rails. *Don't look down.* The water below her churned from prop wash and high seas.

At the top, as she grasped the deck railing, the ladder gave a final lurch and fell into the sea.

Once again, Jenny dangled over the side of the *Intrepid*, her hands slipping off the deck railing.

As if in some déjà vu, strong hands clasped her wrists and shoulder. She was pulled over the rail and deposited on the deck.

She landed on her hands and knees, her breath ragged. She looked up to see two men standing, feet wide apart, machine pistols at the ready.

"Señor Pasqual," one of them said into a walkie-talkie. "Mi hermano and I have a woman ... portside."

Chapter Forty-One

Jenny instantly began formulating an escape plan. She knew that she had but seconds.

She feigned injury, moaning as if in pain, curling on her side.

It wasn't hard to be convincing. Her hands were cut from grasping the crusty ladder, her face and wet suit were coated with oily bilge residue, and the bloodstains on her suit from Velstinevitch were fresh. The more the men looked her over, the more relaxed they became.

"I thought Pasqual said she was dangerous," one of the men said in Spanish. Jenny caught the gist of his words.

"Such a small woman," the second man responded. To Jenny he asked in broken English, "Miss, what's the matter?"

Jenny moaned, "The pain ... it's bad." She used some of her limited Spanish vocabulary.

"Pardon, señorita. ¿Qué estás?" he asked. He slung his machine pistol over his shoulder and stooped to help her. It was the opening Jenny needed.

In a flash, she had her dagger out of its back scabbard and held it at his throat. She caught him while he was off-balance. She pulled him down and twisted him so that he shielded her from his partner.

With no clear shot, and with the speed of Jenny's move, they were both instantly helpless.

"Drop it," she said in English, hoping the words were universal and that she'd correctly understood the Spanish word for "brother." He lowered his pistol.

"Más," Jenny said, moving the sharp dagger a fraction. A thin line of blood appeared on her captive's throat. The brother dropped his pistol to the deck.

When he complied, Jenny wrested away her captive's machine pistol and replaced her knife in its scabbard.

She gestured with the pistol, "Take off your shoes and socks." She pantomimed her message. They both looked at her in disbelief. She fired a shot into the deck. "Now," she said.

Five minutes later they were barefoot and zip-tied to the ship's rail. She'd pocketed the zip ties from the *Greenville's* stores. She threw their shoes overboard. *Slow 'em down without shoes.* One of the brothers started speaking in Spanish.

"Put a sock in it." She stuffed one of his socks into his mouth. She took his walkie-talkie and clipped it to her belt. She also stuck the spare pistol in her belt.

"Manuel, where are you?" Pasqual's voice came over the radio.

Jenny looked across the ship's split stern. A crane in the center didn't hide Pasqual. Across the fifty-foot chasm, they locked eyes. Pasqual fired.

A bullet pinged off the handrail next to her. Jenny had no intention of getting into a gunfight on the fantail of the *Intrepid*. She ducked into the closest passageway.

She ran through open interior hatches, passing work and living spaces. She hid whenever she heard voices or footsteps.

Moving through the superstructure, she noticed that the roll of the ship was much less violent. The storm clouds had mostly passed, and there was a hint of daylight coming through portholes. She checked her watch. It'd been four hours since her short nap on the *Angel*.

The walkie-talkie she'd confiscated crackled to life. The message was in rapid Spanish. She only picked up a few of the words; she understood "stop" and "Army."

She came to a closed hatch. She knew she was approaching the bow spaces. An inner voice warned her to move with caution.

A well-oiled handle moved without a sound. She opened it a slit, then wider.

A guard was standing fifteen feet away from the opening with his back to her, smoking a cigarette. Dressed in a crewman's blue uniform, he appeared relaxed and inattentive. She reflexively pulled the hatch closed.

She guessed that Pasqual pulled all the white-shirted guards to look for her. The crewman didn't appear to have a walkie-talkie. Taking a deep breath, Jenny cracked open the hatch again. She reached for her dagger. *Killing should be the last resort. Doubt he even knows what he's doing.*

She noticed a firebox in the corridor, next to the hatch. It contained a fire extinguisher and fire hose.

She stretched out the hose and turned on the water. The hose filled. She held the fire extinguisher under her arm and stepped through the hatch.

"Hey, big boy," she said. She opened the lever on the fire-hose nozzle. The crewman turned toward her voice and got a face full of high-pressure water. It knocked him against the rail, and he fell to the deck.

She sprinted to his side.

"Señorita ...?" he queried, trying to scramble back to his feet.

Before he could get up, she hit him over the head with the extinguisher. He fell to the deck, unconscious. She hit him again for good measure.

"Have a nice nap, buster." She zip-tied his hands and feet to the rail.

It was then that she noticed that he'd been standing in front of another hatch that looked new. The new hatch led back into the ship's superstructure, toward the stern.

She lifted the hatch lever, throwing caution aside. It was time to get moving.

Entering the space, Jenny found herself on a platform that overlooked an open bay filled with bunk beds stacked six to eight high. The line of beds stretched as far as she could see into the ship's cargo bay.

There appeared to be hundreds of people sitting, standing

and lying in the areas. They were babbling and conversing in several languages. The noise was deafening. She pulled a small camera from one of her waterproof pockets and took pictures as fast as she could.

"You," a man's loud voice cut through the noise. "Stand fast. I want to talk to you."

Jenny looked for the source of the yelling. She spotted a white-shirted man on a catwalk that surrounded the bay of people. The catwalk led to the platform Jenny occupied. Running toward her, the man was speaking into a walkie-talkie.

Jenny backed out of the hatch into the passageway. She grabbed the axe in the firebox and used it to lock the wheel on the hatch cover. "That should slow him down," she muttered to herself.

She took a quick survey of her surroundings. Her mind was racing. *Suspicions about ship confirmed.*

Looking through the open passageway, she could see white caps of waves beyond the rails on both the port and the starboard. To her front, toward the bow, were freight containers stacked five and six high.

Jenny noticed a strange configuration of how the big semi-trailer freight containers were stacked. The first two layers of containers seemed permanent. They were welded to the deck and to each other. A white-shirted man appeared in the passageway. "Alto," he said. "No está ..." He aimed a machine pistol slung on his shoulder. She saw his finger tighten on the trigger.

She drew her pistol and was quicker; her marksmanship perfect. Two holes appeared in the man's chest. He staggered into the ship railing, slowly leaned over and fell into the sea without another sound.

When Jenny fired, she had to let go of a life raft barrel she'd planned to use to escape the ship. The ship's movement caused the barrel to roll away. It hit something on the first layer of welded freight containers. A door slid open.

"Well, how about that!" she said out loud.

She peeked inside the opened container and then stepped inside. Astonished, she found at least fifty cells constructed within the bottom layer of containers. There were toilets and built-in showers. In the cells were women and children—boys and girls. Each prettier than the other.

A white-shirted guard approached from within the cell area. He reached toward her with a stun gun in his hand. "What the hell are you doing in here?" he demanded.

There was no time for finesse. Jenny shot him without a pause. He dropped like a tree. "Serves you right, asshole," she said. Again, she took pictures.

"Help us. Please. Let us out!" the occupants chorused. Others were pleading in languages Jenny didn't understand.

"Calm down," Jenny said, putting her finger to her lips. "I have to go get help. I'll be back."

"Don't leave us."

She pulled a key ring off the belt of the dead guard and threw the keys to a girl in the nearest cell. "I'll be back," she repeated. "Stay in here." She stepped back into the main passageway. The container door hissed shut.

She looked for the life raft barrel and then froze in her tracks.

Chapter Forty-Two

When Jenny exited the *Intrepid's* cargo container, she was stunned by what she saw. Pasqual was standing in the passageway, and a man dressed in a Coast Guard uniform was standing next to him. It was Charlie Watson, her Coast Guard friend … her sailing partner … Brenda's husband. He was holding a pistol to Stephens's head.

She gasped, "Charlie, what the hell?"

"Put down your pistol," Charlie ordered Jenny. To Pasqual, he said, "It's her. I told you she was coming. It's a miracle she got on board, but that's her."

"I'm so sorry, Jenny," Stephens cried. "He knocked on the engineer hatch and said he was from the Coast Guard. He knew your name. I'm sorry."

"Shut up, lady," Charlie said.

"What are you doing, Charlie? How did you get here?" Jenny asked.

"I came out in my pursuit boat to warn my friends about you. That's what I'm doing. Now, put down the pistol, or I'll shoot your friend."

"OK. OK," Jenny answered as she dropped her pistol to the

deck. She slipped her waterproof camera into a pocket. "Why are you doing this, Charlie? I thought we were friends."

"Friends? Bullshit! You're an obtuse, meddling busybody," Charlie said. "It's been right in front of you. You know full well that since the Coast Guard was attached to Homeland Security after 9/11, Brenda and I have been on various task forces for immigrant interdiction. We shared information ... pillow talk. I'd also hear about plans in my meetings. I sold the information. It's that simple. Satisfied?"

"Charlie, I didn't know anything about you and that task force stuff. It's the first I've heard ... and why would you bring the Coast Guard's prototype boat out here in this?"

"Right, Miss Innocent. I suspected you were going to find some way to intercept this ship. You told Brenda about your suspicions the other night. I couldn't just call this ship on the phone. Right? I get paid a lot of money to keep these people informed. More importantly, if it wasn't for you, Brenda would still be alive."

"Charlie, how can you say that? I was nowhere around. Brenda was killed by a hit-and-run."

"God! Are you really that dense? She was wearing your clothes, walked out of your house, looked like you. It's all because of you ..." He choked back a sob.

"Charlie, that doesn't compute. How can a hit-and-run be my fault when I wasn't there?" She watched his pistol waver, his agitation growing.

"It was no accident. It was on purpose. Don't you get it? There's a two million dollar bounty on your head. They thought Brenda was you."

"Bounty. What?"

"Shoot her, goddammit!" Pasqual suddenly ordered.

"I told you to shut the fuck up, Pasqual." He turned his attention back to Jenny. "Somebody wants you dead."

In Jenny's mind, events began to crystallize. Past events began to come together. *Could the assassination attempt of Penfant been aimed at me? Brenda? Me? Bounty? Why?* Her thoughts were abruptly brought back to the present.

"Now, I'm going to kill you," Charlie repeated. "I'll collect the bounty and be set for life."

"Why are you even involved in something like this?" Jenny implored.

"Are you serious?" Charlie answered. "Look at me, a Coast Guard Academy graduate, over twenty-five years of service, still a lieutenant commander running some backwater project. I should be an admiral already ... it's not fair."

"Charlie, are you jealous of me? You've been very successful. The pursuit boat project is high-visibility. Senior Coast Guard and Navy officers visit you every day."

"Crap! Look who's talking? You're going to be promoted *above* my pay grade in a couple of months, and you've got half my time in service. And then you get Brenda murdered."

"Enough," Pasqual said. "Shoot her, or I will. We're getting close to the harbor channel."

"I told you I'd do it," Charlie said. He pointed his pistol at Jenny. His hand was trembling; the gun wavered. He sobbed. "I can't do this."

Jenny had been watching the body language between the two men and had anticipated something would happen.

"Fuck it," Pasqual said. "You have too much baggage." He turned his pistol to Charlie and shot him in the head. Bone and blood exploded over Stephens. She screamed.

Jenny vaulted over the ship's rail.

Chapter Forty-Three

Legs together, knees bent, hands covering her eyes and face.

Jenny braced for the pain—it was a long way down from the *Intrepid's* deck to the water. As expected, the impact felt like a sledgehammer hit her whole body. Choking back a gasp, she nearly drowned in the first seconds.

Ignoring the pain, fighting a coughing reflex, she swam downward to avoid Pasqual's bullets. She could see their phosphorescent path as they whizzed by underwater. When one bounced off her arm, its momentum spent, she knew that she was deep enough.

Not a second after that realization, she felt the vortex from the *Intrepid's* propeller. Even though she was a strong swimmer, she could feel the propeller drawing her toward certain death.

She swam harder, with all her strength. But without flippers, the propeller's magneticlike pull was overpowering.

Out of breath and near exhaustion, Jenny was about to give up and suck in a lungful of water when a hand forced a dive respirator between her lips. She sucked hard at the oxygen flow. A face mask was slipped over her head.

Dizzy with relief, Jenny realized without looking who her savior was. Reimers.

He helped her secure the oxygen mask and air tank harness. He then pointed to her wristband. "Remember? That's got your GPS on it," Reimers said through the underwater talker. "That's how I found you. Hang on."

He gunned the scooter, and they easily broke free of the powerful propeller whirlpool.

"Now the trick is to find the *Angel*."

He revved the scooter to its maximum speed. "We're ten miles from the rendezvous point and have less than thirty minutes to make it on time. I sure don't feel like floating out here for twenty-four hours waiting for him to come back. Let's hope he waits a little longer."

Chapter Forty-Four

Fifteen hundred miles north of Jenny, President Harold Fisher was having a somber breakfast in the White House private quarters. He felt symbiotic pain watching his wife agonize over the news they'd just received informing them of Vanessa Esquedas's death.

"I hope she didn't suffer," she said, choking back her sobs.

"She went over a cliff, honey. She was probably scared for a few seconds and then didn't feel anything."

"I know, it's so hard to think about. I'm just angry at Louis for excluding everyone from her services. Her friends and family."

"You're right. I can't explain his behavior." He gave her a hug. "However, her parents have scheduled a memorial for Friday here in D.C. That'll be nice. I cleared our calendars so that we'll be able to attend."

"You're sweet, and I'm sure the service will be special, but it's not the same," Mrs. Fisher responded. "Besides, I still don't understand the accident report. Why would Vanessa be driving in Argentina? She never drove in the States in her life. Chauffeurs and cabs were her normal transportation. She's never owned a car. It's so unlike her, and she hated shopping and seldom drank, particularly by herself. Something's not right."

"Hmm. Let me look into that. You try to get some rest while I go over to the office."

"OK, Harry. It was sweet of you to have breakfast with me. Thank you for understanding." The First Lady started crying again.

The President kissed the top of her head and patted her shoulder. "I'll come back over in a bit to check in."

Fifteen minutes later, the President was discussing the matter with Augusta in the Oval Office. "Steve, there's a mystery about Vanessa Esquedas's death that I'd like to unscramble." He explained the information that his wife had conveyed earlier.

"Well, sir, you and I could dream up several scenarios," Augusta said. "But maybe when Tavares sends his liaison down to discuss human trafficking, he or she can nose around. I want to check on another mysterious angle too. His deputy said something about Argentina being Esquedas's homeland. That doesn't track with what we've been led to believe."

"That is strange," the President responded. "It was probably a slip of the tongue. Let's make sure Tavares sends someone who can make sense of it all. I was thinking of that O'Shane MP we met. I liked her, and it won't look like we're sending in the FBI to investigate."

"I'll call Director Tavares and twist his arm a little," Augusta responded.

☆☆☆

"I wouldn't mind O'Shane going to Argentina at all," Director Tavares answered when Steve Augusta phoned him. "But she's gone on what you Americans refer to as a boondoggle."

"You're kidding?"

"I wish I were. Unfortunately, it may have a sad ending. Central Command called me today to let me know that they believe that the prototype boat she was helping test may have gone down in the hurricane in the Caribbean. They lost communications with the boat yesterday."

"I'll be damned. That's terrible. Well, I need to give Penfant a call," Augusta said. "The President will want to know details.

He liked that woman."

"Yeah, I could see how she could grow on you. Let me know what you find out."

A few minutes later, Augusta had Penfant on the line.

"There's no good news," General Penfant reported. "Our latest information was that she's on leave. She had plans to go on the Coast Guard test run. She was also discussing with my Chief of Staff about working with Special Operations in SOCOM in regards to her special assignment. I haven't had any reason to find out which one she did until today. Now that the test boat's missing, I will.

"For your information, search and rescue teams are looking for the boat, but there's not much chance. The search is a mess in the storm and especially difficult because the Cubans aren't inclined to be cooperative. We hope she wasn't on it.

"There were some interesting items that the rescue divers found in the water near one of the boat's life preservers. But there are no bodies and no boat so far. I'll keep you posted as they continue the search."

Chapter Forty-Five

Vladimir stared out the veranda windows of the estancia. Wind-slashed rain poured down. Eduardo was standing beside him, sharing bad news.

"Our road down the mountain is washed out, and the helicopter pad is flooded. Reports are that all bridges across the Paraná River are impassable all the way to Rosario," he said.

"This is a disaster," responded Vladimir. "We have deliveries to make and a U.S. dignitary to prepare for. El Toro is going nuts."

"I'm sorry, señor," Eduardo continued. "That's not all. We've been unable to obtain fresh food and our septic system is overflowing. The toilets."

"I know. I know … no bathrooms, no showers, etcetera. Who'd have thought we'd get twenty-four inches of rain in two days."

"Sí, señor. And the forecasters say the weather system has stalled. We could get another ten inches overnight. The storm stretches all the way into the Caribbean."

"My God. Can it get worse?" The question had no more than crossed Vladimir's lips than El Toro walked into the room.

"What have we heard from the *Intrepid*?" he asked.

"As you know, our communications are sporadic. The pirated Russian link is undependable, and the Chinese satellite is not repaired. All landlines are down," answered Vladimir. "The last we heard from Pasqual is that he has an intruder on the ship. We think we know who it is, and it's only a matter of time before he finds and disposes of her."

"You said 'her.' You know who it is? How can someone stow away on one of my ships?" He began to fume.

Vladimir tried to soothe him. "It's all conjecture at this point. Our Coast Guard informant boarded the ship in a mid-ocean rendezvous, before the storm became intense. He reported that he thinks he knows the identity of the intruder. She was supposed to go with him on his boat, but never showed. When she failed to show, he arranged the rendezvous to provide us warning that he suspected she was trying to intercept the *Intrepid*. We lost communications before he could share the identity.

"The informant sank the small boat he used, and Pasqual dumped some contraband over the side at the spot. He thought it would help stymie and confuse any investigation when they do a search and rescue for the lost boat."

"That's good. Tell him 'good job.' I just don't like the idea of someone—"

"I'm not sure it's serious. From what we've pieced together, this is more of a rogue operation. It's not officially sanctioned, and if the intruder disappears, no one will even notice. If she shows up, she'll have a lot of explaining to do."

"Hmm. I still don't like it." El Toro paused briefly as if to contemplate the situation. Then he abruptly changed subjects. "What about this mess?" He waved his arm to indicate the heavy rain.

"As I said earlier, power and phone lines are down," Vladimir answered. "The septic system is out."

"What are the contingency plans?" asked El Toro.

"Señor, no one could've foreseen a sewer back up—" Eduardo started to explain.

"I don't care about that. There are more important matters being disrupted. We have orders to fill, ships waiting instructions, ransom agreements to conclude … besides fifty people on the ranch who need to eat. Fix it." With another imperious wave of his hand, El Toro stormed out of the room.

Vladimir took several deep breaths. He told Eduardo, "Have two of our best riders use the horses to see if our four-wheeler can get down the mountain."

Chapter Forty-Six

General Penfant was in the middle of a late afternoon staff meeting at CENTCOM headquarters at MacDill. Colonel Everett slipped into the room through a side door and handed him a large brown envelope.

It held four items.

First was a message from the Navy search and rescue unit indicating that they'd formally shut down the search for the prototype Coast Guard boat. The message noted that the issue of drugs and money found near the initial search site had not been resolved.

Next was a copy of a letter of protest from the Cuban government that was sent to the State Department. The protest stated that U.S. Navy ships were detected in Cuban territorial waters.

The message claimed that one of the boats was sunk by the Cuban Navy, but that the U.S. forces had killed a number of civilian fishermen before making an escape. "That's bullshit," he muttered silently to himself. "What brought that on?"

The third item in the envelope was a cryptic message from the *Greenville* indicating that O'Shane was returning home that night. He grinned to himself thinking that he knew why the Cubans had protested. She'd somehow been mucking around in their area. He could envision O'Shane's standard reply. Her, "Sir, I can explain," responses were becoming legend. The last item in the envelope was a phone message asking Penfant to call the President.

He scribbled a note on the back of the envelope and gave it back to Everett. He'd written: (1) Call Director Juan Tavares at INTERPOL. Tell him O'Shane's on her way back. (2) Call the White House. See if the President is free at 1800 hours this evening.

Penfant's staff meeting didn't end until just before his scheduled call to President Fisher. He hurried to his secure phone in his office. Colonel Everett intercepted him on the way.

"What's up, Jack?" Penfant asked.

"Sir, I thought I might share some thoughts with you about O'Shane."

"Sure. Go ahead."

"Thank you, sir. First of all, she was planning to go on some test for a Coast Guard boat."

"Hold on, Jack," Penfant interjected. "I told her it was OK to go on leave. She planned to help out a Coast Guard friend. Don't jump to conclusions because you didn't know."

"Yes, sir. Sorry. Nonetheless, the Coast Guard boat is reported lost in a storm. Drugs and cash are found at the scene where the boat goes down."

"The two aren't necessarily connected. Come on. I'm fairly certain she's on the USS *Greenville*."

"Hear me out, sir." Everett paused to catch his breath. "A few days later, out of the blue, we get this cryptic message that she's returning from Cuban territory, which is the hub of drug traffic in the Caribbean. Then the Cubans file a complaint."

"You think the Cuban protest may be some attempt to cover up the truth?"

"Exactly. Let's say she made it in and out of Cuba. How would she do that without official cooperation? Then the Cubans make a big noise about her departure. It's a bit too contrived for me to swallow."

"Hmm. I understand what you're saying, but I think you're

way off-base. She wasn't even supposed to be in Cuba itself and she's somehow linked up with the *Greenville*. That's stretching things—a lot. Let me think on it," Penfant responded.

"Well, sir. Consider that she's been known to be pretty much a maverick in her career."

"Yeah, I hear you. We'll talk more after I speak with the President." In his office, Penfant picked up the secure phone. "Put me through to the White House secure operator," he said into the receiver.

In a few seconds, Penfant heard President Fisher's voice.

"What the hell do you think the Cubans are complaining about?" Fisher asked.

"Mr. President, it may be O'Shane. I was informed today that she may have been either in Cuba or at least in Cuban waters."

"What are you talking about, George?"

Looking at his aide, the General explained about Jenny's trip and then repeated the scenario that Everett had outlined. "Sir, it's possible that O'Shane may have gone over the edge. That may not seem likely, but the information is pretty murky as to what she's been doing."

"I don't know. That's a bit farfetched. I like that woman. Secretary Doakes likes her too. I think you're mistaken."

"I hope so. She's got a fantastic record. I'll let you know what I find out."

"Good. If the misunderstandings get cleared up, I'd recommend she go on the liaison team that Tavares sends to speak to Esquedas in Argentina."

He paused for a second and then added, "That gets to the real purpose of my call. Betty wants to go to the Esquedas residence in Argentina to pay her respects to her friend that died there. You met her at the White House. Esquedas's wife."

"My God, Mr. President. I didn't know—"

"Yeah, it's a sordid story. But I'd like to combine Betty's trip with the Tavares liaison trip so that her visit will be under the radar. How about working with Tavares to come up with a plan on how to make that happen?"

"Mr. President, neither O'Shane nor the First Lady's trip is a good idea."

"I don't know about O'Shane, George. But Betty is

determined," Fisher answered. "I'd appreciate it if you'd help me arrange for her to pay her last respects to her friend."

"Of course, Mr. President. I'll make it happen."

After saying their goodbyes, Penfant pushed the autodial for Director Tavares. While the phone was ringing, he told Everett, "Have my helicopter pick up O'Shane when she gets in tonight. Tell her she's on administrative leave through the weekend. I've got my commander's conference at Ft. Bragg until Saturday afternoon. I'm supposed to play golf with the Major Commanders on Sunday. Tell her I'll see her first thing Monday morning."

"Roger, sir."

Chapter Forty-Seven

At the Argentinean estancia, Vladimir watched El Toro whack another golf ball against the wall. His putter was bent, and the walnut-paneled wall had dozens of splintered holes. Carlotta was sitting on the desk watching her father.

"Carlotta, I can't bear much more of this!" he yelled, savagely hitting another ball.

"Papa, you must calm yourself. This person cannot continue to lead a charmed life. She will pay."

"It seems impossible for her to be alive! To jump off a ship in those seas was suicidal."

"You're right, of course, señor," Vladimir said. "I thought I killed her with the truck. Perhaps our source at INTERPOL also made a mistake. There's a chance it's another case of mistaken identity."

Vladimir wiped sweat off his forehead with the towel hanging around his neck. He'd been kickboxing in the gym when summoned. He was sure the three, big-muscled gauchos that were acting as his opponents were grateful for the reprieve. A fourth had already been taken to the infirmary.

"Perhaps so," El Toro said, calming at Vladimir's rationale.

"However, our previous information from this source has been impeccable.

"Let's talk of something else. What do you know about the *Intrepid*?"

"It's good news. The underwater welder in Cuba did his work. The propeller is repaired, and the ship is cleared to depart Isla de la Juventud today. The second engine is repaired and operational. We expect its arrival in New Orleans in two days."

"Finally! Maybe I can get that stupid ship off my mind. I'm assuming other operations are progressing?" He squirmed in agitation.

"Papa, calm yourself," Carlotta said, kissing the throbbing vein on his forehead. She kissed him again, lightly on the lips.

Despite Vladimir's presence, El Toro pulled Carlotta close and pressed his face against her lower stomach. He began to caress her buttocks. Her breathing quickened.

Just as suddenly, he stopped. He spanked her rear end with a sharp slap. He said, "Later, you naughty girl, my little vixen. Now go—" His face flushed, he turned back to Vladimir.

"Continue," he told him.

"Sí, señor. Here at the estancia, it's back to business as usual. In fact, all of our communications are operational with the Chinese satellites. Every radio and phone message is fully encrypted."

"Good. We were exposed for too long."

"Sí, señor. But I was informed that only a few messages could have been intercepted by any intelligence satellites. The chances are slim."

El Toro waved his hand to indicate Vladimir should move on to another subject.

"Sí, señor. I'm also informed that the girl who escaped from detention in New Orleans has been located. She will either be recaptured or eliminated."

"Perfect. We can't allow her to expose our activities. I'm assuming you have consequences planned for, uhh, what's his name?"

"They call him Stack, señor."

"Yes. Stack. You will see that Stack has some unpleasant encounter? We must send a message about carelessness and inefficiency to our operators."

"I've spoken to him once. Now he will pay a steep price, señor. I will see to it personally."

"Good. On another subject," El Toro continued, "what's this message from the White House?"

"Sí, señor. It's a confirmation of a visit by Mrs. Fisher," Vladimir answered. "The First Lady wants to pay her respects regarding Mrs. Esquedas."

"What a strange culture the Americans have."

"Sí, señor. The exact date is unknown for security reasons. I would guess it'll be within the next two weeks. The U.S. government wants it to be kept unofficial."

"Well, we don't have much choice as to her coming. Let's try to keep it brief."

"Sí. I'll ensure that Mrs. Esquedas is moved out of the detention area in the stables before Mrs. Fisher arrives," Vladimir said. "I've gotten a fake gravesite prepared."

"No, don't," El Toro said, feeling a perverse tingling of anticipation. "It will give me a special pleasure to have her close when Betty Fisher visits the grave. I like that."

Chapter Forty-Eight

On board *Greenville*, Commander Thomas outlined to Jenny and Reimers his plan for their return to Key West. "We have an inflatable raft that you can use to make your way back to shore. My orders are not to come within five miles of the coast. We'll surface tonight to let you off. There's supposed to be heavy cloud cover still from the storm, so overhead satellites will probably not detect us."

"Still remaining covert, huh?" Jenny asked. "It seems like we'd drop the level a bit now that we've gotten off the *Intrepid*."

"The Cubans are still complaining, and we don't want to give them something else to point to such as overhead satellite pictures as proof of allegations. Apparently, when they sent out boats to escort the *Intrepid* into harbor, they detected the ASDS."

"I knew it was a mistake coming in so close," Cullis said. "I must be getting soft."

"We'd have never made it back it you hadn't, Master Chief. Our scooter was running out of juice," Reimers said.

"Yes, thanks again, Master Chief. You're not as hardboiled as you want everyone to believe." A playful, wet smooch on the cheek from Jenny caused him to blush a bright red.

"Yeah, yeah." He pushed her away.

"If you two are done, we need to get on with this. We've only got a few minutes." Thomas got a nod from Jenny to indicate she was done clowning around. "The seas have calmed way down, so you shouldn't have much of a problem. You just follow the channel markers to the Navy Station."

"You think they'll let us in? I thought it was a restricted area."

"It is, but I radioed that you'd be coming. Sorry I don't have better transportation. It's either the raft or swim. We don't carry anything else like that on board that I can spare without breaking into our safety gear. We put a small outboard engine on it."

"That'll be fine, Commander," Jenny responded. "Where did you find the raft anyway?"

"Well, the SAS team actually found it floating loose when they were swimming out to board the ASDS after their exercise. Strange, but it's got Coast Guard markings on it, and says *Hidden Stinger* on the sides. I haven't heard of any distress calls, so ..."

Jenny looked at Reimers. "That's the name of Charlie's prototype pursuit boat. I'll bet the raft self-deployed when he sank the boat ... some kind of safety feature."

"Charlie? Boat sank?" Commander Thomas asked with a quizzical expression on his face.

"I could explain, sir, if we weren't running short on time. I'll send you a report." Fifteen minutes later, Jenny and Reimers were racing through the waters of the Gulf of Mexico, headed toward the bright lights of Key West.

The entry to the Navy base appeared within a few minutes. Two Navy Zodiac patrol boats zoomed out of the entrance.

"Major, I think you better stop," Reimers said. Reflections from city lights revealed that both boats had M240 machine guns mounted and manned on their bows.

Jenny shifted the gear lever of the little engine to neutral. The small craft wallowed in the backwash.

Spotlights came on, and a loudspeaker blared from one of the boats: "Ahoy, Coast Guard vessel. Turn off your engine. Please stand where we can see your hands."

"Ahoy, Navy vessel," Jenny responded. "This is Coast Guard inflatable from the pursuit boat *Hidden Stinger*. I'm Major

Jennifer O'Shane, U.S. Army."

"Yes, ma'am. We know who you are," the voice said over the speaker. A man emerged from the small wheelhouse of one of the boats coming alongside.

"I'm Chief Petty Officer Edwards, Navy Master at Arms. We have orders to apprehend you and to escort you to the Naval Air Station. Please step aboard my boat."

"Apprehend me? Am I under arrest?"

"Not yet, ma'am. Please step aboard." The crew of the patrol boat was in full battle gear. They appeared deadly serious.

"Not yet? What's that mean? What about my friend? This is ridiculous. I'm not going anywhere."

A pair of handcuffs appeared. "Ma'am, you're to come with us," Edwards repeated. Two sailors moved to board the inflatable.

Reimers said, "Major, go with them. I'll manage."

She gave Reimers a hug. She whispered in his ear, "Don't take any crap from these yahoos. Contact Central Command as soon as you can."

Not hiding her annoyance, she climbed onto the patrol boat. "Do you want to handcuff me?" she asked.

"That won't be necessary, ma'am, as long as you behave yourself." The Navy boat accelerated toward the docks. Minutes later, Jenny was transferred to a Humvee that was parked at the dock. Two burly sailors crowded beside her in the backseat.

"What's going on?" she asked. She was answered with silence.

After a short ride in the Humvee, they passed the gates of the Key West Naval Air Station. The CENTCOM commander's helicopter sat at the station's helipad with the blades turning.

The sailors pointed her toward the chopper. The helicopter crew chief handed her a headset and helped her fasten seat belts. There was another passenger.

"Welcome back, O'Shane," a familiar voice said into the headset microphone as they lifted off. "You're not so high and mighty now, huh?"

Jenny turned toward the passenger. "Colonel Everett," she said. "Why am I not surprised?"

Chapter Forty-Nine

Jenny sat snuggled on the couch against Gary Patten at the Cavanaugh house in a happy reunion with her friends. Ex-Command Sergeant Major Jim Cavanaugh and his wife, Ginger, sat in lounge chairs, and Momma was in her rocker. Crystal, the girl who escaped, was sitting at Momma's feet. Jenny's other team members, Big John and Bubba, stood at the front window, glancing outside to watch traffic.

Everyone vied to ask Jenny the next question.

"Enough. Enough," she laughed. "I'm talked out. You guys have to tell me what's been going on here. I've been gone for three days."

"Four if you count yesterday," Patten said.

"I got in late. I was catching up on sleep."

"Is that what you call that ...?" he said with an arched eyebrow. Everyone chuckled.

"All right. You lovebirds want to stop with the bragging," Jim Cavanaugh said. "We've got some serious issues going on. Why didn't you let us know you weren't going with Charlie? We were all worried sick when we were told the boat sank in the storm. And what's with the report of drugs and money found by the rescue team?"

"I wasn't given time or opportunity to tell anyone. SOCOM cloaks everything they do in a web of secrecy. All I'm allowed to tell you is that they got me to the *Intrepid*. I did explain what I did to the CENTCOM staff," Jenny answered. "As to the drugs, Pasqual said something about dropping some contraband overboard to misdirect any investigation. That was probably what the rescue team found. At any rate, I'm stuck on admin leave, restricted to the area. Everett is such a prick."

"I wonder if Penfant restricted you to the area or if it was his super aide-de-camp. That's a strong reaction. There must be more to it than a tenuous drug connection," Cavanaugh said.

"We won't know that until Penfant gets back. That's if he has time to see me. The Chief is out of town too. Dammit!" Her anger smoldered. "I know the *Intrepid* will be docking either today or tomorrow. Neither Director Tavares nor anyone else will talk to me because Colonel Everett's poisoned the well with the drug bullshit."

"It's OK, baby. Don't cry," Momma said.

Jenny looked up, thinking Momma had spoken to her. Instead, she saw Momma patting Crystal's head, smoothing her hair. The girl was racked with sobs.

"What's up, Crystal?" Jenny asked. She decided it was time they talked.

As she started to get up from the couch, something caught her eye on Cavanaugh's muted flatscreen TV. A local channel was broadcasting the news. The camera was focused on two familiar figures exiting an airplane.

"Hey, I know those guys," she said, pointing to the screen. The figures were wearing fancy dishdasha robes. They were Crown Prince Fahd and Minister Kaliq.

Cavanaugh turned off the TV. "Come on, Jenny. Let's stay focused. We need to come up with what you're going to tell Penfant when you see him."

"Yeah, you're right. Sorry. First, I think Crystal and I will take a walk in the park."

"Miss Jenny, that's not such a good idea," Big John said. "I'm thinking some bad dudes are probably still out looking for this girl."

"You worry too much, Big John. Just keep an eye on us." She put out a hand. "Come on, Crystal."

Cavanaugh also started to object, but Crystal jumped up from the floor and grabbed Jenny's hand. They were out the door before he could say anything else.

They walked in silence around the edge of the park. Jenny's hand hurt from Crystal's tight grip.

"Come on. Let's sit over there," Jenny said, pointing to an empty bench in the park center.

She noticed a large black pick-up truck idling in a far parking lot, but she kept her main focus on Crystal.

Stack was in the driver's seat of the pick-up behind tinted windows. He popped another of his specially concocted pills into his mouth and followed it with a giant slug of Red Bull. The truck cab was littered with empty soda cans and PowerBar wrappers.

He shook himself. He'd been awake almost constantly since he'd watched the truckers pick up Crystal in the New Orleans dockyard.

Stack had a perfect vantage point in a parking lot with a view through a community park that fronted the Cavanaugh house. He was determined that Crystal would never get away again. When Jenny and Crystal came out of the Cavanaugh house, he caressed a silenced pistol that lay under newspapers on the seat next to him.

Jenny let the silence build with Crystal. She finally felt the small hand holding hers begin to relax. When it lay without tension, Jenny spoke.

"Crystal, I know this is hard for you," she said. "Let me try to help. I'm going to say some things. Shake or nod your head. OK?"

After a short pause, Crystal nodded.

"Good. You're not from New Orleans, are you?"

Again, there was a short pause. Then a head shake.

"You look Hispanic. Are you from the Southwest?"

While she waited for Crystal to answer, Jenny saw a big man get out of the idling pick-up. She watched him start toward them from about two hundred yards away. He was moving slowly, his head swiveling as if casing the area for observers. The man wore a muscle shirt and had tattoos covering his upper torso.

"New Mexico," Crystal answered.

Jenny tried not to act surprised. "Do you know how you got to New Orleans?"

Crystal nodded her head. She paled as if the memory was painful. "Van, then boat," she said.

"Were you kidnapped from New Mexico?"

Jenny watched the man, now at about one hundred and fifty yards away and who had picked up his pace. He was carrying a silenced pistol along his leg. Jenny eased her dagger from her back holster when Crystal looked away. She laid it on the bench beside her.

Crystal shook her head in response to Jenny's question. "No. Took me from Sarasota, Florida. I was working, saving money to go to New York."

"How did you get to Sarasota?"

"Hitchhiked."

"Could you find where you were held in New Orleans?"

Crystal shook her head. She didn't remember. "Old docks. I have to find it. I promised Isabella." She started sobbing again. Jenny held her close. The man was only one hundred yards away, nearly in range of the pistol.

From nearby, there was a man's yell. "He's got a gun!"

Jenny shoved Crystal to the ground, lying on top, her throwing arm cocked.

She looked up to see Bubba's ham-sized fist crash into the jaw of the approaching man. Big John had his big hands circling the silenced pistol. He yanked it away as if it were a toy.

He and Bubba knocked the struggling man to the ground. Big John gave him a rabbit punch in the ear, and the man lay unmoving.

Jenny looked around the park to see if the man had a back-up. She saw only a couple hurriedly walking away in the distance.

Crystal stood and immediately recognized the man pinned by Bubba and Big John. "That's Stack," she said excitedly. "He's the animal who ran the New Orleans operation." She tried to wriggle from Jenny's grasp to kick the man. He began to stir.

"Look at this," Crystal said, calming. She pulled her blouse off her shoulder. Marks from Stack's stun gun were still obvious.

"Who do you work for, mister?" Jenny asked Stack.

"I ain't talkin' to you, bitch," he sneered.

"Oww!" he yelped when Bubba's size twenty shoe stepped on his hand.

"Oh, you're gonna talk to me," Jenny said. "Bet on it." To Big John, she said, "Bring him to the house."

Chapter Fifty

☆ ☆ ☆ ☆ ☆

Big John deposited Stack on the floor of the Cavanaugh house. Jim exploded. "That's exactly why I said you shouldn't take Crystal outside. Dammit!" he yelled at Jenny.

"That was a near thing, missy," Big John added.

"Yeah ... sorry about that," Jenny said. "But I feel like we're running out of time. I had a hunch someone would be watching us, and I also figured you guys would be watching my back," she said with a wink to Bubba and Big John. "I saw you follow me. You're kind of hard to miss."

"You take way too many chances," her fiancé, Gary, objected.

"I'm always careful." She hugged his arm.

"Right ...," Gary said, somewhat mollified by her attentions.

"OK, you two. Save it. What's next?" Cavanaugh asked.

"Now we take an airplane ride." Jenny pressed autodial on her cell phone.

"Hello, Minister Kaliq," Jenny said when a voice answered. "Welcome to Tampa, Excellency."

Within hours of Jenny's phone call, she was in the Saudi Crown Prince's personal C-17 flying at twenty-five thousand feet. It was fitted with luxurious accommodations for passengers.

Cavanaugh, Big John and Bubba were aboard, as were four burly Saudi security guards that Minister Kaliq had insisted accompany them.

Stack was trussed up in the cargo hold. The plane was headed to New Orleans.

"One phone call and we get a luxury airplane ride. Some friends," Cavanaugh said.

"I told you. I'm a Princess of Saudi Arabia," Jenny answered, enjoying his reaction. "This is one of the perks."

"Right," he answered, shaking his head in disbelief. "Well, I hope your boss understands your absence. You explaining this one will be priceless."

"No worries," she said. "We'll be back before he gets home. In the meantime, let's go talk with Stack."

She led the group to the plane's cargo hold. Inside was a helicopter. Its blades folded so that it fit into the specially constructed compartment.

It was near freezing in the compartment, and Stack was huddled in a corner, shivering.

Jenny hooked a headset into the intercom system. "Captain, can you hear me?" she asked the pilot through the microphone.

"Yes, Princess," he answered from the cockpit. "What can I do for you?"

"Please reduce altitude to five thousand feet over the Gulf. I want to open the rear-loading ramp."

"Minister Kaliq instructed me to do as you asked, Princess. But, with all due respect, it's extremely dangerous in the cargo compartment while engaged in that maneuver."

"We'll all be strapped in crew safety harnesses, Captain. Thank you for your concern. Please do a rapid descent."

In less than thirty seconds, Jenny heard, "We are leveling off at five thousand feet now, Princess."

"Thank you," she answered. "Please lower our speed to just above stall. Put the tail down fifteen degrees. I'm opening the ramp."

After everyone but Stack was strapped in the harnesses worn

by aircrew for in-flight cargo handling, Jenny gave instructions to Big John and Bubba. "Hook Stack to the shackle on the helicopter winch cable."

"What are you doing? You can't do this," Stack yelled over the noise.

Jenny pressed the "ramp down" button. Stack gripped on the fuselage side rail to keep himself from sliding down the slant of the rear of the aircraft.

"I think that shackle will hold over one thousand pounds," Jenny said in his ear. "But, in the slipstream turbulence ... I don't know."

She kneed him in the groin. He squealed in pain and grabbed himself. He lost his balance, tumbling down the tilted ramp.

Jenny had put enough slack in the winch cable so that he dangled half-on, half-off the ramp edge. The aircraft slipstream buffeted his legs.

She released more cable. Stack couldn't hear her voice, so she pointed to her mouth to let him know she wanted him to talk. He began to windsurf.

She reversed the winch. He was pulled back onto the ramp. His shirt was ripped, and he'd lost a shoe. His eyes were wide with fear. A glob of snot was running out of his nose.

Jenny pointed to her mouth again. He didn't hesitate. He nodded. *Yes*, he mouthed.

Two hours later, when the jet began descending into the New Orleans International Airport flight path, Jenny told her team, "I've arranged for an FBI SWAT team to take over the *Intrepid* right after we do our business there. I've briefed the SWAT team leader as to what to expect.

"We've got an hour to take down the ship and to find the operations center on land. Once we find the land-based operation, and after I've got Stack's computer, we'll alert the SWAT team of the operations center location.

"We need to be gone when SWAT arrives there. You can bet we'll play hell keeping the computer after they arrive."

"You think the laptop is that important?" Cavanaugh asked.

"Yeah, I do. Did you see how he clammed up when he let slip there was one? There's something on it he doesn't want anyone to know about."

"I don't understand why that shit bird won't tell us where his land-based operation is located. He told us about the *Intrepid*," Big John commented. "Maybe we should winch him back out?"

Jenny was tempted. Then she shook her head. "No. That's not going to work again, as much as I enjoyed it."

Seeing the frustration on Big John's face, she tried to help him understand. "Look. The *Intrepid* is out in the open, so Stack took little risk in providing us that information. But he knows that his bosses will guess who gave up the land location. He knows we know that it'll be somewhere near the ship. But by giving us anything else specific, he figures that he's a dead man, in or out of prison."

Chapter Fifty-One

Even though nervous about the impending take down of the *Intrepid*, Jenny enjoyed the ride in the Saudi helicopter as they flew toward the harbor from the New Orleans airport. She loved skimming along at treetop level, watching the landscape flash below.

They soon circled the *Intrepid* near the port of New Orleans in the Mississippi River. The ship's lights were blazing in the late night. Its cranes were loading a barge with cargo containers.

Stack had given them good directions. He was still wide-eyed when they'd left him handcuffed to a fuselage strut in the plane's cargo hold at the New Orleans airport.

"You shouldn't have threatened him like that, Jenny. It's not right," Cavanaugh spoke into a helicopter communications headset.

"Well, it wasn't torture," Jenny answered. "There was no blood. You know there are sports called skydiving and windsurfing."

"Are you serious? That was no sport."

"No, but it sounds good. Frankly, I'll claim he slipped off the cargo ramp during a practice release of the helicopter. If anything, I saved his life when I found the reverse button on the winch."

"That's the way I saw it, missy," Big John chimed in.

"Hell, I wanted to do it again," Bubba added.

"Ohh, come on," Cavanaugh started, shaking his head.

"He's not hurt at all," Jenny continued. "On the other hand, look at Crystal. I can only imagine what he and his goons did to her and the others they've kidnapped."

Jenny had sketched out the layout of the *Intrepid* on a pad of paper as best she could recall.

Her team was armed with Uzis that the royal guards packed in the Crown Prince's airplane. Dress was a mixture of civilian black for Jenny and her group and desert camouflage for the Saudi guards. They all had walkie-talkie headsets.

Eight people were jammed into the Prince's six-person helicopter.

"Right. Let's do a recap," Jenny said. She addressed the leader of the bodyguards.

"Captain Faz'el, you take your men. Focus on the berths where the guards stay."

"You want me to keep them boxed in?" Faz'el asked.

"Correct. From what I could tell, they're berthed on the third deck of the superstructure. Find a blocking position on the above and lower decks. That should do it. We don't want to give them a chance to take hostages or maybe kill witnesses."

She next turned to her other teammates.

"Big John and Bubba, you guys clear the portside on the main deck. Herd guards that are outside toward the bow and keep them there. Jim, you do the same on the starboard side. I'm clearing the engineer compartment and wheelhouse."

Everyone nodded in understanding. Cavanaugh reaffirmed, "The security guards you saw were in white shirts with Acme Trans logos?"

"That's what I remember," Jenny answered. "They also wore blue baseball caps with the same logo. The crew wore blue coveralls. They're in the red hardhats.

"If you find the transfer point on the ship, let the staff continue to work. I want to see the operation."

Again, her comments were met with nods. Cavanaugh asked,

"You think Pasqual will meet us on the ship helipad?"

"That's my expectation," she said. "He'll want to know what's going on. Everyone remember that he's a primary target. We want him alive." The helicopter started to descend.

"Here we go," Jenny continued. "Captain Faz'el and his men will exit the chopper first. Seeing the Saudi military uniforms should confuse Pasqual long enough for us to grab him. Once he's secure on the helicopter, we proceed with the rest of the plan."

The helicopter landed. A ship's crewman opened the door. Pasqual was standing thirty feet away, out of the main rotor wash.

Faz'el and his men jumped out. They walked up to Pasqual and began an animated conversation. As soon as Pasqual's back was to the helicopter, Jenny stepped onto the ship.

She walked up behind Pasqual and said, "Buenos noche, Señor Pasqual."

"Buenos noche ...," he started, smiling and turning toward the pleasant voice. He saw Jenny. Recognition dawned.

"What the hell?" He snarled, and began to draw his pistol.

She had her dagger under his chin before he got his hand on his gun.

"Breathe too hard, and I'll put this in your brain," Jenny said.

With exaggerated slowness, he pulled his hand out from under his jacket.

Big John frisked him and bound his wrists and ankles with plumber's tape. He then tossed him into the helicopter as if he were a sack of potatoes. Pasqual's head bounced on a seat strut.

"Oops," Big John said. He handed Pasqual's phone and pistol to Jenny.

Chapter Fifty-Two

Jenny knew that the *Intrepid* was not that large a ship. As she expected, within fifteen minutes, her team reported that they had swept up the surprised guard force. In the meantime Jenny made her way to the engine compartment.

"Jenny!" yelled Stephens when the hatch opened. "Oh my God! You made it." Stephens gave Jenny a rib-crunching hug.

"I told you I'd be back," Jenny said when she was able to pull loose.

She started to tense up again when she saw another crewman in the compartment with Stephens. She couldn't help but notice a fat lip and black eye on his face.

Stephens saw Jenny's look. "Alehandro is my new assistant," she explained. "He's been hired to replace Rocky. He's glad to be out of Cuba, and he seems to be a decent mechanic."

She then explained the marks on his face. "We started out with a misunderstanding. He thought he had special privileges with me. But we're good now."

"Then you'll be OK alone for a while longer?" Jenny asked.

"Sure," Stephens replied.

"Good. Lock up. There should be an FBI SWAT team arriving

on the ship in the next forty-five minutes. I'm headed up to the wheelhouse. Call the Captain and tell him to distract any guards. I'll be there in a minute."

It took less than that for Jenny to open the door of the wheelhouse.

"Wish we could meet in other circumstances, Major," Slovinski said. "Stephens told me about you. Sorry about this." He nodded toward three guards with pistols out that had him and the helmsman hostage. "There's been a lot of chatter on their walkie-talkies."

"I was afraid of that," she responded. "Look," she said to the guards, "I don't have time to mess around. If you guys want to jump off the ship right now, no one will stop you. It's a short swim to shore. Otherwise, I'm going to have to kill you."

They looked at her with initial bravado and smirks. She watched their faces change. She could see them listening to feedback on their own headset walkie-talkies. Glances of fear were exchanged.

First one and then another laid his weapon on the deck. "Perdóneme, Sanchez," one of them said to the guard holding Slovinski. "Es para nada."

He walked out the doorway and jumped over the railing. The second guard followed.

Sanchez was alone. "I will kill him," he said, pushing a pistol barrel into Slovinski's ear. A fanatical look was in his eyes, but fear made his voice quaver. Jenny guessed him to be no more than twenty years old. "I can't swim," he admitted with a whisper.

"You can come with me, Sanchez," Jenny said. "It doesn't have to be this way."

"I'm a known member of the Shining Path," he said. "The Peruvian government would pay a big reward for my capture. I can't." His eyes looked into the distance.

"But ..." She didn't finish. Sanchez had been working his tongue against his teeth. A pained expression came over his face.

Froth developed over his lips. He coughed once and fell to the deck. His back arched. He groaned from deep within his chest. Then his head lolled toward Jenny, and then he lay still, eyes open. The faint smell of almonds permeated the wheelhouse. *Damn! Should have thought. Shining Path must issue death pills to maintain secrecy.*

Within seconds, Faz'el burst through the wheelhouse doorway, his scimitar raised. "Princess, are you all right?" he asked.

Before she could respond, Cavanaugh spoke in her earpiece on the walkie-talkie. "Jenny, I'm at midship, deck one. You need to see this."

Faz'el heard the same message. "Follow me," he said.

In minutes Jenny stood next to Cavanaugh behind stacked barrels, peering through open spaces between the stacks.

In front of them, crewmen loaded people into freight containers. She counted over one hundred men, women and children herded into one container.

Buoyancy tanks were attached, and the container was sealed and lowered by a crane into the water through a hole in the deck. Two men in wet suits and scuba gear were in the water with submersible scooters. It was obvious—they were there to guide the sealed container to its destination.

On the upper decks, she'd seen a normal off-loading operation of freight containers—legitimate business as usual. Jenny was amazed at the simplicity of the movement of the illegals.

"Wonder where they're going," Cavanaugh said, gesturing toward the container settling into the water.

"They're probably going to their land base," Jenny responded. "That's where Stack's laptop computer will be. Let's find out." She started walking toward a crewman in a wet suit who appeared to be supervising operations. A communications headset hung on a bulkhead hook.

"Wait a minute, Jenny. Don't be hasty," Cavanaugh said. He tried to grab her but was too late. "Dammit!" he exclaimed.

The look that crossed the face of the supervisor was a picture of surprise.

"What are you ...?" he started when he saw Jenny striding toward him.

"I need your wet suit," she said.

Chapter Fifty-Three

Given the surprised look of the supervisor in the bowels of the *Intrepid*, Jenny figured the communications headset hanging on a bulkhead peg was his. He appeared unaware of the changing situation on the ship.

His eyes darted about, looking for an escape. He tensed, preparing to dive in the water.

Jenny stepped in front of him and pointed her mini-Uzi. "No," was all she said.

He glared at her.

"Tell them to stop," she added, waving toward the ongoing operation.

He called out. One by one the crew stopped in their tracks, eyeing her and the machine pistol strapped on her hip. One or two had pistols. *Will they fight?*

Cavanaugh and Faz'el stepped from behind the barrels. "Throw down your weapons," Cavanaugh said.

The tough-looking, gun-toting duo sealed any decision by the crew. They tossed their weapons to the deck.

Jenny could see the lights of submersible scooters dim in the murky water of the Mississippi. The scuba team was pushing away the freight container that had been loaded.

"Let me have your fanny pack," she told the supervisor, pointing to a small bag he had strapped around his wet suit.

Puzzled, he took it off and handed it to her. She stuck her walkie-talkie radio inside.

Strapping the pack to her own waist, she told Cavanaugh, "I'm going after that container. There's no time for the wet suit. I'll radio you where to bring the chopper to pick me up."

Once again, moving fast, she gave no opportunity for Cavanaugh or Faz'el to react. She grabbed an air tank and face mask off a bulkhead rack and dove through the deck opening.

Underwater, she grasped the mouthpiece with her teeth and secured the mask over her face. She blew out through her nose to clear the water in the mask, slipped on the air tank harness and kicked toward the receding scooter lights. *Dammit! Should have gotten a flashlight.*

The scuba divers moved slowly at first. She caught up. In the illumination from the scooter headlights, she could see the divers using air tanks on flotation devices to stabilize the container. In the muddy water, the headlights became her only source of reference.

Entering the river channel, she felt the current become stronger. She began to fall behind the faster, battery-powered scooters.

The already dim illumination from the lights began to blink on and off. The intervals between "on" and "off" lengthened.

Then the lights disappeared altogether. She swam harder, thinking she'd catch up.

Her head banged into a hard object in the water. Her face mask was knocked askew and filled with water.

Disoriented from the impact, she started a free fall into the river depths.

Hyperventilating, thrashing her arms and legs, she was near panic.

She clamped down on those feelings, steadied her breathing and reset her mask, blowing out the water that had seeped inside.

Then she hit something with her shoe. Then she bumped

something else with her elbow.

Feeling surrounded, Jenny twisted and turned to escape what felt like an imprisonment. She bumped from one rough, hard surface to another. It felt as if she was in a thick forest at nighttime, blindly stumbling from tree to tree.

She had an urge to rip out her mouthpiece. She wanted to scream. *No ... think!* She willed her mind to be logical.

"These are dock pilings!" She blurted out through her mouthpiece.

To reinforce her conviction, she put her hands around the next object she bumped into. She felt rounded, machined surfaces broken by barnacles and slim.

Her confidence surged. And then, it plummeted. She couldn't see anything. *How do I find a way out?*

At a point when her resolve was at its lowest ebb, a light appeared. One of the underwater scooters was coming back, directly toward her. Another followed.

She ducked behind the piling she'd been holding. The swimmers didn't notice her when they passed; they were focused on pushing and pulling a freight container through a passageway in the pilings.

She strained her eyes, looking in the direction from which the scooters had come. She saw a faint glow—light reflected in the ripples and bubbles of the wake of the passing scooters.

She swam forward, guided by the gleaming bubbles. Within minutes they led her to a small rectangle of light on the water from a source above, an opening cut in the dock. She swam to the edge of the rectangle of light. With her head above the surface, she remained in the shadows. Peering upward, she saw a chain with a large hook on the end hanging in the center of the dock opening. A steel ladder extended from the dock's edge into the water.

She was certain she'd found the container destination.

Treading water, she heard voices recede away from the dock opening. And then the lights went off.

Disoriented by the sudden darkness, she tried to focus on her quick visual of a nearby ladder. She dog-paddled in that direction. The side of her face, and then her hand, brushed the rusty ladder rail.

She grasped a rung in a tight-fisted grip, hanging motionless, letting her heartbeat return to normal, allowing the pounding in her ears to subside.

"God, I hate the dark," she said half-out-loud. She recalled being traumatized as a child when an elevator stuck her alone mid-floor for hours during a power blackout. The experience had caused her nightmares for years, and her palms still sweated at the memory.

She stood on the first rung of the ladder and shrugged off her air tank, hoses and mouthpiece; ditto for the face mask. The equipment floated away in the eddies of the current.

She unslung her Uzi machine pistol. By feel, she ensured the bolt, receiver and clip were seated.

Earlier, she'd used duct tape to disable the pistol's primary safety on the grip. Now she thumbed the secondary safety switch to the fire position.

She chambered a round. Her pistol had the L-clip configuration, so she had two twenty-five round magazines.

"Not much at four hundred fifty rounds a minute," she muttered. But she didn't plan on a gunfight. She peeked over the top of the ladder—she was set to rock and roll.

Chapter Fifty-Four

Jenny pulled herself over the dock edge of the New Orleans wharf. The roughened planks of the pier felt warped and splintery. Everything smelled like decay. Despite the moisture in the air, the boards seemed tinder dry.

A shaft of light pierced the darkness, stretching from beneath a nearby doorway. It provided enough light to keep her from tripping. She crept silently in its direction.

Voices sounded from outside the door, a low rumble of conversation. No one seemed close.

On the wall behind her next to the doorframe, she found a switch box. She ran her hands over the device and flicked the lever. Lights flooded the pier.

In an instant she turned them off hoping that the lights went unnoticed. She crouched and moved closer to the door's side, expecting visitors at any second. No one came.

"Whew!" she silently breathed.

But in that brief glance at her surroundings, she'd gotten the picture of how the human cargo was unloaded. She was in a dilapidated warehouse built over the dock.

Cut in the center was a large hole. The cable she'd seen from the water hung from a ceiling crane mounted in the rafters.

Hooks on the wall had a variety of clothes hanging on them. She assumed they belonged to the scuba divers that were moving the freight containers through the water. She fumbled her way to the wall hooks.

She grabbed a ball cap to cover her wet head and pulled a button-down shirt over her shoulders. She hoped the clothes would help conceal the fact that she was sopping wet and would help hide the mini-Uzi slung on her shoulder.

She silently opened the door and did a quick scan to check for guards. Left ... right ... behind the door. Clear.

Twenty feet down the hall on her left, several people were lined up next to the wall.

Acting casual, Jenny walked out of the door and joined the line.

An older Hispanic man stood in front of her. He looked askance at her when she moved behind him.

"Why you all wet?" he asked in broken English.

"I fell in," Jenny answered.

"Not good start," he responded, turning his back, dismissing her.

In front of the line, Jenny could see a strobe light flashing. She tapped the man on the shoulder. "What's going on up there?" she asked.

"You no listen to instructions?" He shook his head. "You not make it in U.S. if no listen. They tell us they take photo for ID and give Social Security. Give you for you show Immigration. No arrest. Comprende?"

"Yes. I understand," she answered. Her words coincided with the opening of a corridor door opposite the one she'd used. Two men came out holding weapons she recognized—tasers—stun guns with fifteen feet of wire coiled inside with prongs attached to the ends. When triggered, compressed air cylinders mounted in the gun shoot the wire toward the intended victim. The prongs penetrate fabric and skin, and the wire transmits electric current to shock targets from an extended range.

The men were escorting three young girls and a blond-haired boy. The four children were handcuffed and chained together. All were wearing short-sleeve, brown-colored shifts. Jenny guessed their ages to be between twelve and eighteen.

The group went through the same door into the warehouse that Jenny had exited. She watched one of the men push a girl and say, "Come on, Isabella. Move."

Hearing that name, Jenny's mind jumped back in time to her conversation with Crystal in the park across from the Cavanaugh's.

"I promised Isabella," Crystal had said. "I promised."

Jenny made a snap decision.

"Save my place," she told the old man in front of her in the line. The man gave her a disbelieving look as she followed the guards.

The faces of the two guards gave Jenny renewed confidence in her decision—surprise and shock at her unexpected boldness would slow their reaction.

"Hey!" the one who had pushed Isabella exclaimed. "Get your ass out of here."

Jenny continued walking toward the man, shrugging her shoulders, feigning a lack of comprehension. She didn't want to use the hidden Uzi unless she had to.

"You have bathroom?" she asked with a heavy fake accent.

"Not in here, dummy," the man said.

She continued to approach. "Get away from me, dammit," he said when she got close.

Jenny didn't give him time to act. Quick as a cat, she was on him. She hit his forearm with the edge of her palm, jarring loose his taser.

Before the gun hit the dock's surface, she'd hit the man three more times: throat, solar plexus and groin, in that order. He collapsed, gagging and groaning.

The second guard fired his taser. Jenny watched the prongs arch toward her and fall harmlessly to the dock at the end of their tether. He'd misjudged the distance.

He backed away, scrambling to reload. Jenny launched herself across the space to reach him before he could insert a new cartridge.

She didn't make it.

Instead, with a fury and abandon only an angry child knows, the boy jumped at the guard.

"No more, asshole," the boy screamed. He headbutted the man in the midriff.

Led by the boy's example, all the children swarmed over the man. In that instant, it was as if the guard had stepped on an anthill.

Feet, fists, elbows and knees pummeled him.

Knocked to the ground, he curled into a fetal position, moaning.

Within seconds he was silent. Heedless, the children continued clawing, kicking and stomping, growling and raging in an animalistic frenzy. The thud of blows on human flesh echoed off the walls.

"That's enough," Jenny yelled, overcoming her initial shock at the violence of their reaction. "Get off him." She began pulling on their chains.

With reluctance, the children allowed themselves to be pulled off the still form. They were panting from exertion.

"He was the worst," one of the girls said. She spat on him. "He's mean as a snake."

"Well, it's over. Let's not kill him," Jenny said. She checked his pulse. "He's still alive. We'll cuff him. The FBI will be here in a few minutes, and they'll handle this." She kept a wary eye on the group.

"The handcuff keys are in his shirt pocket," the same girl offered. She helped Jenny unlock the other children.

Their lust for revenge sated, they rubbed their wrists, watching silently. Jenny cuffed the two guards, but still kept an eye on the youths.

"Be careful. There are more guards through the door across the hall," one of the girls said.

"Are you Isabella?" Jenny asked the girl.

"How do you know my name?"

"Crystal told me, but I don't have time to explain now," Jenny answered. She started back out the door. "You guys wait here. An FBI SWAT team will be here in a few minutes. I have to do something."

A look of panic crossed their faces. "No. Don't leave us," they chorused. "Please—"

"Trust me. The FBI is coming. Wait right here."

Fighting guilt pangs, she went back into the corridor. She wanted a copy of the IDs, to see the whole process, and she wanted Stack's computer. She stood in line behind the old man again. She kept an eye on the second door across the corridor. If another guard showed, it could get ugly.

"Where you go?" the old man asked. "You no behave, we all have big problem." He gave her another disapproving look.

"Bathroom," she answered. She noticed a woman sobbing in front of them in the line. "Why is that woman crying?" she asked.

"You know deal. She know too. We pay ten thousand dollar for ship ... for fake ID ... we pay another ten thousand. Or we agree work one year. She agree work. Her husband and son agree work. They go Florida ... be crop picker. She go Indiana chicken farm. She sad. Why you ask so many questions?"

Jenny didn't have to answer because the photographer called the man next. A minute later, it was her turn.

A cameraman told her in a bored monotone, "Take off your hat. Stand on the line." The camera flashed. He waved Jenny toward a nearby table.

A husky woman at the table was laminating cards from pictures a printer was processing off the camera.

When it was her turn, Jenny was given two cards—one card was a Louisiana driver's license with her picture on it and the other was a Social Security card. She pocketed them both.

Jenny must have had a look of surprise on her face because the woman told her, "Williams—that's your new name, honey. Get used to it. Go get in the truck in the alley."

Jenny still had her hat off, and the woman took a closer look. She said, "Hey, Pete. This one's too cute to go on a work detail."

"We don't have much time, Fran," the man called Pete answered. To Jenny he said, "Take off that shirt, sweetheart. Let me get a good look at you." The rest of the people who had been in line had moved outside to load on the truck. Inside it was only Jenny, the woman named Fran, and Pete the photographer.

Jenny stood mute at Pete's directions, stunned at the cold, callous attitude. It pissed her off. The woman made another mistake.

None too gently, Fran jerked off the shirt that Jenny had

draped over her shoulders. "Dammit, he said to take the shirt off."

Then Fran's eyes grew wide. The Uzi was pointed at her chest.

"Jesus Christ!" she exclaimed, backing away.

Jenny's anger almost bubbled over. Her finger tightened on the trigger.

"You even twitch wrong," she said, "and I'll blow you apart. I swear. Now get down on your knees."

Fran fell to her knees without hesitation. "Please don't kill me," she pleaded.

Jenny pointed her machine pistol at Pete. "Get your ass over here and tie up your friend. Use the laces on her tennis shoes." After Pete was finished, Jenny tied him, hands and feet, with a zip tie.

Unable to restrain her anger, she kicked Pete in the chest, which sent him sprawling into Fran. They both fell to the ground.

"I hope you rot in hell," she told them. She removed and pocketed the memory card from their camera.

She ran through the door that she'd seen Isabella and other prisoners exit. The door led to another dilapidated warehouse that had an open staircase in the middle of the floor.

She jumped down the staircase three and four steps at a time into a narrow hallway. A man looked up from a small desk centered in the middle, surprise written on his face.

"What the hell ...?" He reached for a pistol in a shoulder holster. Jenny shot him with a three-round burst to the chest. He toppled backward. The gunfire reverberated in the confines of the hall.

She didn't pause, expecting the noise to alert any backup guards. Racing down the hall, Jenny passed four open doors that led into rooms resembling prison cells. *Isabella and those kids must have been in there.* Scared faces peered out small windows of other closed doors. "I'll be back!" she yelled.

She skidded around a bend in the hallway. Two men were running toward her. "Wait a minute ...," one of them started.

Jenny didn't wait. She fired two more bursts. The men collapsed with the impact of the bullets stopping them in their tracks. They were still twitching when she leaped over their bodies, heading up a stairway they'd come down.

She burst into a ratty-looking office area. It was empty. The front door was hanging open.

She could hear an engine fading in the distance. "Run, you bastards!" she yelled out the open door. "I'll find you. Bet on it."

Surveying the room, she saw two beat-up desks, unmade bunk beds and a dirty-looking microwave oven. One of the desks had a hard-wired PC on it. The other had an open laptop.

She smiled. "Thanks, Stack," she said into the empty space.

Opening the sealed fanny pack, she pulled out her walkie-talkie. "Jim, can you hear me?"

Chapter Fifty-Five

Vladimir was relieved that El Toro reacted calmly to news about another loss of communications with the *Intrepid*.

"When do you think you will reestablish contact?" El Toro asked.

"Based on the past, I'd guess within the hour. There's probably a tower down in the New Orleans zone."

El Toro got a distant look on his face and said, "I don't think so. That's not supposed to happen near a major metropolis. Something's wrong." He paused for a minute.

For the first time, Vladimir saw the workings of the brilliant mind that had formed a criminal empire. In the silence, he reflected on how different El Toro acted without Carlotta nearby.

"Why hasn't the New Orleans operations center checked in?"

"Same reason, I suspect. That link has been trouble since Katrina," Vladimir answered. "It's always come back."

El Toro shook his head. He said, "I disagree. My intuition tells me we may have been compromised by that girl."

Carlotta came into the room. "What girl?"

El Toro brought her up-to-date. He became agitated in her presence, shifting in his seat, his eyes darting around the room.

The characteristic vein bulged in a steady beat on his forehead.

"Papa, you're getting upset," she said, smoothing his hair. "Why don't I handle this?" She glanced at Vladimir, as if flaunting her power.

Vladimir knew her response would be excessive and unpleasant. Nonetheless, El Toro waved his hand for her to continue.

With that encouragement, her eyes bored into Vladimir's. "Get rid of that ship. Destroy all evidence of our contact with New Orleans and the *Intrepid*. Kill everyone involved. Make it particularly painful for Stack and Pasqual ... and that stupid ship captain, whatever his name is."

"Señorita, aren't we overreacting?" Vladimir answered. "That ship cost a fortune."

"I don't care," screamed El Toro, his face contorted with rage. "We have *Endeavor, Enterprise, Voyager* and the *Atlantis* making us millions. This one ship has been a nightmare."

Carlotta added, "And if that conniving bitch that escaped from Stack brings authorities back to New Orleans, it could be a disaster. Get rid of it. We have other facilities."

"She's right. Do it! Do it," El Toro ranted, bouncing up and down in his seat, hammering the desktop with his putter.

"Shhh, Papa," Carlotta said, pressing his face to her breast. "Shush, now. You must calm yourself."

"Mmm," he responded, his voice muffled. "You're so good for me." He began to nuzzle and caress her. Carlotta motioned with her head that Vladimir should leave.

"Wait," she said, changing her mind. "The servants tell me you've instructed them to prepare for a visit from the U.S. President's wife."

"That's correct," Vladimir answered. "Mrs. Fisher confirmed that she will be visiting next week."

"I don't like the idea. Cancel the visit."

"No, Carlotta," El Toro said. "I told him to go ahead with the plans. It will be fun. I will enjoy it." He was unbuttoning her blouse, pushing at her bra.

She looked down at him. Her breathing was becoming unsteady.

"I'm told that she will be traveling on a private jet and that she intends to stay here less than twenty-four hours," Vladimir said.

"Good. The shorter the better. I assume she's bringing a security detail?" El Toro asked.

"Sí, señor. But only five people. We should be able to host them all in the main house. Again, names aren't provided for security reasons."

"Who cares? Did you prepare the mock gravesite?"

"Sí, señor."

"Excellent. It will give me a perverse pleasure to know that when she pays her respects at Vanessa's grave, her friend will be under guard one hundred meters away."

When Vladimir gave him a quizzical look, El Toro explained in a child's peevish tone, "She and the President have always treated me like a second cousin. Betty Fisher has never liked me even after I married Vanessa. And I've contributed heavily to President Fisher's political campaigns. This will be my small payback to them for all of their social slights."

"Didn't the President provide you a special award for civic service?"

"It was a meaningless trinket, and it was embarrassing," El Toro responded, referring to the questions asked of him about his Cuban ancestry by Director Tavares right after the ceremony. He gave a dismissive wave and pawed at Carlotta's skirt.

Vladimir turned on his heel and walked out of the room. He gave an involuntary shudder in disgust at their behavior. He decided to hold off on the order about the ship and operating center until he could reason with El Toro at a later time.

☆☆☆

Ten thousand miles to the northeast, President Fisher was having a mild argument with his wife after dinner in the White House.

"George, I would never forgive myself for not respecting Vanessa's memory," Betty Fisher said.

"I understand. But the interior of Argentina is not secure. The Secret Service is going to be very difficult about this."

"Sweetie, they work for you."

"That's not the point and you know it. Couldn't you at least take Air Force One?"

"How could I do that and keep a low profile? That's ridiculous. The world would know that I was there and soon find out why. The whole story about Vanessa would become public. I can't bear to be a part of tarnishing her memory."

The President nodded his head. "I can understand that. Would you at least use the normal Secret Service detail? I can probably arrange an aircraft from a corporate friend."

"George, I'm not going down there with twenty-five men and women trailing me at every corner. That's not going to happen. It would have exactly the same result as using Air Force One."

"There's only ten agents on the detail—"

"I'll take two. That's it."

"Christ, Betty. You're not being reasonable." He paused for a minute and looked at her attractive face. She seldom asked for anything and had put up with a lot given his job and political career. He shook his head in resignation. "All right, but I pick the agents. This whole thing is against my better judgment."

She stood and hugged him. She said, "Thanks, Harry. I knew you'd understand." She kissed him on the forehead, trailing her hand over his shoulder, walking away. "Come to bed early tonight. I'll make it up to you."

"You don't play fair," he smiled.

"Never have, sweetie."

Chapter Fifty-Six

Jenny waited in Penfant's outer office at CENTCOM headquarters. She'd been summoned via three e-mails, two text messages and a handwritten note taped to the front door of her apartment.

The messages were all the same. "Meet the CG in his office at 0630 Monday." Colonel Everett had signed all the notes. He'd been checking to see if she'd followed his instructions, and she was certain he'd discovered she hadn't.

The rush of elation she'd felt over the success of the weekend mission in New Orleans was quashed by the terse messages.

The physical demands and tension of her two-day trip had taken their toll. She felt exhausted. She'd arrived back in Tampa on a civilian red eye flight at two a.m.

The Prince's airplane was down for maintenance. After she heard the first phone message, she decided not to wait for any repair to be complete.

"Don't worry about it," Jim Cavanaugh had said when she told him about her summons. "Wait until you show them what you found. They'll forget all about your breaking that bogus restriction that Everett imposed."

She wasn't as confident. When Director Tavares came in at seven with barely a nod in her direction, she became even more apprehensive.

Ten minutes later, a smug-looking Colonel Everett called her into the CG's personal office.

She walked in, stood at rigid attention in front of Penfant's desk and popped her best salute.

"Sir, Major O'Shane reporting as ordered," she said.

Penfant returned her salute. She could feel his eyes boring into her. He didn't say a word for a full minute. When he did, he spoke in a silky tone Jenny recognized as preceding bad news.

"O'Shane, I don't think there's much hope that you can explain your actions sufficiently to stop me from having your name pulled off the command list that's scheduled to be published next month."

Her mouth dropped open. She started to answer, "Sir, I—"

"I know you didn't know about the list. It's not public yet. However, if it was released, you'd be the youngest Army battalion commander appointed since World War II."

He paused to let those words sink in, and then added, "And you would have been the only woman MP battalion commander in Afghanistan. There are six hundred soldiers in the unit you were designated to lead."

He started to sign a letter on his otherwise empty desk.

"Sir, I can explain," she said.

He looked up at her with a face that was lined by fatigue and stress. There was a sadness in his eyes.

"Not this time, O'Shane. There're too many questions. It's not the simple matter of breaking restriction to spend a weekend in New Orleans with your friends."

He held up his hand to stop her protest. He started ticking off items on his fingers.

"One, there's an unexplained issue of drugs and cash where the Coast Guard boat sank. That will require an investigation. Two, there's a missing Coast Guard officer that'll require another investigation. Three, there's an alleged military incursion into Cuba waters that resulted in a State Department protest. Four, the Coast Guard insists that their prototype boat be replaced. Five, you go missing for three days without telling anyone where you're at."

Penfant rubbed his forehead and shook his head in exasperation. "How can you possibly explain these things away, O'Shane?"

He sighed, but still didn't give her time to respond. "Let's see where the investigations go, and maybe we can revisit a future command assignment. This letter will temporarily remove you from the list."

He bent to finish signing the document. A phone at his elbow buzzed. A red light on it blinked. He picked it up immediately.

"Yes, Mr. President?" he answered.

He listened for a moment and then said, "No, sir. I didn't know about a SWAT team in New Orleans. I was at Bragg until last night."

She heard the buzz of a reply in the receiver. "Holy shit," Penfant said.

Penfant listened for a minute more. His facial features softened. He even smiled. "Well, I guess she had the code word for a reason, Mr. President. Yes, sir. I'll tell her." He hung up.

He arched an eyebrow toward Jenny and said, "The President and the Secretary of Defense send their regards. Apparently, the Director of the FBI also extends a greeting. He credits you with the bust of a human smuggling ring in New Orleans."

"Sir, I apologize for not—"

"For not keeping me informed as to what you were doing?" Penfant finished for her.

"Uhh, yes, sir. Sorry, sir. I used the code word in a phone message for you on Saturday morning. I didn't get a response. So I used a fallback option."

"By calling the President of the United States?" Penfant asked, incredulous.

"Yes, sir. Sorry, sir." She stood even more stiffly at attention.

Penfant pursed his lips and got a far-off look on his face. Then he focused back on Jenny. "You left a message for me with the code word?"

"Uhh, yes, sir. I said that it was a Griffin message for General Penfant."

Penfant shifted his steely gaze to Everett. "What's up with that, Jack? You were answering my phone messages for me."

"General, I thought it was bogus."

"So, you decided to ignore her? This is the only woman in U.S. military history to be awarded two Silver Stars for valor. Yet you virtually arrested her on Friday in Key West, you restrict her to quarters in Tampa in my absence, then you ignore a phone message of that precedence?"

He let his comments sink in. Then he continued. "I have to get a call from the President to learn about her rescue of kidnap victims in New Orleans. Jack, your judgment seems to be really warped regarding O'Shane." He waved away Everett's protests.

"We'll talk about it later." He turned his gaze back to Jenny. "OK. Speak to me, O'Shane. And, for God's sake, would you please stand at ease. This isn't the West Point parade ground."

"Yes, sir. Sorry, sir—"

"And knock off the 'sorry' shit," Penfant interrupted again. "You're driving me nuts. Tell me what happened."

Jenny briefed the highlights of her story. She told about the ASDS interception of the *Intrepid*, Charlie's death, and her findings in New Orleans. She ended by putting the fake IDs and the camera disk on Penfant's desk. "There are witnesses to verify what I've told you."

Penfant was silent until she mentioned the witnesses. "You have witnesses? Why didn't you bring—"

"Sir, at first there wasn't room on the Prince's helicopter," Jenny interrupted. "Then the Prince's plane broke, and I needed to get back here for this meeting."

"Prince? Jenny, you left out the part about the Prince," Penfant said.

She explained about using the royal airplane and helicopter, and the plane still being in New Orleans for maintenance.

"You see what I mean, General?" Everett interjected. "There's the 'I can explain' crap. The Saudi Crown Prince has a personal C-17? Bullshit! And the airplane has a helicopter on it? Come on, sir."

His comments were rewarded with a baleful glance. Ignoring Everett, Penfant said to Jenny, "You mentioned witnesses?"

"Yes, sir. I left several key people in New Orleans. Because the helicopter was small, we had to shuttle them back to the airport from the wharf. I flew out on a commercial flight before we got them all moved."

"There you go again, O'Shane," Everett interrupted. "Another cock-and-bull story with no witnesses."

"Jack, put a cork in it," Penfant said. He directed another question to Jenny. "So how do we substantiate your story with witnesses at this point?"

"General, I said I don't have all the New Orleans witnesses," Jenny responded. "But Reimers, the British officer, will confirm most of what I've shared, and there are people downstairs in the lobby you may want to meet."

Jenny felt herself blush as she saw the baleful look he directed toward her. "I apologize again, sir."

Penfant held up his hand. He shook his head in disbelief. "I shouldn't be surprised, I guess," he sighed.

He took a deep breath. "Jack," he continued. "Go downstairs and bring up our visitors."

Everett lifted his chin and his lips thinned. He glared at Jenny, clearly blaming her for his demeaning gofer assignment.

When he'd gone, Director Tavares asked his first question. "Major, I've listened carefully, and I wonder how you could do this by yourself?"

"I had help, sir," Jenny admitted with hesitation.

"You used the people you spoke to me about? That man Cavanaugh, someone named Little John and Bubba?" Penfant asked.

"Uhh, yes, sir."

"Great," Penfant explained to Tavares. "She took two ex-criminals on a mission sanctioned by the President."

He rubbed his forehead again and asked Jenny, "How do you think this is going to play out for the public, O'Shane?"

"Well, sir," Jenny added. "There were four Saudi palace guards."

"Palace guards?" Tavares asked.

He and Penfant exchanged open-mouthed looks. Penfant shrugged his shoulders. "What can I say?"

Jenny then laid a paper on Penfant's desk with numbers scribbled on it. "General, those numbers probably explain the problem in INTERPOL that we discussed with President Fisher."

"You mean the President's special mission?"

"Yes, sir. I got those numbers off a cell phone that belonged to the leader of the thugs on the *Intrepid*. He seems to have been getting information from the director of the Cuban Intelligence Service. It's a long story, but I think you'll find that two of the numbers connect to key INTERPOL offices. One of them is a European phone number, and one has an area code in the U.S. I tried the U.S. number on my way to New Orleans."

"What are you two talking about? What the hell have you been up to, Major?" Tavares asked with indignation in his voice, his brow knitted.

Penfant interceded on Jenny's behalf and explained the President's mission in brief detail. Jenny watched Tavares become more and more agitated.

"Why wasn't I told?"

"Because we weren't sure of anyone, Juan. It was better this way," Penfant said.

Tavares was pissed and completely disbelieving until Jenny told him, "Director, I spoke to a Veronica Fluentes at this number. I think she works for you?" She handed him the paper.

"My God. You can't be serious." He looked at the sheet of paper and then collapsed back into his seat on the office couch. "I've suspected there were issues within our INTERPOL organization, but a leak out of my own office, by my most trusted assistant?"

Before anyone could say more, there was a knock on the door, and Colonel Everett trooped in with three people—Crystal, Reimers and Pasqual filed in behind him.

Chapter Fifty-Seven

A few hours after her meeting with Penfant, Jenny sat on the couch in her apartment holding Nikki on her lap. Another "war council" had been convened with Jim and Ginger Cavanaugh, Momma, Gary, Big John and Bubba.

"That cat gets more attention than me," Gary said.

"Don't tell me you're jealous of a cat?" Jenny asked.

"Well, I sure don't get to sit on your lap getting my belly rubbed," her fiancé retorted.

"Aww, come here Big Boy. I'll rub your belly." Gary's face lit up, and he started to move onto her lap.

"Hey, you guys. Did you remember there are other people in the room?" Jim Cavanaugh said. That generated a general chorus of laughter.

"What's your point?" Jenny asked. Her straight face, and Gary's big frame on her lap, caused more laughter.

Seconds later, Jenny's comments turned the room serious again. "I think our trip tomorrow is a waste of time," she said.

She had finished packing and was preparing to leave for Argentina. "I know little about INTERPOL's organization or operations, and we've about wrapped up the human trafficking investigation. What can the big shot Women's Resources chairman offer at this point?"

"Lighten up," Cavanaugh said. "If I'm reading the cards right, my guess is that the First Lady doesn't want a contingent of Secret Service goons surrounding her while she makes this pilgrimage to the gravesite of her friend. Did you notice the flight lists only two agents?"

"Yeah, I saw that. I'd bet that's partly why you and Big John are also going."

"That's my guess and it's why we got temporary Secret Service credentials. We're sort of a backup to keep a low official profile."

"Whatever, it certainly doesn't make me any happier about the assignment."

"I know you wanted to be on point here with INTERPOL to clean up the loose ends of the investigation," Cavanaugh said. "But Stack and Pasqual will spend the rest of their life in a prison somewhere. And Tavares can handle the rest of the heavy lifting now that you uncovered the mole in his shop. You've done more than your part."

"You can think of it as a sort of paid vacation. You've never been to Argentina before. Remember also that Director Tavares owes you big time," Gary offered.

"It wasn't that big a deal," Jenny responded.

"Right," he scoffed. "You memorized numbers in the address book on that thug Pasqual's cell phone. What was the name of that Cuban Intelligence Service he contacted?"

"The Cuban DGI," Jenny answered. "Its full name is Dirección General de Inteligencia. Apparently they were blackmailing Tavares's assistant by holding her family hostage in Cuba. Her cell phone number was the other one I called."

Cavanaugh shook his head. "Right. No big deal," he parroted. "What made you think of checking numbers on his phone's address book?"

"I was bored on the airplane. I scrolled down the list on the phone I'd taken from him and saw there were U.S. area codes. I thought they might be important. I kind of have a thing for remembering numbers."

Momma said, "Girl, you seem to do more things by accident

than most people do on purpose." Everyone laughed at her remark.

Jenny felt a blush creep up her face again.

Momma scolded her. "You need to stop being embarrassed at being so smart!" That evoked a full round of laughs that even Jenny had to share. After the laughter died down, Jenny said, "I'm glad Tavares found out about the information leak in his own office. That woman must have been passing INTERPOL secrets for years."

"You have to feel sorry for her," Cavanaugh said. "Having your entire family held hostage would be tough. The DGI must be real bastards. I hope it's over."

"I hope so too. There's probably a lot we'll never know about the situation," Ginger said. "I hope a judge will show leniency for her and the *Intrepid's* captain and engineer. They got in way over their heads."

Another somber silence enveloped the group.

"Director Tavares must have been pleased," Cavanaugh said, trying to brighten the mood. "It was sure convenient he was in the CG's office at the right time to make the whole thing fall into place. When did you connect that he and Crystal were related?" Cavanaugh asked Jenny.

"I wasn't sure until she got to Penfant's office. She recognized the Director because he looks almost identical to her dad. The Tavares brothers were placed in foster care when their parents were killed on a freedom boat from Cuba. They'd lost touch. The familial reconnection made the issue about the office spy go down a lot easier."

"Yeah, and you made two lifelong friends."

"It was a guess," Jenny responded.

"Right," Gary said. "You uncover a mole in the U.S. and in Europe for INTERPOL, reunite a family, and, oh yeah, bust up a human smuggling operation ... all guess work. You should play the lottery."

She felt her face flush for a second time.

"That's a nice color," Gary teased her. "It goes well with your hair."

"Stop it," Jenny said. She tried to cover her embarrassment by an exaggerated closing of the cover of Stack's laptop. She'd been fiddling with it and talking at the same time.

"I don't think we're ever going to get into this thing. Stack won't tell us his password and I can't crack it."

"Tell me again why you decided not to give that up to the FBI techies to work on?" Cavanaugh asked. "The CG specifically took you off the main investigation. He's going to have your ass when he finds out you have that thing."

"I know. I know," Jenny answered.

Gary rumpled her short hair. "Face it. You want to stay in front of it all."

"No. It's more than that, dammit. The thugs involved in this operation are despicable. I can't bear the thought of one of them escaping. No witness protection deals and the like." She pushed the computer across the table. "This thing is the secret, I'm certain of it. No one will follow up like I intend to."

"OK. OK. Sorry I said that." Gary put his hands palm out into the "I surrender" motion.

"You're not going to go vigilante on us, right?" Cavanaugh asked.

"Of course not, Jim. But these assholes are going to be brought to justice. Of that you can be certain." She could feel her Irish temper starting to flare. Her anger at the abuse and destruction of human lives for purposes of profit ran deeper than she could explain.

Cavanaugh seemed to understand. He suggested a compromise. "Why don't you leave the computer here? My stepson Bobby can take a look at it. He's a computer genius."

"That's an idea," Jenny agreed, curbing her outburst. She glanced at Ginger. "But you have to promise to call me if he finds anything."

"It's a deal," Ginger answered. She stood and pulled Cavanaugh to his feet. "Now we need to break this up. Three of you have an early flight in the morning—you'll be living the high life, traveling with the wife of the President no less."

Jenny rolled her eyes. "Thanks for reminding me," she said. Her feelings of being sent on a fool's errand returned.

Chapter Fifty-Eight

Jenny walked with Mrs. Fisher to the Saudi royal airplane parked at a secluded runway at the Ronald Reagan National Airport. She'd flown with Cavanaugh and Big John from Tampa and was already feeling jet lag.

Saudi Crown Prince Fahd bowed when the First Lady arrived at his plane's stairway. "Mrs. Fisher, you do me a great honor traveling with this humble servant of Allah," he said.

The President's wife was equally gracious and provided a genuine Southern curtsy. "It is my honor, Your Highness. I consider it a privilege," she said.

Secret Service Agent Alan Palmer, appointed to lead Mrs. Fisher's security, preceded them into the aircraft. Captain Faz'el met him at the top of the stairs. He was head of the Crown Prince's security detail.

In an unprecedented accord, the Crown Prince hooked his arm through Jenny's and pulled her toward him so that they walked up side by side. Jenny could feel his right hand under her left breast, gently rubbing as they ascended the stairs. She pulled away slightly to break contact. *That's all you'll get, buddy*. The Prince didn't appear to notice.

They were followed up the stairway by Mrs. Fisher and Minister Kaliq. The remaining entourage followed.

The dignitaries, including Jenny, were guided to seats in a luxurious VIP section. The First Lady flashed Jenny a questioning look.

Jenny started to explain. "Ma'am, I was—"

"Allow me, Princess," the Crown Prince interrupted. He must have seen the same look and didn't give Jenny a chance. He explained the circumstances of Jenny's title. "Mrs. Fisher, Major O'Shane will act as if her recognition is undeserved, but the fact is that her heroics saved my life. I crowned her a Princess of Saudi Arabia in reward. Our protocols would have her second only to me on the aircraft."

"Is it safe to assume that Princess O'Shane may have arranged my transportation?" the First Lady asked quizzically.

"I offered to assist the Princess whenever we could, Mrs. Fisher. She need but ask," the Crown Prince answered.

"Ma'am, General Penfant asked for suggestions," Jenny added. "And I knew that the Crown Prince was going to South America."

"It made perfect sense, Mrs. Fisher," Minister Kaliq interjected. "The Crown Prince is headed to an OPEC meeting in Caracas. The plane would have been sitting idle for two days in Venezuela, and you needed a means of travel that could go unnoticed."

"This is very generous of you. Thank you."

"It's but a small token of Saudi friendship, Mrs. Fisher."

They sat in silence for a few minutes. Then a look of chagrin slowly came over the First Lady's face. "Do you have your security detail with you?"

"Yes, we do," Minister Kaliq answered. "They are in the rear passenger area."

The Crown Prince added, "Minister Kaliq smiles because he insists on bringing many more guards than we require."

"Will the extra guards remain with the aircraft when I travel to Buenos Aires?" the First Lady asked.

"Most will," answered Kaliq. "Captain Faz'el has been assigned to accompany the Princess for her protection."

The First Lady directed another look to Jenny. "I'd bet you

were given an additional mission as an alternate bodyguard for me at the estancia when you go about your other duties?" she asked.

"Uhh, ma'am …"

The First Lady shook her head. "It's OK, Jenny," she said. "The President always seems to get what he wants. It's convoluted, but he's ensured that I've got a security detail without violating our personal agreement. It's sweet, but sometimes he goes so overboard."

She smiled again and looked out the window of the plane.

After dropping off the Crown Prince and refueling at Simón Bolívar International Airport in Caracas, the plane was on its way to Buenos Aires. The lights were dimmed for sleep.

During the six-hour flight, Jenny was handed two messages relayed from the cockpit. One was from Ginger Cavanaugh. The other was from British Captain Reimers, who was back on the job at Central Command headquarters.

Jenny had but a few minutes to glance at the messages before Agent Palmer asked for her in the galley. It was obvious he was unhappy.

"Listen, Major," he started as soon as they had some privacy, "I'm not thrilled that you're here. I overheard your conversation earlier with the First Lady, and you need to understand. I'm responsible for the First Lady's security. The President may have directed that you receive interim Secret Service credentials so you don't have to go directly through customs and so that you can carry a weapon through security, but this is my detail. You, Cavanaugh and that character named Big John are temporary help."

"Take it easy, Agent Palmer. No sweat. Remember, this wasn't my idea. I'm window dressing as far as the First Lady is concerned. Do what you have to and let me know if we can help. We're here primarily on INTERPOL business.

"Don't let your shorts get twisted. I don't think we should be here either. We're following orders like you. In fact, I may use other transportation to get to the estancia as a diversion.

I'll meet you there." Jenny gave him a short jab on the upper arm. "Come on, Agent Palmer. Same team and all that. I'm here for the ride. Relax." He gave her a look that conveyed he was unconvinced. However, he turned and walked back down the aisle.

Instead of following Palmer to the VIP section, Jenny sat beside Jim Cavanaugh. She showed him the two messages she had received. Ginger's message said, "Bobby broke through one of the firewalls on computer ... Found reference to Women's Resources International ... E-mail exchanges with an organization called Acme Trans in Argentina. That's all we got before the hard drive did a self-destruct."

Jenny filled in some gaps for Cavanaugh. "Acme Trans was the owner of the *Intrepid*. I saw a trawler called *Gotta Girl* in Tampa Bay registered to Acme Trans. According to Crystal, a fishing trawler transported her from Tampa to New Orleans."

"I'm getting a bad feeling," Cavanaugh said.

"That's not the half of it," Jenny responded. They read Captain Reimers's message together. "Received reports from National Security Agency that they intercepted radio/phone conversations from *Intrepid* and a ranch in Argentina. NSA phone intercepts match intercepts made by Russian Intelligence. We're working to triangulate a fix on the exact Argentine location. So far we have rough coordinates in a mountainous desert area in Argentina on the edge of a dry lake bed. It seems to be near the estancia you are traveling to. The data isn't that precise. However, nighttime satellite photos show many more lights there than are normal for that remote region."

Jenny exchanged looks with Cavanaugh. "Are you thinking what I'm thinking?" she asked.

"We could be headed to the headquarters for the syndicate that ran the *Intrepid* and the New Orleans operations," Cavanaugh answered.

"Exactly. This looks suspicious as hell. I want to check the place out before the First Lady gets there. We need to abort the visit if it's a hot zone."

"How're you going to do that from thirty thousand feet? And, oh, by the way, the Secret Service is supposed to do that kind of thing."

She flashed her newly minted Secret Service badge. "Ha! I am one," she said.

Chapter Fifty-Nine

The cargo compartment of the Prince's C-17 was noisy and cold, just as she remembered. Cavanaugh balked at her idea when she showed him the gear and air tanks for high-altitude parachute jumping. She'd seen the equipment stored in the compartment when she'd questioned Stack.

"High Altitude Low Open jumps are for professionals, Jenny. I've done this dozens of times when I was in Special Forces, but you're asking to get hurt or killed," Cavanaugh protested.

Only after she'd told him she was "going with or without him," did he relent to help.

Captain Faz'el fitted Jenny into a HALO jumpsuit. Both he and Cavanaugh gave instructions.

"After we jump, keep an arch with your back and arms, with your legs spread apart. I'll be holding you here and here," Cavanaugh said. He grasped her harness on her shoulder and leg and had her practice the arch position.

"Jim, you don't have to do this," Jenny said. Her voice shook.

He looked her in the eye. "You're not going without me. It's been years, but HALO jumping hasn't changed much."

"I also have made many jumps, Princess. This is the Crown

Prince's favorite hobby," Faz'el said.

"I'll have an altimeter, and I've set a handheld GPS for the coordinates," Cavanaugh continued. "I'll give you instructions on your helmet communications headset as you descend."

His frown deepened. "I want to go on record that I think you're nuts, Jennifer. You've got just enough parachute jumps to be Airborne qualified. This type of jumping is dangerous business. Why don't Captain Faz'el and I do this and report back to you?"

Jenny gave them a hard look. "Come on, guys. It isn't that difficult. If that old man can do it, I sure as hell can." She pointed to a picture of the Crown Prince taped to the fuselage.

"Why not make a low altitude pass for a normal jump?" asked Cavanaugh. "It would be a lot safer and easier."

Jenny squared her jaw. "I don't want whoever's down there to have any warning. This is going to be hard enough. We'll only have a few hours head start on the First Lady's arrival as it is."

Cavanaugh pursed his lips. "OK, but don't say you weren't warned. Here we go. I'll deploy your main chute by pulling this handle at about five thousand feet. If your chute doesn't open, punch this release and pull this handle."

He pointed to the release and the backup rip cord that was strapped across her chest. He had Jenny practice the emergency sequence until he was satisfied that she understood.

He proceeded with the briefing. "I'll land before you and guide you down to the landing area." He strapped a strobe light to her ankle. "Turn this on if I tell you. There's a bright moon, but this will help me direct your descent if we get some cloud cover."

He then explained that the parachute had steering toggles on both sides of the chute.

"Pulling one will turn you in that respective direction. Pulling both will flare the chute and slow your descent," he said. "The theory is that you land softly by doing a complete flare of the parachute before your feet touch. But when you get ready to land, remember to have your feet together and your knees bent. Place your arms over your chest and hands over your face. Clear?"

Jenny nodded once more. Again, he insisted that she practice the landing position.

"The ground wind is about twenty knots. It'll be rough even with a good flare," Cavanaugh continued.

"Normally, professionals wouldn't jump with this wind," Faz'el said. With those not so reassuring words, he helped her put on a tight-fitting helmet and face mask. He pulled on his own and handed her a silenced Uzi. He must have detected a puzzled look on her face as she looked over the weapon because he said, "It's the only silencer we have. I'm told you're an expert marksman. You can ensure a silent approach."

He then handed her a spare magazine of bullets striped red.

He must have detected another quizzical expression on her face as she looked at the magazine. He explained, "The Crown Prince insists we keep a supply of rubber bullets for crowd control purposes. In this case, we're not sure what we'll find down there. We should probably not kill anyone in a friendly foreign country until we're certain of cause."

Jenny was glad he was on her side. She gave a short nod of affirmation.

Faz'el asked her one more time, "Are you certain you want to do this?"

"Yes, dammit. Let's get it over with. One more thing though. Ask the pilot to have the Prince's helicopter hovering near the estancia if we need a quick extraction."

"As you wish, Princess," Faz'el said. He continued instructions. "Make sure your mask is secure. The airplane is especially configured, but the pilot can only slow to about two hundred miles an hour. Be prepared for a blast from the slipstream."

Jenny pulled on her straps to make sure they were snug. "Got it," she said, shivering from more than the cold cabin.

"The oxygen feed is similar to scuba diving. The tank is just smaller," Faz'el added. "Breathe normally." Jenny nodded her head again. Swallowing hard, she tried to ignore her stomach's flip-flops.

"OK, Princess. It's summer here, so we'll only be cold for a minute. But keep your gloves and mask on so you won't get scraped up on the ground if the chute pulls you overland.

"The pilot is already flying into the wind and says he's within twenty miles of the coordinates. He's descended to twenty-five thousand feet and has reduced speed. We'll jump together on my call."

Cavanaugh had a look of concern pasted on his face.

"Don't worry so much, Jim," she said with more confidence than she felt. "Call the pilot, and tell him we're dropping the ramp. Big John can come back and retract it after we jump."

Soon they heard the pilot over the speaker system.

"Ladies and gentlemen, we'll soon experience some turbulence. Please fasten seat belts."

Committed, Jenny pushed the down button for the ramp. Freezing air engulfed the cabin.

A green light came on.

"Now!" Faz'el yelled.

Jenny jumped into space, tumbling head over heels into the black void, mesmerized by a kaleidoscope of spinning stars.

Chapter Sixty

In a surreal moment, when Jenny tried to assume an arch to her body, the jet's slipstream blew her and Cavanaugh upward.

For a millisecond, she floated above the level of the aircraft. The next instant, they were plummeting toward the earth.

It was gut-wrenching—the shift from seeming weightlessness, to plunging at speeds in excess of one hundred miles an hour. Jenny couldn't envision the wildest carnival ride duplicating the free fall.

At the same time, there was an indescribable serenity. The plane's engine noise disappeared, and all she heard was the high pitch keening of rushing wind.

The view was spectacular in the cloudless sky. Lights twinkled in the far distance. Whole cities were spread out beneath her; the bright moon provided mountains in full relief; roads and rivers were clearly visible. She thought she could see a slight earth curvature.

The sights were hypnotic, and the dangers minimalized in her mind. She glanced at Cavanaugh to see if he was enjoying the thrill.

He paid her no heed. His eyes were on the altimeter on his

wrist. The hand gripping her shoulder harness crept down to her breast.

She looked at him, stunned. "What the hell are you doing?" she yelled into the headset.

Her words were lost in the noise of the wind, but he looked up at her. He pulled the rip cord for her main chute and let her loose.

There was a pause. They both flew within feet of each other. Then Jenny's chute unfolded. She was jerked upright.

She thought that the harness had cut her in half. "Ouch!" she couldn't help shouting at its tight grip between her legs.

She saw Cavanaugh fall away, continuing his high-speed descent. Next came Faz'el, who flew downward in a blur. Jenny watched them for a second and then looked up.

She mouthed a silent prayer when she saw that her parachute had deployed.

Looking down again, she watched Cavanaugh release his own chute and then Faz'el. She dangled at about two thousand feet, and the first sensation she realized was the complete lack of sound. No noise at all. It was beautiful. At that altitude, the sun started to peek over the horizon.

Disregarding instructions, Jenny unsnapped her face mask. Crisp, fresh air never tasted so good. The exhilaration of being alive in the moment overwhelmed her. "Hooah!" she whooped out loud. "Hooah!" She looked down.

The earth rushed toward her. She didn't remember falling as fast during Army Airborne training. She heard Cavanaugh over her helmet headset, "Jenny, you're doing fine. The wind is blowing you west. Pull on your right chute toggle."

She did as instructed. She could feel the parachute dip and change direction. It also sped up.

"It seems faster because it's still mostly dark out," Cavanaugh reassured her, his voice calm. "There's a stiff breeze, so you're slipping sideways. You'll do a right-side landing in about ten seconds."

Jenny braced herself. She tried to remember instructions about landing. Then her feet hit the ground.

She landed topsy-turvy. With the blowing wind, she bounced three times—chest, side and back—before her chute started to collapse, but then it instantly reinflated from the crosswinds. The chute dragged her across a meadow like tin cans behind a car. She came to an abrupt halt on her stomach when the chute snagged a rock and deflated

She twisted onto her back and hit the harness release button between her breasts. Excruciating pain radiated across her chest. The chute didn't release.

She looked down to find the plastic release button cracked and bent. It was broken. "Damnation!" she muttered, "Must have busted it when I landed." She pressed on the button again. No luck.

She heard Jim's voice. "Jenny, I'm about one hundred yards behind you. I can see you're having trouble with your quick release. Run toward your chute, and step on it so it can't refill. Then pull the harness off from your shoulders."

Jenny did as instructed and soon had her chute and harness on the ground. She covered the equipment with rocks and knelt down to catch her breath. While resting, she did a visual recon of the landing area. She was bruised and sore, her heart still pounding. She flexed her hands and legs. Nothing seemed broken.

The scene before her was washed by dawn's early twilight; she could see clumps of pampas grass that came up to her shoulders in some places. The grass was interspersed with rocks of varying sizes. She'd been fortunate to have missed the larger boulders.

She was on a knoll that overlooked a narrow road. The road wound up a hilltop where lights streamed through windows of several buildings. She guessed the buildings to be about two kilometers away.

She spotted Cavanaugh's parachute on the ground and hustled toward it. He was sitting nearby massaging his ankle. "Sorry," he explained. "My foot twisted on a rock when I landed." She looked at Faz'el. He waved to indicate he was fine. He joined them and then crouched, watching the road.

"No sweat," she responded to Cavanaugh. "We'll find a vehicle to pick you up later."

"No," Cavanaugh said. "I'll be fine." He paused and cocked his head. "Do you hear that noise?"

Jenny listened. She heard a faint whining sound moving toward them. Fast. She could also hear the rapid click of animal toenails hitting a hard surface.

"Guard dogs coming down the road," Faz'el said. "I'd guess Argentinean mastiffs. Their voice boxes are removed so they can't bark and warn intruders. We have them guarding oil complexes in my country. These will be killers."

"I see them. They're four," Jenny said.

Jenny had the only silencer; she would have to take out the dogs if they were to maintain a silent approach. Cavanaugh pulled his Ranger knife from its scabbard, and Faz'el unsheathed his scimitar.

Jenny loaded the rubber bullet magazine. She didn't want to kill the animals unless she had to. She worked the Uzi bolt. She was grateful that the machine pistol had only a few dings from her bumpy landing.

Switching the selector to single shot, she knelt and fired at the leading dog. She missed. The bullet pinged off a rock in front of him. He kept coming.

Seventy-five feet—pphft ... pphft; the silenced Uzi could barely be heard. The lead dog went down this time, skidding across the road on his nose.

The second dog was now only fifty feet away. Pphft ... pphft. The dog dropped, falling in a somersault of fur and dust.

The remaining two dogs were huge, running pell-mell at them.

Jenny fired once more. She saw a puff of fur when a rubber bullet thumped off the third dog's shoulder.

The shot knocked him sideways. He tumbled, sliding to a halt only feet in front of her. His neck was twisted at an impossible angle. He was dead.

The fourth dog attacked. He ignored Cavanaugh and Faz'el, who'd both bravely stood to present themselves as the bigger threat.

Showing that he was trained to attack the person with the gun, the dog leaped toward Jenny from a distance of fifteen feet.

The big mastiff knocked her sprawling. With fangs bared, he jumped for her throat.

She thrust the barrel of the Uzi into his mouth an instant

before his jaws snapped shut. His teeth closed on the silencer instead of her neck.

Pinning Jenny to the ground with his huge front paws, he shook his massive head. She could feel his chest rumble with a deep, ominous growl.

Out of the corner of her eye, Jenny saw Cavanaugh raise his Ranger knife to strike the dog. He hesitated; the thrashing figures gave him no opening.

Jenny tried to kick the dog off. It was wasted effort. She had no leverage

Her finger was still on the trigger. His jerking, twisting movement caused the Uzi to fire. The top of the mastiff's head blew off.

He collapsed on top of her, crushing her breathless.

"Jenny ... goddammit," Cavanaugh gasped in a panicked voice. "Are you all right?"

"Princess ...?" she heard Faz'el ask.

They struggled to pull the dog off.

"I'm OK," she answered, muffled by her furry cover. "Get this monster off me. Please!"

Between the three of them, they pushed the dead weight of the lifeless animal to the side. Cavanaugh helped Jenny sit.

"Are you hurt?" he asked.

"No, I don't think so," she rasped, still short of breath. "A few more bruises."

She put her hand on the side of the beast. "Poor thing. It's a shame to kill something so beautiful."

"I've never seen a mastiff that big," Cavanaugh said. "They must breed them."

"That sure as hell tells me there's something going on here besides ranching. Why else would they have guard dogs that vicious?" she asked.

Faz'el nodded his head and began to wipe her face with a neck scarf he wore. She pushed him away.

"What are you doing?" she demanded, indignant at his attentions.

"You are covered from the remains of the dog. You look demonic."

She looked at the stains on his scarf. "Yuck!" she exclaimed.

Cavanaugh put his hand on her shoulder. "Here, take a drink." He handed her a canteen of water.

Jenny took a long drink and then wiped her face with her sleeve. "Jim, how's the ankle?"

"I can't keep up with you, but I'm not staying here," Cavanaugh said.

"Right. Well, I'm going to check out that smaller outbuilding. Whistle if I get too far ahead. Captain Faz'el, you keep rear guard."

She started down the road at a trot. The sun was beginning to peek over the distant mountains. She figured they had about four hours before the First Lady's arrival.

She decided to approach in the open, surmising that outer security was probably made up of the guard dogs.

Jogging from dog to dog, she pulled each one off the road and hid them in the pampas grass.

Soon cresting a hill in the road, Jenny could see the outbuilding more clearly below. It looked like a horse stable. Beyond it, the outline of what looked like a helicopter pad was in view.

She heard a whistle. It was a signal from Cavanaugh—a warning. The next instant she heard a vehicle engine approach from behind. She ducked into the roadside brush.

An enclosed van drove by. It stopped at the stable, and two men got out. They were dressed in traditional gaucho garb of flat-brimmed hats and brightly colored, loose-fitting shirts. She saw pistols on wide belts around their waists.

Another gaucho came out of the stable to greet them. He carried a shotgun.

As if on cue, three other men dressed as gauchos rode out of the stable on horses, cantering up the road toward Jenny.

Chapter Sixty-One

Jenny wriggled deeper into the brush when the gauchos rode by on horseback. She could see their faces, burned dark brown by the arid sun. They were armed with rifles in saddle sleeves and holstered pistols—a tough-looking bunch.

Jenny stepped out of hiding after they passed. The Uzi coughed three times. She hit each man in the center of his back in less than two seconds. From only twenty feet, the rubber bullets knocked all three men off their horses.

One of them was only stunned. He raised his rifle and spun toward Jenny. "Damn," she said out loud. "Don't need noise ..."

She pulled the trigger of the Uzi again, confident she'd put him down. The trigger clicked.

She'd run out of special ammo in the clip. She dove for cover.

Out of the corner of her eye she saw Cavanaugh, his knife flashing. He'd stepped out of a bush behind the gaucho.

He hit the man in the back of the head with his knife pommel. The gaucho keeled over without a sound.

"Good job, Jim," Jenny said, running back to help ensure all three gauchos stayed down. Faz'el joined them. They all crouched in place, listening, watching, all senses on alert for indications they'd been seen.

Breathing easier as it became apparent that there was no alarm, Jenny said, "Let's tie these jokers up and switch clothes with them. It'll be a good way to get close to the stable without a major fight. For sure we need to find out what they're up to. Armed men at every turn ... this smells really bad."

Jenny soon led Cavanaugh and Faz'el toward the stables on the gaucho's horses, wearing their flat hats and shirts.

When they rode up, the two men from the van were escorting a young boy out of the stable. The boy had a dirty bandage wrapped around one hand.

"That was quick," one of the men said, not looking at the riders. "Did you find the dogs?" And then the driver looked up. "Where's Eduardo?" he asked.

His eyes widened when he took a closer look, and then his mouth dropped open when Jenny dismounted and aimed her Uzi at his stomach.

She'd reloaded with a magazine of live ammunition, and she was prepared to shoot. The man and his partner apparently understood her body language. They'd also glanced over at Cavanaugh and Faz'el, who both had exposed their own pistols. The men raised their hands.

The gaucho in the stable wasn't as smart. He came outside in time to see the hands rise. He cocked the shotgun. "Alto," he ordered.

Jenny's silenced Uzi coughed again. A hole appeared in the man's forehead.

He died in place, but he fired the shotgun into the ground in a reflexive response.

Jenny, Cavanaugh and Faz'el exchanged looks. "Shit!" she said.

They hid behind the van and waited for someone to come. They could see the main house two hundred yards away on a small rise. No one came.

"Thank God," Jenny said for them all. "Hopefully, they thought the guards were shooting at rabbits. Tie these jokers up in the van," she instructed Faz'el. To Cavanaugh she said, "Come on. We'll check inside the stable."

She ran to the door's edge and motioned Cavanaugh to

the other. Peeking around the frame, she saw the center aisle empty. She gave a hand signal that she was going in. She dove to the ground in the middle, hoping anyone inside would expose themselves.

No one did. It was quiet except for an unexpected sound. Someone was singing.

Chapter Sixty-Two

Vladimir watched the baby blue Women's Resources International helicopter approach on time in the late morning sunshine. The Sikorsky settled on the Argentinean estancia's helipad with a gentle bump.

Vladimir cursed himself, realizing too late that floodwaters had washed mud onto the pad. Baked by the hot sun, the mud had turned to a heavy layer of loose silt.

He stepped back to escape the whirling cyclone effect of dirt and debris blown up by the rotor wash. The dust, combined with the bright sun angled behind the helicopter, made it impossible to see more than a few feet to the front—hardly more than a bare outline of the helicopter. In the WRI helicopter, Agent Palmer looked out the right side door at a single man standing alone, shielding his face from the blowing debris.

"That's not Louis," the First Lady said to Palmer over the communications headset. "For God's sake, Esquedas doesn't even have the decency to personally meet me."

She had no more than spoken when Palmer felt the left side door of the helicopter suddenly jerk open. A dirty, disheveled woman was shoved into the cabin.

"What the hell?" Palmer exclaimed. He drew his pistol as if to shoot the woman.

"Wait. It's Vanessa!" the First Lady shouted. She grabbed the woman in a bear hug. They both began sobbing. Palmer couldn't have separated them if he wanted to.

He uncocked his pistol and looked at Big John, who was seated next to him. "What's going on?" he said into the headset.

"Beats me," Big John answered.

Then another face appeared in the open door. Palmer cocked his pistol once more.

He relaxed his trigger finger just in time. A preteen boy was shoved into the helicopter behind Vanessa.

In that instant, Palmer saw Big John's eyes shift to outside the aircraft. He followed his gaze.

Cavanaugh was next to the cockpit window, pointing a shotgun at the pilot. The look on Cavanaugh's face left no doubt that he was prepared to shoot.

Palmer shifted his pistol toward Cavanaugh. "What are you doing?" he yelled.

Next, in a burlesque affect, a demonic-looking, blood- and dirt-covered face appeared in the left doorway. Big John knocked Palmer's arm aside as he took aim at the new figure.

"It's Miss Jenny," Big John shouted into the microphone.

"Get out of here," she mouthed to Palmer, urgently waving her arms upward. She slammed the door and disappeared.

"Go! Go!" Big John yelled.

Palmer could see Cavanaugh motioning upward with the shotgun.

Palmer ordered the pilot, "Take off. Now!"

The pilot didn't wait one second longer. He pulled maximum pitch. The helicopter nearly leaped off the landing pad.

When the dust settled, a surprised Vladimir wiped his eyes and attempted to brush the dirt and dust off his clothes. He watched the helicopter disappear into the horizon. "Something happened," he muttered. "What?" He looked around the empty helipad. Nothing moved.

He looked out at the stable building. The van was still there that was to have picked up the boy. He flipped open his walkie-talkie. "Eduardo, are you there?" he paged the foreman. No answer.

Chapter Sixty-Three

Jenny watched the WRI helicopter become a speck in the distance. Faz'el was in a pampas clump on the forward edge of the pad, assigned to keep an eye on the man greeting the helicopter. She'd told him to shoot the man if he interfered with their plan.

She and Cavanaugh had seen to the loading of the boy and Vanessa Esquedas onto the helicopter. The blowing dust had provided them excellent cover. Now they held perfectly still in a tall clump of pampas grass until the man on the other side of the helipad finally started walking back toward the main house.

"Whew!" Jenny whispered. "I didn't think he'd ever leave. He has to suspect something."

On the helicopter Vanessa Esquedas cried with relief, telling the crew members about her heartrending story.

"I sang every morning so that my rescuers would know where I was," she said. "I sang as a way to keep my chin up, to tell myself there is hope."

She described her bleak cell and the treatment from her husband. She talked about hearing others crying and the taunts from guards. She knew her husband was a vicious man, she said, but she never knew just how evil and murderous.

"He's a walking Satan," she said of El Toro. "He's pure evil."

The boy's story was equally chilling. He was the only child of a Brazilian industrialist. He was abducted in Buenos Aires during a field trip with schoolmates.

His captors had chopped off and then mailed his little finger to his parents with a ransom demand. The parents paid the ransom with no questions. The van that had arrived at the stable was to deliver the boy to a pre-planned drop point.

The boy wiped his tears as Vanessa gave him a comforting hug.

☆☆☆

Jenny, Cavanaugh and Faz'el regrouped and hid in tall grass and desert shrubs by the helipad. They all did a quick check of weapons. They kept somewhat separated to minimize target profiles. Cavanaugh caressed the automatic shotgun he'd taken from the guard at the stables.

"Don't get too attached to that thing," Jenny said. "I'm still hoping we can do this without anymore serious gunplay."

"Bullshit. These people have a prison on the property, guard dogs trained to kill and staff armed to the teeth. They're not going to give up easily," Cavanaugh responded.

"You're right. I was trying to be optimistic," Jenny answered, nodding her head. "I'm still amazed at the stables doubling as a prison. The cells looked like a regular jail. Steel beds, toilets and sinks—the whole works. Esquedas imprisoned and planned to sell his own wife. That's a sick mind at work."

After listening to the stories of the two prisoners and seeing them safely on the helicopter, there was no doubt in Jenny's mind as to her next step.

She was going to take down Louis Esquedas.

Chapter Sixty-Four

When Vladimir returned to the estancia's main house, he found El Toro practicing his putting in his office. Carlotta was clapping in encouragement. "Have you shown Mrs. Fisher to her quarters?" El Toro asked.

"No, señor."

"Well then, where is she?" he asked, missing an easy putt. "I'm not going to stand around all day waiting for her."

"I'm afraid she didn't stay," Vladimir explained. "The helicopter touched down but then left immediately. I'm not sure what happened."

El Toro looked up from his putter. "Did they signal anything? I don't understand."

"I couldn't see any signal from inside the helicopter because of the dust from the prop wash. I'll radio them from operations downstairs and see what happened."

Vladimir started to leave and then thought he should share his observations. He explained about the horses and van at the stable. "I also tried to reach Eduardo on the walkie-talkie."

El Toro thought for a minute, his eyes shifting back and forth. He touched Carlotta's arm and stroked it. Then he said,

"You worry too much. The helicopter probably left because of some perceived breach of security identified by the Secret Service. They'll be back."

He paused for another few seconds. "You're getting paranoid about possible intruders," El Toro added. "We'd see trespassers coming up the road from miles away. And those dogs of Eduardo's ..." He realigned for his next putt.

"Nonetheless," Vladimir said, "I think I'll take the golf cart down to check,"

El Toro waved him away.

Vladimir ignored the brush-off and went down to the operations center. There was no response when he radioed the WRI helicopter.

"They're probably behind a hill. Communications will pop back up in a minute," one of the operators said.

Vladimir wasn't so sure. Unsettled by the seemingly unrelated coincidences, he became even more certain that something was amiss.

He climbed down a small stone stairway to a garage adjacent to the house. He pushed a remote to the roll-up door and turned the ignition key of the golf cart.

The gasoline engine started without hesitation, its noise loud inside the garage.

He looked down at the dashboard gauges and then laid his head on the steering wheel hub.

The gas gauge reading was on empty. "Govno!" he cursed in Russian, venting his frustration. "Shit! Shit!"

He looked over to the hand pump that was hanging on the wall. It led to a drum of gasoline outside. The rule of the house was that the last one using the cart was to refill the gas tank.

Cranking fuel into the cart, he said out loud, "Carlotta, you're one lazy, disgusting pervert." She had used the cart the previous night to go down to the stables to watch the gauchos with Vanessa Esquedas. Distracted by his negative thoughts, he forgot to close the garage door behind him after he gassed up and headed down the road.

Chapter Sixty-Five

Vladimir's golf cart sputtered past Jenny's hiding place in the pampas grass near the helipad.

"We're toast as soon as he finds those guards we locked in the van," she said. "Jim, you handle him. Faz'el and I will take down the main house."

"Consider it done," Cavanaugh said, already following the cart, limping slightly from his twisted ankle.

"Be careful," Jenny cautioned. "Let's go, Captain."

She and Faz'el sprinted to the garage door. In the open approach to the house, Jenny felt exposed and vulnerable; she thought it was the longest two hundred yards she'd ever run.

She glanced back every few seconds as she ran toward the garage, checking to be sure the man in the cart didn't turn around. He didn't.

When they got inside the building, she gulped a huge lungful of air. She had to smile when she realized she'd been holding her breath.

She looked at Faz'el. He was panting in the shadows of the garage doorway. He was leaning over, hands on his knees, wheezing.

"You need more time in the gym, Captain."

"With respect, Princess, I'm not the only one breathing hard."

Jenny grinned at him while she checked out the small garage. She noted the fuel nozzle and then the four stone stairs leading down to a doorway into the house. She nodded at Faz'el.

Together, they leaped down the stairs to the stairwell. Faz'el kicked the door open. They were into the house in a flash, guns at the ready.

☆☆☆

Vladimir approached the stable with his senses on full alert. After years of living the dangerous life of a KGB spy, he'd learned to listen to his intuition.

Shouting and a sudden banging from inside the van caused him to look up from the driveway's rutted path. That's when he saw something in the rearview mirror of the golf cart.

A figure darted into the shadows of the garage of the main house. Vladimir skidded to a stop, jammed the shifter into reverse and wheeled the cart around in a sharp turn.

Before he could accelerate back up the drive, a man dressed in a gaucho shirt and armed with a shotgun moved into his path.

"Get out of the cart," the man ordered, the gun pointed at Vladimir's chest.

Surprised, Vladimir forced himself to keep his mind calm, to analyze the situation. He'd noticed the man favoring an ankle, a tall, black man who seemed forceful but calm. *This guy's a pro*, he thought.

"Please don't be hasty. Who are you? What do you want?" Vladimir asked in heavily accented English. He raised his hands, climbed out of the driver's seat and tried to appear submissive, but kept his eyes glued to the trigger finger on the shotgun.

Chapter Sixty-Six

Inside the doorway of the house on the estancia, Jenny and Faz'el stood on a landing with stairways leading up and down. Jenny motioned downward.

Opening another door at the base of the stairs on the lower level, Jenny gasped at what she saw. Below them was a full-blown operations center. Computers, extra-large flatscreen monitors, telephones and people were crowded together. It looked like a miniaturized New York Stock Exchange.

Maps of every continent and major city lined the walls. Oceans were also depicted. Various colored pins were stuck in the land maps, and small boat symbols were positioned on the oceans areas.

There was a flashing LED sign; numbers with a dollar sign were displayed—Jenny guessed it represented cost associated with the acquisition of merchandise.

On the flatscreen monitors, she saw hair and skin color, weight, height, age and full-size pictures of nude women and children.

Instead of stocks, bonds, merchandise or other goods sold in a normal stock exchange, the brokers standing on the floor of the basement were selling humans. They were talking on phones and radios taking bids, yelling numbers that would change the LED sign. A melodic voice announced the current bid on a speaker system.

Jenny felt a level of disgust and revulsion unlike any she'd ever experienced. It was a stunningly sophisticated operation—and frightening.

She noted that there didn't appear to have been an alarm concerning intruders. Operations continued without interruption. "Way too overconfident. Intruders definitely unexpected," she muttered to Faz'el.

She recognized one of the men in the center of the room as the Sudanese general from the Saudi reception. He wasn't in uniform, but she was certain of the identification. He was sweating profusely, the dome of his head a bright sheen.

The general nudged a broker standing beside him who made a bid on a woman pictured on the big screen TV. It was Vanessa Esquedas. Others were present who also appeared to be bidding.

Tethered to the general was the Italian girl Jenny had met at the reception. This time she wasn't wearing the attire of a Muslim woman. She was bare-breasted and only wore a thong. There were welts on her back and buttocks.

She had a dog collar around her neck. A leash was attached to it that the general was holding in one hand. She wore a dazed expression and carried herself as would a broken animal.

Jenny could feel a fury building within—a volcano about to erupt. Her jaw clenched so tightly that she thought she would break teeth.

She took a deep breath. Faz'el must have sensed her anger. He put a hand on her arm. She knew he was sending her a message to calm down and to be rational. She nodded. He was right. A fit of temper wouldn't do it.

She took another breath and surveyed the room again. The noise level from voices of brokers competing for merchandise was high. Din from fax machines and printers added to the volume.

She saw two guards on a platform that was above and surrounding the room. The stairwell landing on which she and Faz'el stood was on level with the platform. The guards were armed, and Jenny assumed they were present more to maintain order in the operations center than to deal with intruders. They were relaxed and had AK-47s slung on their shoulders.

"You take out the guard on the right, I'll cover the left," Jenny instructed. "Let's try to take them without gunfire. I'd like to surprise the crew downstairs. On the count of three. One ... two ..."

Chapter Sixty-Seven

Jenny and Faz'el circled the ramp over the operations center at a dead run. They had the guards bound and gagged in short order without commotion. The noise and hubbub going on beneath them obscured any noise they made in their attack.

Perfect, Jenny thought. She was concerned that if someone gave an alarm, many of the operators would escape out the doors before she and Faz'el could corral them. She wanted to capture every single person. She was determined that each one would pay for the suffering they caused. Jail was too good for any of them.

She also wanted to capture information on the computers. If one of the operators below was able to erase data, the chances of tracking down the entire organization would become much more difficult. Many people involved at remote locations might escape justice altogether. That wasn't going to happen if she could help it.

She and Faz'el entered the center from two sides. Their joint effort worked to perfection. The group was caught completely unaware—they milled about like stampeded cattle, squealing and mewing as they were herded into one corner.

The only resistance was the Sudanese general. "You'll never capture me, you meddling whore."

He held the Italian woman in front to prevent Jenny from having a clear shot, and began backing toward an exit sign on a far wall. The only clear target was his sweaty face. And he kept shifting from one side of the Italian's head to the other.

Moving backward, the general struggled with something in the waistband of his pants. Jenny assumed he was reaching for a gun. Between his huge gut, his overflowing shirt, and trying to hold the girl close, he couldn't pull it loose.

With barely a pause, Jenny told Faz'el, "Watch the others. He's mine."

She ran straight toward the Sudanese. Even in the short distance crossing the floor, she gained enough momentum to launch a flying kick.

The shock at seeing her running attack caused the big man to hesitate momentarily. It was enough for Jenny to have a clear angle. His face became a perfect target. One boot heel hit him dead on the nose; the other struck his shoulder. She bounced off and landed back on her feet. He staggered back and dropped the leash. Blood gushed down his chin. His eyes widened in disbelief.

With the released tension on the choke collar, the girl screeched. She spun around and raked her nails across his cheek. He grunted in pain and pushed the girl to the floor. A look of dismay crossed his face as he realized his mistake.

He was unprotected. He struggled again to pull out his gun. Jenny had a clear shot. Two bullets landed in his chest within centimeters of each other. The big Sudanese staggered back ... one step ... two. Then he toppled to the floor with a thud.

He lay on his back gulping for air. Jenny could see bubbles forming over the holes in his chest. His lungs were filling with blood.

He reached a hand out as if to ask the Italian girl to help him. The girl walked up and spit in his face.

A bloody froth formed on his lips. His body convulsed in one last gasp and then sagged as he collapsed into death.

"I hope you rot in hell," Jenny said to his still form.

She took a sport coat hanging on a nearby chair and put it

over the girl's shoulders. Jenny could feel the girl trembling. "Don't worry," she said. "He won't bother you ever again. We'll get you home soon."

She guided the young girl to a chair and turned her away from the body. "Sit here. I'll be back."

Jenny looked over at Faz'el. He pointed to rolls of duct tape on a counter. She nodded.

He said to one of the male operators, "Tie up your colleagues, hands and feet. Make it tight."

"Anybody else want to help?" Jenny asked. Two women brokers raised their hands.

"Good. Copy what's on these computers onto a thumb drive," she told them. One of the girls hesitated. "I mean now!" Jenny said, giving her a shove. "You have one minute. Move!"

Jenny then told Faz'el, "Use the radio and contact the Prince's chopper pilot. He should be hovering nearby. Tell him to be here inside fifteen minutes. Then notify the Argentinean Bureau of Internal Security. I'm sure they'll want to send a team here.

"Once the computer information is transferred onto the thumb drive, tie the rest of this pond scum up. Let's not let one person escape."

She pointed to the Italian. "Take her outside with you. I'll meet you at the chopper pad. I'm going to go get Esquedas."

"Be careful," said Faz'el.

"We don't have time."

Chapter Sixty-Eight

Jenny crept up the stairs out of the operations center and into a large, well-appointed house. Two people met her before she got ten steps into the foyer. One was dressed as a butler and the other, a maid.

"Can we help you, miss?" the butler asked in perfect English. He had a pistol held at his side. The maid moved to his left about five feet in the wide hallway.

Jenny had no doubt that the couple was a security team. *Must have been alerted by interior cameras.* She didn't have the time to use finesse.

Pphft ... a bullet hole appeared in the butler's forehead. He collapsed in a pile.

The maid moved quickly to take advantage of Jenny's preoccupation with the butler. A knife appeared in her hand, and she quickly showed she knew how to use it.

The maid lunged at Jenny, who tried to back off, but the woman followed. She jabbed upward. The Uzi magazine deflected the blade, and Jenny felt a nick of the blade next to her belly button instead of what would have been a killing blow.

Deflection of the jab overextended the maid to the side.

It was an opening. Jenny punched the woman in the ear. The maid's head snapped around, and she shifted sidewise, providing separation.

It was enough. Jenny pointed the barrel upward and pulled the trigger. Pphft. The bullet entered under the chin and blew the top of the maid's head off. She bounced off a wall and then fell to the floor, a red pool spreading beneath.

Jenny crouched against a wall and listened, tense, ready for the next encounter. There was silence. *If there are others they just must not know I'm here*, she thought, breathing easier.

Walking quietly down the hall, Jenny heard heavy sighs and giggling in a front room. She peeked around a door and found a couple having sex on a desk. She didn't get a clear look at their faces.

She kicked the doorframe to get their attention. "Hey! Tell me where to find Louis Esquedas," she commanded in a no-nonsense tone.

"You found him," the man panted, not really looking at her. "Who in the hell are you? You with the security team for the First Lady? How about giving us a minute here?"

"Sorry, Esquedas," she responded, watching his every move. "Not this time. You're under arrest. Now, put some clothes on."

He pulled away from the woman and began to fasten his pants. Esquedas and Carlotta stared at Jenny's blood-and dirt-caked face. Recognition dawned. "YOU!" they exclaimed in unison. Expressions of hate filled their faces.

At that moment, Jenny recognized the couple from the airport—and the man from the White House. She was still mystified by their combined malevolence.

"Before I put you both in jail, please explain. What did I ever do to you?"

Esquedas answered in his silky voice, "You killed my son, you ignorant and stupid woman. Does the name Lieutenant Esteban Histaves mean anything?"

"Histaves? Sure I remember him. He was torturing me."

"You deserved it. You involved yourself in other's affairs, just like you're doing today. Besides, he shouldn't have died at the hands of a peasant like you."

His face projected insanity. "You've been very lucky to date.

Now I'll see to killing you myself. You've lived on borrowed time."

"You're both crazy, and now you're the one out of luck, Big Shot."

"Maybe not," Esquedas said, looking over Jenny's shoulder. A sledgehammerlike blow landed on her neck. Everything went black.

Chapter Sixty-Nine

Jenny awoke to find herself spread-eagled on the floor in the estancia study. Three people were standing over her—Esquedas, Vladimir and Carlotta. Jenny started to get up. Esquedas hit her in the thigh with his putter.

She screamed in pain and grabbed her leg. "You bastard," she said. He hit her in the side. Again, Jenny yelped in agony. She looked over and saw Cavanaugh sitting on the floor, his back against the wall, his right leg bent at a grotesque angle.

"Sorry, Jenny. I'm losing my touch." He grimaced.

"Not your fault, Jim," Jenny said. She braced for another blow from Esquedas's putter.

"Papa, wait," Carlotta said. "The putter's too easy. Let's have some fun before we kill her. I want to see more pain. Let's have Vladimir work her over. It will be great entertainment."

"You are a demented woman, my love," Esquedas said. "Vladimir, what do you think? Are your kickboxing skills up to it?"

"Of course, señor," Vladimir answered. "It will be my pleasure. This tiny woman has caused us a lot of grief."

He pulled Jenny to her feet. She pretended to be groggier

than she felt.

Vladimir swung a side kick intended for her head. She sidestepped. His foot whistled by her ear. She punched him in the groin while his foot was in midair. She missed his testicles, but she could tell by his expression that the blow still hurt.

She followed with an elbow to his throat, and she jabbed a finger at his eye.

Dodging her finger, a look of surprise appeared on his face at her unexpected quickness and technique.

He backed away and bowed. "I should have known. Nice," he said, rubbing his throat. "This will be more fun than I thought."

"You enjoy beating up women?" Jenny retorted.

Her words seemed to infuriate Vladimir. He attacked with a flurry of punches and kicks. Jenny blocked most of the blows, and she landed her fair share.

She could tell that she was hurting him, but he was bigger and stronger. Although she was faster, her speed wasn't enough. He landed several punishing blows.

She began to feel her strength ebb from his never-ending onslaught. His power finally prevailed. A full-fisted blow got through her block and collided with her forehead. She went spinning away, dazed by the impact.

Vladimir followed with a front kick to her chest. She felt his heel land on the exact spot that was already bruised from the parachute release button.

Jenny screamed, fell to the floor and curled in a tight ball. The pain was excruciating. She thought he'd broken her sternum. She could hardly breathe.

Through eyes glazed with pain, she could only watch a sweating and bloodied Vladimir look at El Toro. "Enough?" he asked.

El Toro nodded his head. "Kill her," he said. He and Carlotta were crouched beside Jenny with gleeful looks on their faces.

Vladimir gripped Jenny's head in both hands and prepared to snap her neck with a sharp twist.

Chapter Seventy

Vladimir held Jenny's head in a death lock and smiled as El Toro looked on approvingly. "Snap it!" El Toro commanded.

A bellow emitted from the hallway. Faz'el stormed into the room, startling Vladamir. Faz'el had no time to shoot ... no clear target without hitting Jenny.

So he charged, bowling into Vladimir, Esquedas and Carlotta, knocking them all to the floor like pins. Faz'el raised his scimitar to strike Vladimir.

Lying on his back, Vladimir used a perfectly executed, ballerinalike heel kick. His foot struck the handle of the sword. It went spinning away and planted itself point first into the wooden floor near the doorway.

Vladimir jumped to his feet and faced off with his new opponent. Even as groggy as she was, Jenny realized that Faz'el was seriously outclassed.

With Vladimir's attention diverted, Jenny slowly began to regain her senses. She reached behind her neck to draw her own dagger. It was gone. *Damn, they must have searched me.*

All eyes in the room were watching the merciless assault. All except Cavanaugh's.

"Jenny," he called. She looked over. He'd pulled a Ranger knife from his boot.

Cavanaugh flipped the knife to Jenny.

She grabbed it midair and struggled to her feet. Staggering, still not fully with it, gritting her teeth against the pain between her breasts, she approached Vladimir from behind, plunging the dagger upward into the base of his skull.

For a second, it had no effect. Then, in slow motion, he turned toward Jenny as if to determine his latest source of irritation. He smiled his ugly, crooked smile. "You have the karma," he said and fell to the floor.

Jenny and Faz'el collapsed next to him, exhausted.

"You'll never take us," El Toro shouted. He and Carlotta raced toward the door. Jenny summoned another shortlived spurt of energy. She yanked the knife out of Vladimir's head and threw it at Esquedas.

The blade did its work, slicing the side of his neck. His carotid artery spewed a fountain of red. He staggered, grasping his neck. Blood pulsed through his fingers. He fell to his side, convulsive in trying to stop the bleeding.

"Papa," wailed Carlotta and knelt beside him. "Noooo!" She cradled his head in her lap, unsuccessfully trying to staunch the spurting flow. He died in her arms.

Covered with his blood, she looked up when Jenny tried to stand.

"You did this," Carlotta screeched. "You killed my brother and now my precious papa. You will pay!"

Her face was contorted and had a demented intensity that was bloodcurdling. She jumped up and ran out the door.

Jenny leaned against a wall for a minute's rest. Then she remembered that she'd told Faz'el to call Argentinean Internal Security. They would be inbound. *Let her go for now. Have to get out of here. Never explain ...*

She looked for her dagger. It was on El Toro's desk. She grabbed it and, using the last of her reserve of energy, she leveraged the bloodied Faz'el to his feet. Between them they dragged a groaning, limping Cavanaugh to the helicopter pad.

She heard an approaching chopper. She saw the Saudi emblem on the fuselage. *Thank God.*

"Captain, do you have the thumb drive?" she asked.

He patted a pocket. "Yes, Princess. Right here."

"Good job. How did you know to come back for me?"

"I brought the woman to the helicopter pad as you asked. We heard the golf cart go by toward the house. We were sitting in the tall grass, so they didn't see us. But I caught a glimpse of the driver. When I saw it wasn't Cavanaugh, I knew it was trouble."

"You did great. Thank you."

"My orders were to guard you with my life, Princess. I failed. You saved me."

"I think we're even in that area," Jenny answered. She gave him a hug of gratitude. She sensed he was embarrassed by her attention. Rotor wash from the landing helicopter drowned out his reply.

She helped get Cavanaugh and the Italian woman onto the royal helicopter and then Faz'el. She gave the area one last look. Then, satisfied, she jumped into the passenger area and gave the pilot thumbs-up.

He took off immediately, flying a low-level ground-hugging egress toward the airport and the waiting royal jet.

High above them, Jenny watched four Argentinean Internal Security helicopters painted in mountain camouflage heading toward the estancia.

Chapter Seventy-One

President Fisher stood in the wings when the White House Press Secretary announced, "Ladies and gentlemen, the President of the United States." The packed room of reporters rose to their feet as one when the President entered. They were assembled in the White House Press Room.

"Good evening, ladies and gentlemen," the President said, glancing out from the podium at the crowd of curious reporters and blinking at the bright lights of television cameras. "I'm here to announce the successful conclusion of an investigation into an international syndicate involving human trafficking. I have a statement and then I'll take questions."

He began reading. "A special team led by INTERPOL, working with the U.S. Central Command, uncovered a worldwide syndicate dealing with illegal immigration and human trafficking in the slave market.

"The international syndicate included elements of the police, military, government leaders, health agencies, maritime shipping groups and nonprofit organizations from multiple countries. Bribery, murder and extortion were their primary weapons.

"Analysis of captured documents indicates that billions of dollars in profits were being funneled to Al Qaeda terrorists.

"Diligent police work was the key to success and INTERPOL is to be congratulated on its triumph in exposing these criminals. This successfully closed yet another source of terrorist revenue. A special commendation should go to INTERPOL North American Director Juan Tavares.

"Critical to this investigation was civilian and military cooperation. My thanks go to the CENTCOM commander, General George Penfant, for his active role in this cooperation.

"The U.S. Coast Guard, DEA and the FBI also played major roles in solving these crimes. I want to thank all the key players in those organizations for their contribution in bringing this matter to a successful conclusion.

"I'm also extremely proud that, as part of this effort, Mrs. Fisher was asked to participate in a covert operation to help rescue a close friend. That operation was also a complete success.

"I would be remiss not to mention the assistance rendered by our good friend, the Saudi Arabian Crown Prince Abdul Fahd. His security team provided a ruse that allowed infiltration and ex-filtration by Mrs. Fisher's group to accomplish the rescue. It was brilliant.

"In this facet of the operation, you may rest assured that everything possible was done to maintain Mrs. Fisher's security. An elite team was handpicked to protect her at all times. Senior Secret Service Agent Alan Palmer was the leader of that team.

"I would also like to congratulate and thank the Argentinean Bureau of Internal Security for their active participation. They arrested and will bring to trial the core of criminals that ran the syndicate's operation center.

"One ringleader escaped, and in cooperation with Argentina and INTERPOL, a Ms. Carlotta Esquedas, aka Carla Histaves, is listed as one of the world's most wanted fugitives. Pictures will be distributed later.

"Lastly, let me add that the claims by the Cuban government that U.S. military personnel invaded their sovereign waters and killed innocent civilians in pursuing this operation are completely false."

The President looked up from the podium. "I will now take

your questions."

He was inundated.

Jenny was watching the press conference on television in her apartment with her fiancé. She had a heating pad between her breasts, Nikki on her lap, and she was snuggled up to Gary.

"You didn't think you would get any credit did you?" Gary asked her.

"I don't care. I'm glad it's finally over."

"Not quite. When are you headed back to Saudi?"

"Prince Fahd's coronation is next month. It's sad about the King dying. I never met him. But I'll bet Fahd will be a great king for his country and people."

"The coronation should be quite an experience for you as part of the Royal party."

"I hope they don't stick me into a lot of the hoopla. That sounds so boring. The good news is that the prince asked me to assist Captain Faz'el in coordinating security for dignitaries at the ceremonies."

"That's actually cool. But then you immediately ship out to Kabul for your new assignment. So I won't see you for a while. I guess this is what life's like for a military husband."

"Don't remind me." She snuggled tighter into his side.

"I'll miss you, Major Jenny, or, I should say, Lt. Colonel O'Shane."

ACKNOWLEDGMENTS

I wish to especially thank the PJ Parrish sisters, Kelly and Kristy, for their generous help in the initial editing of this work. They were exceptionally kind to a beginner. Also, many thanks to: my agent, Susan Gleason, who was tireless in promoting my effort; Frank Tiffany who is a brilliant senior ship engineer who happens to be my son-in-law. He patiently tried to help me describe ships and submarines (any mistakes are all mine); Sherrie Kahley of Southern Exposure Photography for donating her time and efforts to take pictures for the cover; my great friends Bob and Anne Clancy for their support and insights as we struggled through final editing of the manuscript; Sergeant First Class John Ledbetter (U.S. Army, Ret) who was super and infinitely patient in helping me explain HALO parachute jumping; and Debra Stowell, owner of Circle Books, who insisted I keep working on this novel. Most importantly, my deepest appreciation goes to my wonderful wife, Peg, who has steadfastly supported my ambition to write. Her review of every page was critical and a blessing.